DEAD THINGS

ANTHONY GIANGREGORIO

OTHER LIVING DEAD PRESS BOOKS

DEAD THINGS

Table of Contents

DEAD GRAVE: A DEADWATER STORY

The ghouls were everywhere, and Henry Watson raised his Glock and shot another zombie in the head.

The 9mm round struck the zombie in the right eye and blew out the back of its head in a glorious spray of blood and bone matter. But for every one he shot, there were five more to take its place.

"Jesus Christ, Henry, where the fuck did they all come from!" Jimmy Cooper yelled by his side as he let loose with a barrage from his twelve-gauge shotgun.

Only a few feet in front of him, bodies disintegrated into red mists filled with viscera that fell to the ground, to then become crushed by the approaching dead.

"We can't keep this up forever!" Mary Roberts yelled from behind Henry.

"No shit, we need to find a way to break free from these bastards or it's all over!" Cindy Jansen replied.

"Get off, get away!" Sue Anders shrieked as she shoved a decayed body away from her. No sooner did the ghoul fall away then it was coming back at her, but then its head was practically severed from its shoulders by a dark vision with long black hair and fingernails honed to a razor's edge. As the ghoul fell away, clutching at its exposed throat, Sue let out a sigh of relief and said, "Thanks, Raven, that was a close one."

The dark-haired teenage girl nodded. "Just stay close to Henry," Raven said and then was dancing into the ghouls once more. She moved fast, a blur amongst the slow undead, and each time her nails connected with decayed skin, a slice of flesh was missing from the ghouls. She knew how to use her natural weapons well and each time she dove in, an eye was plucked from its socket.

More ghouls were rendered blind with each passing second, but though a warrior spirit thrived in her small frame, even Raven knew their chances of surviving the battle were slim.

Henry shot three more ghouls in the face, each one becoming unrecognizable as once human, and as the bodies dropped to the ground, he heard the click of an empty weapon. Popping out the spent clip, he reached into his pocket for another only to find himself looking into the eyes of a zombie.

This one had seen better days, the flesh on its face all but peeled away, the faded bone beneath peering through. The nose was gone, only two open slits that dripped pus and mucus. One eye had rotted from the socket and the other looked like it would be joining its mate soon enough. But the ghoul could still see, and as Henry wrapped his hand around the new clip, he felt the ghoul's teeth sink into his wrist.

The teeth were like steel and he cried out, but more in revulsion than fear. Dropping the empty Glock to his feet, he reached down and drew the sixteen inch panga from its sheath riding his hip. As the zombie worried at his wrist, sinking its fetid teeth deep into his arm, Henry raised the panga and brought it down so hard it sliced the ghoul's head in twain, as if it was made of nothing more than paper.

The body dropped to the ground, but the head was still attached to his arm by clamped teeth, and as he raised his arm high, Mary let out a gasp between shots at the closing zombies, to stare at the severed head hanging from Henry's wrist. "Henry, oh God no!" Mary screamed.

"Forget about it, just keep shooting!" Henry yelled as he used the tip of the panga to pry the yellow teeth apart. As he did, the head fell away to roll between his feet, and he raised his boot and brought it down on the head, crushing it to mush as brains spilled out around the sole of his boot.

He glanced down at the wound to see it bleeding freely, and he knew what that bite meant, but for now he needed to deal with the undead, save his friends, and what happened later would be dealt with.

By his side, Jimmy fired another barrage of death at the closing horde, his blast slicing a ghoul in half. The legs continued onward for three more feet as the severed torso began to crawl across the ground, its insides dragging behind it as the other zombies stepped on its entrails and halted it, that is until the trodden feet were lifted and the ghoul could move again.

"So, Henry!" Jimmy yelled out. "How 'bout a plan that's gonna get us out of this shit!"

"I don't have one!" Henry replied.

"What?" Jimmy yelled back as he kicked a ghoul in the balls to no effect and followed it with a shot to the face. "You always have a plan!"

"Not this time, pal."

Behind Henry, Sue yelled again and Henry spun to see her surrounded by five zombies. Bending over, he picked up his Glock and quickly popped in a fresh clip, but as he looked around at his fellow companions, each one trapped in their own war with the dead, he saw only he was close enough to save her.

But as he readied the Glock and prepared to fire, he saw with that sinking feeling of dread that is absolute fact, that he was going to be too late.

Though he raised the Glock and fired four shots, two double-taps each, the remaining, fifth zombie managed to get its teeth into Sue's throat, and with a growl like an animal, it clamped down and pulled back.

As the ghoul snapped its head back, Henry was already firing and the shot took the zombie in the forehead. Its skull disappeared and its mouth fell slack as the large piece of Sue's flesh in its mouth dropped away.

Sue, reaching for her throat, turned and stared at Henry, their eyes making contact despite the carnage around them. Henry could see the blood spurting from between her fingers, and as he watched, he saw the flame die in her eyes as she slumped to the ground.

"No!" he screamed, kicking and punching the ghouls aside as he fought to reach Sue, but he knew before reaching her that it was too late. He had seen it too many times to count and he knew what would happen next, though it broke his heart to admit it.

But he didn't reach her, because before he was halfway there, half a dozen ghouls blocked his path. Firing from the hip, he shot three of them before the others came at him. He raised the panga and began dancing and darting back and forth, always moving so pale, claw-like hands couldn't seek a hold on him. As he did this, the panga was a blur, slicing hands and arms off like a scythe to wheat.

His wrist stung where he was bitten but he ignored it, concentrating on the battle at hand. He tried to peer over the sea of shifting heads, but it seemed to go on forever. As he wracked his brain to remember how the six companions had ended up trapped with no hope of escape, it eluded him, but he knew whatever predicament had gotten them here was irrelevant, the only thing that mattered was escape.

Mary fired her .38 S&W at the rotting faces that came for her, and as Henry turned, he saw three ghouls coming up from behind her, her attention focused only in front of her.

"Mary, behind you!" Henry yelled, but no sooner did he speak, then Mary was overrun by bodies. He caught sight of her scared face before she was lost under a sea of rotting corpses. He heard her scream once, more frustration than fear, and then the scream went into a high-pitched shriek, and a second later he saw her decapitated head dancing amongst the ghouls like a beach ball at a rock-and-roll concert.

"Oh, Christ, no!" Henry screamed as Mary's mouth still opened and closed, the blood seeping from the neck wound. That was when a zombie grabbed the severed head and jammed its hand into the open neck stump, pulling out the muscles and tongue from within.

Something inside Henry broke then, something that could never be fixed. Mary had been the daughter he'd never had and without her, plus Sue, now gone, there just didn't seem to be a reason to go on.

He heard yells to his left and he turned to see Jimmy and Cindy back to back, Cindy firing her M-16 on full auto as Jimmy now used his .38, his shotgun empty and hanging over his shoulder. Each of them fired into the undead crowd without stopping, but there were just too many bodies.

Henry punched a zombie away from him, then kicked another in the face, and as he managed a second of breathing room, he was able to watch as Jimmy, then Cindy, were swarmed by the dead, both fighting to the very end. Cindy was ripped in half, nails digging into her chest to tear it open. As her organs were pulled from her still heaving breast, he saw her blonde hair turn scarlet as her blood exploded out of her to bathe everything in the vicinity. Jimmy had a rougher time as each of his limbs was grabbed by pale hands that were like small vises. He spit and yelled at the undead faces, that is until they began to sink their teeth into the joints of his arms and legs, causing him to yell out in absolute agony.

One at a time, with the flesh and material of his clothing torn by teeth, his arms and legs were separated from his torso, Jimmy was conscious the entire time, and though he begged for death or at least to pass out from shock, his mind refused to acquiesce.

As Henry raised his Glock, he locked gazes with Jimmy, and the young man yelled out, "Kill me, Henry, for Christ's sake, fucking kill me!"

With tears in his eyes, Henry raised the Glock higher, and though he couldn't save his best friend, at least he could grant him peace. One shot rang out and the 9mm round struck Jimmy between the eyes. His head snapped back and his eyes closed, the ghouls never ceasing their feeding.

Henry felt something tug on his left leg and he looked down to see that a zombie had crawled up to him. It was the one Jimmy had blown in half, and it had crept up like a soldier in the forest. Before Henry could kick it away, its teeth clamped down on his left calf, sinking in to the bone and causing Henry to cry out.

With the panga in his hand, he brought it down like he was chopping wood and the blade sank into the skull more than halfway, the head ceasing to bite him but now trapping his blade in the bone.

As he tried to free it, he spotted Raven through a crowd of zombies. She was like a dervish, bouncing from place to place, her hands slashing at any ghoul stupid enough to come too close. But then she met a zombie her nails had no effect on. The ghoul had been a member of SWAT when he had lived and he was still decked out in riot gear. His face was nothing but a white skull and Henry knew this ghoul was one of the originals. This dead man must have been caught out in the rain back when it was still deadly and had died only to come back as one of the undead.

As the ghoul came at Raven, her nails did nothing to its armored body, the Kevlar able to stop a high impact round, let alone a teenage girl with fingernails for weapons, no matter how sharp.

As Raven fought off the zombie, it came at her and grabbed her by the throat. She kicked and scratched at its eyes, taking out both of them, but the ghoul never ceased its attack. It didn't need eyes to kill her, and once its hands were locked onto her, she couldn't escape. As she became trapped, more ghouls surrounded her, and as Henry watched helplessly, Raven was torn apart by teeth and nails. He spotted her ebony hair once in the crowd of the dead, and then she was lost from sight. He realized the entire time the ghouls killed her, she never so much as screamed once. She had always been quiet and had stayed that way to the end.

Henry was alone now, the only one remaining, and as he let go of the hilt of the panga, realizing he couldn't free it from the zombie's skull, the mouth still clamped on his leg, he fired the last rounds in his Glock.

As he was surrounded, he fired the last bullet into a pale face and then raised his fists, prepared to take as many of the undead bastards with him as he could.

But as he kicked and punched, he spun around and then halted, too shocked to strike the ghoul before him.

For the ghoul was none other than Sue. Her flesh was pale now, the jagged wound in her throat still seeping blood. Because of the wound, her head was slanted to the side, her teeth now bloody and clacking up and down as her dead eyes stared at Henry.

His fist had stopped an inch from her face, and though he knew it wasn't her any longer, he just couldn't hit her. For he loved her, even in death.

And what was the point? All his friends were dead and he was bitten, soon to either turn or he would eat a bullet to spare himself the suffering to come.

"Sue, I'm sorry, I told you I would always protect you," he said as the undead surrounded him and hands reached out and wrapped around his body, fingers grabbing at his face. "I failed you, and I give up."

If she understood what he was telling her, she gave no inclination, but instead dove in, and with mouth open wide, prepared to rip his throat out.

He closed his eyes and prepared for the end, but at the last second, his instinct to live overrode his sorrow and he opened his eyes and pushed her away. Punching and kicking, he fought his way through the horde, never ceasing his movement. He felt teeth take bites from his flesh again and again but each time he made it a foot further from the horde.

But though he fought a valiant battle, he tripped over his own feet and fell to the ground, and when he rolled onto his back, he found himself staring up at his five friends. Mary was there, her severed head now held in her hands, her torso nothing but a gaping cavity. Jimmy was there, too, his arms and legs missing as he rolled across the ground, a jagged black hole in his forehead. Raven came up next to him, her body torn and ravaged by dozens of teeth and hands, and then Cindy came up behind Mary, her body all but unrecognizable, only her blonde hair letting him know it was her. And in the middle of the pack, was Sue, her body now ruined and mutilated.

As his undead friends closed in on him, Henry raised his hands up to stop them, but their open mouths, dripping with blood, came forward, blotting out the night and smothering him, as if he was in a blanket.

He couldn't breathe and he felt the air grow hot, his arms trapped like he was tied up, and as he let out a scream, he jumped up, tossing the blanket off him to stare around the dark room, only the one small candle in the far corner to break the absolute blackness.

Jimmy glanced up from his post at the window where he was playing solitaire to see Henry looking around frantically.

"Hey, old man, you all right? You look like you just saw a ghost."

"I, uh, Jimmy, you're okay." He turned his head to see his other friends also alive, each sleeping silently. To his left, lying beside him, was Sue, her eyes closed as she slept. As Henry's heart slowed its frantic beating in his chest, he blinked the fear away and stood up, leaving his bedroll where it was spread out on the floor.

"Of course I'm okay, why wouldn't I be?" Jimmy asked as he looked at Henry with a quizzical look. "Hey, you're not getting senile in your old age, are you? I mean, more than usual."

Henry rubbed his face with his hands, the images of his nightmare falling away, and he shook his head no. "I'm fine, I just thought..." he waved his right hand in a *forget it* gesture. "Never mind."

He went to the corner they had decided would be used for a bathroom and he pissed in the small hole in the floor. There had been a collapse in the foundation and the large crack had become exposed. It was as close to an outhouse as they could ask for and it would do until the next day when they planned on heading out again.

"How is it outside?" he asked Jimmy as he zipped up his fly.

As he turned to look at his young friend, Jimmy shrugged. "The storm's slowing down and with luck we can head out in the morning, like you said."

Henry nodded. "That's good." He stared at Jimmy, the image of his friend with no arms or legs pressing in his mind and he shook the vision away. "Look, I'm up now so why don't I take over for you."

"You sure? You've got another hour before you have to relieve me."

"Nah, go 'head and grab some sleep, I've got this," Henry said with a smile.

"Okay, fine," Jimmy said and jogged across the room, took off his boots, and was under the bedroll with Cindy in less than a second. She grunted and yelled at him, saying his hands were cold and to leave her alone, and he chuckled like a school boy. Then the two settled down and were quiet.

Henry let his eyes play over his sleeping friends as his nightmare flashed across his mind, and he realized though he tried not to admit it, those fears had always been there. His worst possible nightmare was seeing his friends torn apart or worse, and though he tried to keep those feelings repressed, there were times he couldn't leave them bottled up.

He supposed it might have had to do with the fact he was hungry. Hell, they were all hungry.

After leaving the mountains of Colorado, they had found themselves in the middle of an early snowstorm. Luckily, they had found a small hunting cabin and for more than two weeks had been holed up inside its worn walls as their meager supplies of food had waned.

But now it looked like the storm was finally passing, and the hope was that in the morning, they could set out and seek food. Though water was in abundance thanks to the frozen snow, they still needed food and he knew whether the storm ended in the morning or not, they would have to set out or else they would end up too weak from hunger to leave later.

He reached inside his jacket and took out a small map he'd found in the cabin. It was hand drawn and Henry was fairly certain the owner of the cabin had illustrated it. It showed what the owner had believed was good hunting grounds, as well as where the best natural paths were. Henry didn't know how reliable the map was but seems they were lost, it was better than wandering around aimlessly until they died of exposure. Folding the map neatly, he slipped it back into his pocket.

As he pulled his jacket closer around him and stared out at the high snow drifts, the wind howling like a banshee, he did something he didn't do often, as he felt the situation was just that desperate.

He prayed.

Hours later, with the storm finally abated, the companions set out across the snow-covered landscape.

Because the storm had come so early in the season, it wasn't that much of a surprise when the sun came out and began to warm the land. But no sooner did the sun appear than it was lost behind thick clouds that looked as if they would open up once more at a moment's notice. A light drizzle began to fall, and with the temperature rising slightly, the snow turned to slush in many places, soaking each of the companions' boots. The slush splashed when they walked and soon they were all miserable.

"This sucks," Jimmy said flatly, summing it up for the rest of them.

But with little choice, they marched on, avoiding the deeper drifts as Henry used his panga to feel the frozen ground ahead of them.

"Shit, I'm so hungry I think I'm gonna eat my boots before the day is through," Jimmy said as he trotted behind Henry, Cindy by his side.

"Just hang in there, Jimmy," Henry said. "Our luck has got to change soon."

"Hey, Henry, heads up," Raven called as she pointed to the left.

Henry turned to see four zombies stumbling over a rise, plowing through the snowdrifts as if the snow wasn't there. Henry had to admit, right now, he envied the dead just a little as he pulled his collar tighter around his neck. Being dead, the ghouls felt no cold and the snow was nothing but a nuisance to them.

"I thought the deaders would freeze in the snow," Jimmy commented.

Mary nodded. "You're right, but it's not cold enough yet."

"You think they'll just freeze up till spring?" Jimmy asked.

"I don't know," Mary replied. "From what we've seen so far, yeah, but no one's been able to find out for sure. They go dormant it seems and then wake up when the snow begins to melt and the temperature rises."

"Still, we could just go somewhere like Alaska and live there till they all rot away." He turned to Henry and called out, "What do you think, Henry? How 'bout going to Antarctica, maybe?"

Henry chuckled. "Sure, Jimmy, just hop onboard my flying carpet and I'll run you right over there. Maybe if we can find a plane and someone to fly it we could give it a try, but until then we're stuck in the good old U S of A.

The ghouls were closer now, and they let out a moan, their noses and brows dripping with small icicles. Jimmy raised his shotgun to take them out when Henry reached out and pushed down the barrel.

"What are you doing, Jimmy? You fire that shotgun and anything in a mile radius or more will know we're out here. No, we gotta take 'em out with silence. You up for it?"

Jimmy grinned as he spun the shotgun around and prepared to use the butt like a club. "Bring it on, Henry. I'm always ready for a good fight."

Henry looked at the girls. "We got this ladies, you stay here."

Mary crossed her arms over her chest as she shifted her feet in the snow. "Oh, thank God we have you big strong men to take care of us, what would we ever do without you?"

"Why, you think you could do better?" Jimmy asked, the zombies now only twenty feet away and closing.

Cindy stepped up and pushed Jimmy to the side as she handed him her M-16. "Just watch us, sport," she said and looked to Mary, Sue and Raven. "Shall we girls?"

"Ah, I'll stay here with the men, if it's all right," Sue said. "I'm not much on fighting, you guys know that."

"Suit yourself," Cindy shrugged.

Mary, Cindy and Raven stepped away from the rest of the group and made their way towards the zombies.

"You think they'll be okay?" Jimmy asked Henry as he watched the women move away and up the slope the zombies were on.

Henry chuckled. "Are you kidding me? I feel kinda bad for the deaders now."

Cindy was in the lead, followed by Mary and Raven. As she walked up the slope, she let her eyes take in the condition of the four approaching zombies.

They were a decrepit quartet, that was for sure, and Cindy wondered if they were some of the originals from when the rains first came.

Nearly two years later and the first people to die and reanimate were still shambling around what was left of America. The cities were the worst and had picked up the nickname, deadlands. Only fools went close to cities, and most who did never returned.

Cindy let her eyes play over the first ghoul in line. It was female, she could tell, but that was where the identification ended. The face was rotted to the point there was no flesh left and the hair on the scalp had fallen out long ago. The clothes were so filthy and matted with blood and dried gore that Cindy couldn't tell the make or style of the outfit. Most of the material was nothing but rags and more brown, dried and rotting flesh peeked through.

The second ghoul was in the same shape as the first, only this one had been a man. It was obvious due to the size of the ghoul's arm and width of the shoulders. The face was in a similar state of disrepair; only this one still had a nose, though by the looks of it the nose wouldn't be there for too much longer if it was allowed to wander away.

The third and fourth zombies were also sexless, both of medium height with matted, greasy hair and milky-white eyes that seemed to see nothing, yet everything at the same time.

"How are we going to do this, girls?" Mary asked as she pulled a hunting knife from a sheath on her hip. Her brown hair, past her shoulders, blew out behind her in the wind. Her cheeks were red from the cold and her eyes wide with the excitement of battle and she was a far cry from the secretary who had once worked in the lobby of Pineridge Labs.

Cindy had also pulled a knife from her waist, an eight inch, razor-sharp blade to be exact, and she gripped the hilt tighter.

Raven spoke up, cutting off Cindy. "I'll take the big one, you two can have the other three."

Mary glanced at Raven to see the sixteen-year-old's face was serious. Raven was so taciturn and this was a long speech for her. Ever since meeting Raven, Mary had tried to get to know her better but each time Raven had politely refused. Mary quietly realized she knew as much about Raven now as she did when first meeting her and Sue after finding them inside a bus the companions had stolen from a tribe of cannibals.

But Mary also knew though lacking in personal information, she trusted Raven with her life and had done so on many occasions. The young girl was an excellent fighter and could kill with nothing more than her hands, thanks to her long fingernails which were sharpened to razor tips.

"Okay, fine. Mary, you and me will take the three on the left and Raven can have the big one," Cindy said and looked Raven in the face. "You sure?"

Raven only nodded, her long, ink black hair blowing out behind her, looking for all purposes like she wore a cape.

Mary touched her .38, just wanting to know it was there. Cindy carried a small sidearm as well, but both knew if they had to use them, then anyone in the area would be alerted to their presence. Plus, she didn't want to have to fall back on using her gun, for if she did, it would only help perpetuate the stereotype that she and Cindy needed help by the men.

After all they been through together, Mary still shook her head each time Henry tried to coddle her. She knew he only did it because he was overprotective, but still, after all the battles she had fought with him, she would think he would consider her an equal by now.

The ghouls were only a few feet away and the wind shifted, causing the aroma of rotting meat to touch Mary's nose.

Mary exhaled through her nose to then begin to suck in air through her mouth. She was used to the redolence of death, but that didn't mean she welcomed it.

Before she was close enough to deal with one of the ghouls, Raven suddenly took off at a sprint, dashing past her and Cindy as she headed toward the large zombie like a heat seeking missile.

The zombie moaned loudly and raised it hands to grab Raven, its teeth already preparing to tear her apart, but as Raven reached the ghoul, she darted to the left, the zombie overreaching her and falling into the snow. Raven spun around like a gymnast and jumped onto the back of the ghoul, her arms wrapping around the zombie's face, her fingernails pointed directly at its eyes.

In one fluid movement, she stabbed both eyes with the index finger on each hand, her nails slicing into the milky-white orbs like a hot knife through butter. Though the ghoul felt no pain, it sensed the world go dark, and it reached up and grabbed Raven by her jacket, pulling her off its back with one yank of its large arm.

She fell into the snow, sliding for a few feet, until she rolled onto her side and popped back up. She turned to see Mary and Cindy reach her and she grinned widely as she shook ice crystals from her hair.

"That should slow the bastard down," she said proudly.

Both Mary and Cindy nodded, then looked back at the oncoming zombies. The large one, now blind, had grabbed the female zombie and was tearing the ghoul apart with its meaty paws.

The three women watched silently as the large ghoul pulled the female zombie's arms off and raised one limb to its mouth, chomping down messily. But as soon as it tasted the decayed meat, it spit it out, resembling a child who didn't like what he had eaten.

Tossing the limb away, it stumbled away to disappear over a snow drift, its moans and crashing carrying on the wind before it was lost from sight.

Mary and Cindy weren't listening however as they still had two healthy zombies plus an armless one to deal with.

"Mary, you go left and I'll go right. Raven, take care of the one with no arms," Cindy told them as the women charged at the ghouls, their blades held high.

Mary was the first to dispatch her opponent. As the arms of the ghoul reached for her, she knocked them aside and jammed her knife into the milky-white left eye. She felt the tip slide into the eye socket, grating on the sides of the skull to plunge into the brain. The ghoul twitched for half a heartbeat and then dropped to the snow, very dead.

Raven was next, and she snap-kicked the female ghoul in the chest, knocking it into the snow. She followed the kick with a jump onto its torso, where she reached down, placed a hand on each side of its head, and twisted sharply, snapping the neck and severing the spinal cord. The ghoul's legs immediately stopped moving, though the head was still active. Still, it was harmless and forgotten as she rolled to her feet.

Cindy wasn't as lucky and had a bout of misfortune as she reached her zombie. Mimicking Mary, she had knocked the outreaching arms aside and was about to plunge her knife into a milky eye when her right foot came down on a patch of ice that was hidden under the snow. As her arm was raised for the killing blow, she found her feet and legs swinging out from under her as she fell onto her back, her body horizontal for a brief moment before gravity pulled her to the earth. She landed so hard she had the wind knocked out of her, and she blinked to clear the fog that descended over her mind.

As she shook her head, she looked up to see the zombie she was about to kill coming at her, the head directly in a path for her face.

In the brief instant before the ghoul would land on her, she realized no matter how fast she moved, it wasn't going to be quick enough to save herself. As if it was in slow motion, she saw the ghoul falling onto her, its mouth opening wide, as it got ready to sink its yellowed teeth into her nose or cheek.

All she could do is close her eyes and wait for the inevitable pain, knowing once bit, she would end up on the last train west.

As the zombie leaned down to sink its teeth into Cindy's face, she heard a sharp crack of a gun, the report rolling across the hills like thunder, causing a few birds in a nearby tree to take flight. She recognized it instantly; it was Henry's Glock. No sooner did the sound of the gunshot reach her, then a loud squelching sound overrode it and she felt bits of bone and brains splash onto her face, the snow around her head turning a dark shade of brown thanks to the rotting brains.

Half of the zombie's head was blown off and the body twitched on top of Cindy, before going slack and dropping onto her like a spent lover.

As she felt a gelatinous substance ooze near her lips, she opened her eyes to see the zombie was very dead.

Jimmy was only a few feet from her now, and before she could move, he was grabbing the zombie by the scruff of its collar and yanking it away from her, tossing it to the side like errant trash.

"Cindy, are you okay?" Jimmy asked, the worry in his voice apparent to her.

She nodded, feeling a piece of brain slide into her collar and touch her neck. "Yeah, I'm fine. Where's Henry?"

"Here," Henry replied while walking up to her. He stopped when he was four feet away, looking down on her as Jimmy crouched beside her, touching her hair tenderly with his gloved hand.

"Thank you, Henry. I don't even want to think about what might have happened."

He waved her gratitude away. "Don't worry about it, honey. Hell, you've saved me enough times; it's nice to return the favor."

"Are you sure you're okay?" Jimmy asked her again.

"I will be if you'll help me up. There's snow in my pants and my butt is freezing."

"Huh? Oh, yeah, sure, sorry," Jimmy said and pulled her to her feet. She used her sleeve to wipe her face clean, Jimmy picking away a few choice gobbets that had stuck to her hair.

Mary and Raven joined them, as did Sue, who saw the action was over for the time being.

Mary grabbed Cindy's arm and squeezed it, the gesture saying she was glad her friend was unharmed.

"So much for us women being mighty warriors," Cindy said, embarrassed by what had happened, as she cleaned off the rest of the brain matter. "I can't believe I let some ice almost get me killed."

"Hey, speak for yourself," Raven said. She had kicked butt and she knew it.

"Don't beat yourself up, Cindy," Henry said. "It happens; next time be more careful. Remember, when fighting in the snow, ice can be anywhere." He grinned as she touched her shoulder like a father. "Besides, that's why you have us...to watch your back."

"And backside," Jimmy grinned lecherously trying to shake off the worry he'd been feeling. When he saw her fall, his heart had skipped a beat. After being with Cindy for more than a year, he couldn't imagine life without her. He made a mental note to tell her as much when they were alone later that night.

Cindy smiled. "That's my Jimmy, always thinking of sex."

Henry clapped his gloved hands to get their attention. "All right, people, Cindy's fine and we need to keep moving. That shot I took will alert anything in the area we're here, and when it arrives, I want to be long gone."

They each gathered themselves and turned to head out, but as they passed the zombie Raven had paralyzed, Jimmy took an extra second to stomp on its still animated head. The heavy sole of his right boot heel came down on the decayed forehead, pushing it deep into the snow. Jimmy raised his boot again, and when he brought it down, he used the rear edge of the heel.

The heel caved in the face, shattering the jaw and puncturing one eye, but it still didn't destroy the brain. But without a mouth and only one eye, the head could do no damage if an unwary traveler came across it. Plus, Jimmy liked to dish out what he hoped was pain to a zombie whenever possible. If he had his way, he would kill every one he came across, though he knew that was impossible. There was simply not enough ammunition in the world to get the job done.

"Was that really necessary?" Cindy asked as she walked beside Jimmy. She was wiggling a little, trying to get the ice out of her ass crack. It was already melting and that helped, but now the rear of her pants and lower part of her shirt under her jackets was wet. She was already looking forward to when they could build a fire so she could dry off.

"Yeah, it was," Jimmy said as if that settled the matter.

Looking around as they walked away from the destroyed ghouls, Henry said, "I hope there aren't any more roamers in the area."

"If there are, we'll deal with 'em, old man," Jimmy replied. "And next time we'll use our guns, and what happens, happens. This stealth shit almost got my girl killed."

"Jimmy," Cindy said, wanting him to stop, but Henry raised his hand for her not to continue.

"No, it's okay, Cindy, he has a point, though I still think silence is better. Besides, we all know Jimmy, shoot first and deal with the aftermath when it comes."

"No way, not Jimmy," Mary said sarcastically. "Why, he's the most level-headed among us."

"Hey, that was a crack against me, wasn't it," Jimmy said, not quite getting he was the butt of a silent joke.

"Oh, no, baby," Cindy said. "Mary meant what she said. You're the most practical one in our little group. We all want to be more like you."

"Well, I should hope you would, I..." then Jimmy stopped as he figured out Cindy had a wide smile and was messing with him. As he looked at the others, each wore a wide grin, that is except for Raven who was not paying attention but instead was watching their surroundings.

Jimmy frowned deeply. "Hey, that's not funny, quit pickin' on me!" He said it like a middle-schooler who was being made fun of by his friends.

Cindy began to laugh and soon the others were, too, Henry slapping Jimmy on the back.

Cindy came up and kissed a pouting Jimmy on the cheek. "Don't worry, lover, you're still my man," she said so only he could hear. "And I'll prove it tonight if we can get a chance to be alone and find a place that's warm. That perked him up, and as his cheeks turned a deeper shade of red, the group climbed a snow dune and trekked deeper into the forest.

A full five minutes passed before the first of the coyotes appeared from the surrounding brush and trees.

Their muzzles sniffed the air but there was no longer the scent of the six humans.

They had been attracted to the fight between the women and the zombies, but were too scared to come out of hiding.

The last time the pack had tried to attack humans, two of their number had been shot. So they had lied in wait, hoping one of the humans might be left behind, perhaps a weak one in the group.

As they padded out onto flattened snow made by the companions' feet, they slowly crept up to the destroyed ghouls, carefully sniffing to make sure they were truly dead. As they crept closer with heads down, they prepared to run at a moment's notice.

Eventually, they came to the conclusion that the zombies were inactive, and as the leader went in and tore some of the decayed meat from a shoulder blade, the others quickly followed suit.

The meat might be old, but it was sustenance, and in the harsh winter the coyotes had learned to adapt.

Ripping and tearing at the corpses, they fought over what scraps remained on the bodies, the circle of life ever revolving.

* * *

Mid-afternoon, hours after the battle with the ghouls, the six travelers came upon a small glade. The wind had scoured the area clear of snow, though the south side had snow piled more than five feet high. It was still an excellent place to rest and build a fire.

After Jimmy and Cindy gathered what wood they could find buried under the snow, the pickings slim, Henry pulled out a package of fine-mesh steel wool. This was his last bag, the other three he'd found in a hardware store at the last town they'd gone through, the bags now gone, having been used, and he was glad for this remaining one.

As he began to separate the mesh into a wider cloud of wool, it parted, and he reached inside his jacket and took out a 9-volt battery.

"Here ya go, Henry, this is all we could find," Jimmy said as he and Cindy walked up with a few sticks and twigs.

"It'll have to do," he said as they dropped the kindling into a small circle dug in the frozen ground.

"Need any help?" Mary asked.

"No, thanks, I can do it," Henry replied.

When the kindling was set up, he took the top of the 9-volt, the leads exposed, and began to touch it to the steel wool. Almost immediately the wool began to glow and soon it was burning. When he had it going as well as possible, he set it into the kindling, then added a few pieces of newspaper taken from his pack to help get the blaze going.

Sue and Raven gathered close, each of them hoping the fire wouldn't go out, for they had been traveling for hours and all were cold and needed to rest.

"Come on, baby, you can do it," Jimmy coaxed the flames as he leaned in closer, feeling the first hint of warmth.

It looked like it would go out, the kindling too wet from being in the snow, but then it began to snap and crackle and the flames grew hotter. Henry, feeling desperate, took a handkerchief out of his backpack and set it into the fire. This was enough to add to the blaze to get it going and all sighed with relief as the flames began to burn with more strength.

Soon, the fire was casting a circle of warmth as each of them surrounded it, warming their hands and face as the heat penetrated their clothes to their chilled bodies.

"This is the last one, guys, after this we freeze," Henry said, referring to the steel wool.

"Shit, Henry," Jimmy grunted. "There's got to be an end to this damn forest, we've been walking forever."

"I hope you're right about that, Jimmy," Henry said. "Or else they're gonna find six frozen bodies in the spring."

"Oh, Henry, you're so morose," Sue said as she snuggled up next to him. "We'll be fine, you need to have faith."

"A little luck wouldn't hurt either," Mary added as she rubbed her arms.

"Sue, the only faith I have is in myself and you guys, my family. Anything else is up for grabs."

"So, what? We just keep walking and hope for the best?" Jimmy asked.

Henry nodded, the fire turning his cheeks a shade of red. He had taken off his hat and his white hair, once damp from sweat, was now drying. The ash-gray hair still had a few strands of brown in it, but over the past two years, since the dead began to walk, it had almost turned completely gray; which added to Jimmy's affectionate nickname of 'old man' all the more fitting.

Henry shook his head as he used a branch to stir the flames. He wasn't looking forward to leaving the warmth of the fire and trekking on, but he knew soon that was what he and the others would need to do if they wanted to survive the frozen wasteland he and his friends now found themselves in.

"I'm afraid that's all we can do, Jimmy," Henry replied.

"And what if we don't find anything out here? It could be miles before we come across something to help us. What if there are no towns or cabins like the one we just left?" Jimmy pushed.

Henry paused before speaking, as if he was considering the answer. He looked each of the companions in the eye, and said very simply, as if he was chatting about the weather, "Then we die."

Jimmy blamed the map, but Henry blamed Jimmy. Mary blamed the snow and Cindy said it was just bad luck. Sue tried to support everyone and Raven had no opinion other than that she was hungry.

Secretly, Henry was wondering if they would have been better off staying back at the cabin, for though they would have run out of food and possibly starved to death eventually, at least they could have done so in a relatively warm environment.

Though blame was tossed around left and right, at the end it didn't change the fact that they were very lost.

The sun had disappeared for good, now replaced by heavy clouds that looked as if they were going to open up at any second. With nothing else to do but go on, the six companions trudged through the snowy wasteland, their heads down and jackets pulled tightly around them.

As dusk was falling, and Henry was searching for a spot they could set up a cold camp—something he wasn't relishing—the group found themselves in a region of steep, but shallow valleys, where the drifts of snow covered only one side, allowing the walking to be much easier.

Though they trudged on, Henry tried to console himself with the fact that they weren't truly 'lost'. He knew if he wanted to, and the others agreed, they could turn around and trek back to the cabin again. But he also knew that was a mistake, despite their dire circumstances.

Their only chance at survival was to continue forward.

As the clouds opened up with a cold, driving rain, each of them hunched over just a little more, trudging on.

Soon, snow was replaced by slush and all their boots were soaked through. Though military grade footwear, the boots couldn't handle complete immersion for so long, and more often than not, one of them would step into a puddle that turned out to be a small pond, more than a foot deep.

As they continued on, Henry decided stopping would be foolhardy, so they walked for the entire night, six ambiguous shapes blending in to the shadows of the darkness.

They had seen no other signs of life, human or animal, and they all felt as if they had fallen back in time to a place on earth where life didn't exist yet.

Many times, in the darkness, they found their path blocked by heavy snow or land fall and they would have to retrace their steps until they could find a way around the altercation, and the constant exertion was tiring them out to the point each of them looked as if they would fall down, to never rise again.

Even Henry's indefatigable spirit was waning, and with Sue on his arm as he helped her walk, he wondered just how long it would be before the first of them fell over in exhaustion.

Finally, with the night half over, they came upon a large copse of trees with dense branches standing alone at the base of a hill. As they gathered under the trees, huddling together for what little warmth they could take from one another, the rain still fell, turning the ground to slippery mud and freezing them to the bone.

The temperature dropped once more, close to freezing this time, and it was one of the worst nights any of them could ever remember having to endure. Sleep wasn't an option, as each of them needed to stay awake and focused. Jogging in place was the favorite activity, and all wished desperately for a fire, but with everything soaked through, it wasn't an option.

It was one of the longest nights any of them could ever recall living through.

Eventually, dawn arrived, and as the sun touched the gray sky, the rain finally ceased, though a heavy drizzle persisted.

Without saying a word to one another, the companions moved on, their clothes soaked thoroughly and frostbite only hours away.

Jimmy fell back to walk with Henry and Sue, and as the others plodded on, he whispered so only they could hear him. "Cindy's not doing so good, Henry," he said. "We need to stop and get a fire going."

"Yeah, I know, but if you see anything that'll burn, I'm all for it," he replied as he gestured to the sodden trees and brush, the mud and slush all around them.

"Tell me about it," Jimmy replied. "But I'm just sayin', if we can't get warmed up soon...I'm worried about her, Henry."

"Look, Jimmy, we're all in a bad way. Don't you think I'd stop and do that if we could? Just keep an eye out, maybe something will come along soon."

Jimmy nodded, knowing Henry was right, and he picked up his pace and caught up with Cindy. She leaned on him and he helped her along. Mary and Raven walked side by side, though neither spoke. Henry could see Mary's face and where her skin was once vibrant and fresh, it was now pale and her face drawn. He had no doubt he looked the same.

With no other options, he pushed on, hugging Sue tighter as he helped her through the mud.

It was mid-afternoon when Jimmy, on point, came across something of interest to him. Holding up his hand, he went off the natural path and slowed when he came to what looked like a large boulder covered in wet snow.

"What are you doing?" Henry called out as he watched Jimmy stepping through the foot high snow. All of them were about ready to fall over for good. Even Raven looked to be at the end of her rope. All their bellies were full of snow, but even with all the water they could consume, they were still undernourished and needed food. As Henry watched, Jimmy moved through the snow to stop in front of the large drift, and he wondered if his friend was seeing things, perhaps had gone crazy.

"I saw a reflection, Henry, like metal, just give me a second," Jimmy called as he began to study the snow pile. The others had now stopped and each of them wanted to sit down, but all knew if they did, they would probably never get up again. Henry could feel the tips of his fingers going numb and the end of his nose tingling, and knew frostbite was just around the corner. That is if he didn't have it already.

"Ha! I knew it!" Jimmy cried out as he began to brush at the snow pile.

"What's he doing?" Sue asked Henry.

"He's gone nuts," Mary said as she hugged herself. Her cheeks were so red she looked like a Christmas tree ornament, her breath fogging out in a white cloud as she breathed.

As Henry watched Jimmy brushing at the snow pile, he quickly realized there was something of color underneath the snow other than a boulder. He saw the color green!

"No, I think Jimmy found something," Henry said and trudged through the snow to join him. Together, the two began brushing at the object under the snow until more than half of it was exposed.

As the two men worked, the four women joined them, helping where they could until Cindy declared, "It's a car!"

"So?" Mary said. "If it's out here in the middle of nowhere, I doubt it still runs. And even if it did, there're no roads to drive it on."

Henry finished wiping off the trunk and he turned to Mary. "You're right, Mary, but if there's a car here then there has to be a road nearby. We just can't see it because of the all the slush and snow."

"Good point, old man," Jimmy cracked. "But I was hoping maybe we could get it started and have some heat."

Henry's eyes lit up at the possibility. "Well, let's see what we can do, then." He turned to the women. "Come on, ladies, help us out. If Jimmy's right, we can get it running and sit inside and enjoy some warmth."

Though the women all made a face, they joined in and five minutes later the car was exposed.

Mary called out that it was a Toyota when she brushed off the medallion on the license plate, the top of the plate establishing the car had been bought at Al's Toyota dealership in Detroit.

"Detroit? Man, this car's a long way from him," Jimmy said as he finished brushing off the trunk and went to the driver's door. "Let's see if its unlocked." Pressing the button on the door handle, the door popped open and snow fell into the interior from where it had been in the rain well.

Jimmy, not wasting time, climbed inside and called out, "Hey, the keys are still in it, too!"

It was then that he detected the stink of rot and decay, and as he glanced at the rearview mirror, he saw the pale, desiccated, half-frozen face glaring back at him...just before it snapped forward, yellow teeth ready to bite.

The next three seconds passed in slow motion for Jimmy. As he considered what was happening, his mind went in two different directions as he weighed the outcome of his next action.

If the zombie managed to bite him, then he knew he was dead. First infection, then weakness, then death, to be followed by his *return*. Of course, he knew Henry wouldn't let that happen to him and that his friend would put a bullet in his head to spare him from walking around as one of the *things*.

He thought of Cindy and how sad she'd be when he died, and about how his body would be left buried in the snow somewhere and in the spring, when the thaw began, he would become exposed to then become nothing but meat to the scavengers of the forest.

In the blink of an eye, he decided he didn't like that outcome, so as the zombie's head snapped forward, its mouth open wide to take a bite out of him, Jimmy spun around and used his arm as a muzzle, jamming it into the ghoul's mouth. Fetid teeth clamped down hard on his arm but the thick material of his jacket prevented his flesh from being torn, though he did feel the pressure of the front teeth.

Without thinking, his instincts honed after two years of fighting the dead, he reached down with his free hand and pulled his nine inch Bowie knife from the sheath on his hip.

As the ghoul worried at his arm like a dog to a bone, Jimmy brought his arm around and jammed the knife into the zombie's ear. The blade slid in like a warm knife into butter, the blade hesitating for a moment before puncturing cartilage and penetrating the brain. The ghoul began to twitch in spastic movements as Jimmy forced the blade deeper.

To make sure of his kill, he twisted the knife to the right, carving the brains to mush. The teeth let go and the zombie fell back onto the rear seat, like a tired passenger on a long drive.

Henry was reaching into the car now, his eyes wide with surprise. With the ice covering the windows, they had all been caught off guard, the zombie hidden from view.

"Jimmy, are you all right?" Henry asked.

Jimmy lowered his arm, looking at the indentation where the ghoul's teeth had left an impression in his jacket sleeve, and he nodded. "Yeah, Henry, I'm fine, got damn lucky, though."

Jimmy climbed out of the car and Cindy ran into his arms. She had seen it happen and was helpless to do anything as the event had happened so fast.

"I'm okay," he told her. "Got careless is all."

Mary walked up next to him. "Thought we were going to lose you, Jimmy. Who would I have to tease then?"

"Don't worry, Mary, I'm not going anywhere. Hey, if I did, then there wouldn't be anyone around to give you a hard time, right?" he chuckled.

"Right," she said and squeezed his shoulder with a smile on her lips.

Henry was dragging the dead zombie out of the car, and he tossed it a little ways to the side, the body landing in a heap. The corpse wore a flannel shirt, jeans, and a down vest. Its boots were tiny, giving him the impression the zombie had been a teenager, probably male. Sue came up to him and they both gazed down at the corpse.

"I wonder who he was," she said, always the mother hen. "Was he alive when he became trapped inside the car? Then turned later? How horrible, to die alone like that."

Henry shifted to look at her, turning her around slowly to see the others as they milled about Jimmy, glad he was okay. Raven said something that had Jimmy laughing and Cindy and Mary joined in. Raven only smiled, subdued as ever.

"See that, Sue? That's all I care about right now. This deader, it's the past. I don't care who it was or why it was out here. Them, and you, that's all that matters to me."

She smiled and kissed his cheek, feeling the scruff of his forming beard on her lips. Splashed with gray, it gave him a look of wisdom.

"I understand what you're saying," she said.

"Good, now let's get back to the others, I want to see if this car can help us or not."

Henry studied the vehicle as he moved around to look into the car now that it was empty. "Maybe some campers owned it. Figured they could leave the keys in the ignition if they were camping or hiking in the area. After all, who would've known it was here? Hell, maybe that deader was one of them and he died and got trapped inside."

Jimmy was in the driver's seat again and he looked at Henry as he placed his hand on the ignition key still in the steering column. "I don't care how it got inside, I'm just glad it's dead. So, you ready for me to try this?"

"Go for it," Henry told him.

Jimmy closed his eyes briefly and his lips moved, fog blowing out of his nose as he breathed. To Henry it looked as if Jimmy was saying a silent prayer. Jimmy opened his eyes and turned the key, but there was nothing. Not so much as a click. He turned it off and tried again, as if that would magically charge the battery, and when still nothing happened, he punched the steering wheel, no horn sounding when his gloved fist hit the center of it.

"Damn it, I swear we're the unluckiest people on the fucking planet."

Henry pushed off from the car, looking at the women. "No go," he said sadly.

"So what now?" Mary asked. "Do we keep going?"

Henry leaned against the car again as he considered for a moment, then his brow furrowed as his mind worked. Countless times in the past, Henry had managed to get them out of tough scrapes with clever ideas and wild plans. Able to think on his feet, he could look at a problem and come up with a solution almost instantly. Sometimes the plans were more dangerous than the problem at hand, but so far he had managed to keep his people alive, so when Mary saw that look on his face, she took a step closer to him.

"I know that look, Henry, what's going on in that mind of yours?"

He pulled his panga and he stood tall. "I'll tell you in a second. It won't matter if it's empty." He then went to Jimmy. "Pop the hood, will ya, buddy?"

"Why?"

"Just do it, and save the twenty questions for later, all right?"

Jimmy shrugged and did what Henry wanted.

Henry went to the hood, opened it, and peered inside. A standard engine, everything looked to be there. He quickly took off the air filter, using the plastic covering that encased the filter, then he went to the fuse box and did the same. The fuse box was square and the covering, when flipped upside down, resembled a rectangular bowl. Then he slammed the hood closed and went to the back of the car. Going to his knees, he began to use the fuse box cover as a shovel and dug out the snow. When he was through a few minutes later, he was able to crawl under the rear bumper, leaving the fuse box cover in the snow.

Everyone watched as he used his panga to puncture the lowest part of the gas tank. It was made of plastic and it took him a few scrapings and twisting of the tip, but a few minutes later, now colder than ever, he managed to make a small hole.

No sooner did the panga slice into the gas tank, then a slow trickle of gas began to seep out of it.

"Hey, give me that fuse box cover, hurry!" he yelled as Mary went and kicked it under for him. He took it and began fidgeting under the car some more, and when he called out for the air filter cover, Sue was there to hand it to him.

The five friends stood for another seven minutes while Henry worked under the rear of the car. All were freezing and wanted desperately to get moving, if for nothing else than to move their bodies to generate some body heat.

Then, Henry began to crawl out, and after he did, he reached back under and slid out the two plastic car parts.

"Jimmy, come take one of these, will ya!" Henry called out as he went to his knees. His back and legs were covered in snow and the slush had soaked him to the bone once more. He could already feel the shivers coming.

Jimmy reached down and picked up the fuse box cover. Inside it was less than a cup of gas. As Henry stood up, he held the air filter cover in his gloved hands, which contained another cup or so of gas.

"What do you plan on doing with this little bit, Henry?" Jimmy asked. "We gonna start a fire?"

Henry grinned as he walked to the interior of the car. "Yeah, you could say that," he said as he set the fuse box cover on the seat and then took Jimmy's from him. He poured Jimmy's gas onto the front seat, then he drew his Glock and pushed everyone away from the car.

"Stand back, I don't know what's gonna happen exactly," he said.

Everyone stepped back, and when they were far enough away, Henry looked up at the sky and mumbled a prayer of his own that his idea would work. Then, he aimed at the fuse box cover sitting on the seat, the gas still in it, and he fired one round directly at it.

The bullet went where he wanted it to and the gas was hit by the speeding round. Friction or a small spark was enough to ignite the gas and a second after he fired, the inside of the car whooshed into a glowing fireball, resembling a small funeral pyre as the fumes ignited.

"Hot damn, it worked!" Henry yelled as he turned to the others. "I don't believe it. Well, come on, come get warm before it goes out. Don't worry, there's no gas left in the tank and I drained the fuel line, too, so there's nothing left to explode."

Sue and Mary were hesitant at first, as if they expected the car to burst into a massive fireball at any moment, but as the others gathered around the flaming car within a few feet of it, they found they couldn't resist its warmth, and so scooted closer.

Henry had his gloves off and had stuck them on a small tree branch he jammed into the slush and snow near the car. Like a clothes line, the gloves soon were drying, as was his clothes as he moved as close to the flames as he dared. Steam rose from his clothes and he felt so hot he wondered if he was cooking, being steamed like a lobster, but he endured it, knowing the time to dry off was short, and the fire would fade when the seats and other burnable items inside the vehicle were used up.

Jimmy, rubbing his hands together, a big smile on his face for a change as he was glad to be warm, moved up next to Henry and said, "Hey, aren't you worried about the fire being seen by someone? Deaders see it and we'll have a shit load of 'em on us and if there're humans around then this is a beacon to our location."

Henry gave Jimmy one of his patented shrugs. "It doesn't matter, Jimmy. What does is that we need to rest and warm up." He patted his younger friend on the shoulder. "One problem at a time, pal."

Jimmy nodded, realizing Henry had a point. All the safety in the world wouldn't matter if they ended up freezing to death.

Raven had slipped away from the group and now she popped back up again. In her hands she held a rabbit, its neck now broken.

As she moved into the circle, she dropped the rabbit in front of Henry, who looked at it and then her with a surprised look.

"I caught it, so you can clean it," she said flatly and then moved away to warm up by the fire.

"Sounds fair," Henry said as he pulled his panga out again and got to work, knowing time to cook it was short.

Soon, one lone rabbit was sitting on a spit a few feet from the fire, the flames licking out the open driver's door and cooking it one side at a time as Henry turned it.

Jimmy, already licking his lips, was rubbing his hands in expectation.

Ten minutes later, as the flames began to recede; the six companions shared the single rabbit. It was burnt in some places and still rare in others, as was the case with an uneven open flame, but it tasted fantastic.

Though it was hardly enough to fulfill them, it did quiet their hunger pains for a small time, and with more snow eaten to fill their empty bellies, for just a little while, they were relatively fed and warm.

When the fire died down to nothing but embers and there was no longer enough heat to stay warm, the six companions set off once more.

Though their hunger was still there and exhaustion was prevalent, for the moment, they were in high spirits. Their boots had been dried in the fire, though Jimmy's were a little singed when he had put them too close to the flames, and each of them was now relatively warm and dry.

After an hour of leaving the burnt car behind, the cold set in once more and the warmth of the blaze was just a memory.

Plodding through the forest, they continued onward, single file the easiest way to traverse the path Henry had found. Signs of life were spotted, spores from deer and coyote.

Henry was on point, with Mary, behind him, followed by Sue, Raven, Cindy and then Jimmy, who was the rear guard.

Three hours of continuous walking later, and everyone on the verge of collapse, Henry came out of a dense tree line to find he was on the remains of an old road.

The pavement was cracking and flaking away on the edges and there was just the hint of a white double line still visible running down its middle.

The road led two ways. Higher up into the mountains, or downward to parts unknown. Given their state of exhaustion, downward was the direction Henry chose, the others all agreeing completely.

As they marched side by side in pairs of two, Jimmy kept turning around. He had the feeling he was being watched, but each time he turned, there was nothing there.

"You okay?" Henry asked him one time when he saw his friend spin around abruptly.

"Yeah, I just...I think we're being watched."

Henry nodded. "Yeah, I have that feeling, too, but then I caught a look at what it was."

Jimmy gripped his shotgun tighter as he began to flick his eyes back and forth. "Shit, really? So what's the plan? When do we double-back and get them?"

Henry smiled as he shook his head. "There's not a *them* to get, Jimmy. It's one deader. It's off to our right and for some reason it hasn't come out of the brush." He gestured to the right, at the edge of the tree line, and nodded to a large patch of shrubs they were passing, most of the branches flattened by the heavy snow.

"Look past those bushes and you can see it. It's a sorry specimen if I ever saw one. The only reason I haven't taken it out is it's not worth the trouble."

Jimmy flicked his gaze to where Henry was gesturing, and sure enough, he soon spotted a lone ghoul staggering through the snow. From where he was on the road, Jimmy thought the ghoul looked like a lost child in the woods and he could see why Henry wasn't bothering with it.

"So what? We just let it follow us?"

Henry nodded. "Yeah, if it comes too close we can deal with it, otherwise, leave it be." He turned to look Jimmy in the eyes.

"We've been through this before, Jimmy. We can't kill all of 'em, so we need to have some restraint."

Jimmy's face took on a serious look and his voice grew low as he said, "That's your rule, Henry, not mine. If I have my way, then every damn one of those fuckers will be put down by my hand sooner or later."

Henry raised his left hand, his index finger pointed at Jimmy. "And I respect that, just as long as your plan doesn't endanger the rest of us."

"Understood," he replied. "Then you have no complaint if I wanna take care of that bastard?"

Henry looked at Mary and Sue who were walking together. They had both heard the conversation, but were staying out of it. Henry turned back to Jimmy. "It's your choice, Jimmy. If you want to expend the energy to take down one lone deader then knock yourself out."

Jimmy grinned widely. "Can I borrow your panga?"

"Sure, he ya go," Henry said and pulled it from its sheath and handed it to him hilt first. "But make sure you clean it before you give it back."

"Done," Jimmy smiled, turned to look at Cindy, pointed to the forest, and said, "I'm gonna get me a dead one." Then he jogged off the road and into the brush as the others watched him go.

Cindy moved up next to Henry, with Mary and Sue already gathered close to him, but Henry hadn't stopped walking to wait for Jimmy to deal with the zombie.

"Aren't we going to wait for him?" Cindy asked as she began walking backwards so she could keep Jimmy in sight.

Henry shook his head no. "If he wants to do this, then he can, but I'm not gonna stop and wait. I told him it was a waste of time. I'm not his father."

"But you're the leader of us, aren't you?" Mary interjected.

Henry glanced over his shoulder to Mary; he shrugged. "If I'm the leader then he would've done what I said. So there's your answer, I guess. Now, I'm gonna keep going, you can stay and wait or come with me."

Cindy stopped walking and crossed her arms over her chest. "Well, if there's a choice, I'll wait for Jimmy, in case he needs some help."

Mary and Sue looked at Henry, then at Jimmy's back as he stomped through the snow and then back to each other.

"Henry's right, Cindy," Mary said. "Jimmy was asked to leave it alone and he didn't. You stay and watch his back, the rest of us are going to keep walking. Catch up when he's done."

Cindy looked to Raven as the girl walked past her. "Raven, are you going, too?"

Raven shrugged. "Waste of time, it's not bothering us, not worth the risk. I'll keep going, too."

"Fine, then go, we'll catch up," Cindy said.

Henry was ten feet away and still walking. But he stopped and turned around. "Hey, Cindy, watch his back good, you know how he gets."

Cindy's visage softened at his words and she nodded. "It wouldn't be the first time I had to save his ass," she said with a grin.

"Okay," Henry said. "If you take too long we'll see about taking a break down the road if we can find a good place to stop, give you a chance to catch up. If you run into real trouble fire off a few shots and we'll come running."

"Done," she said, and began walking back the way they'd come, wanting to reach Jimmy before he did something stupid.

Henry watched her go, then he turned and continued on, his boots slapping the slush and snow, careful not to slip on the hidden ice beneath the crust of white.

He felt a pang of regret for continuing on, but if he gave in this time, then before he knew it there would be an argument about this and that and soon there would be a discussion about everything. Though they were basically a democracy, he was still the leader and any good team knew only one person could call the shots. Too many decision makers and there was no time to act, only discuss, and in the end that could get them all killed.

As Henry walked along a bend in the road, he glanced over his shoulder one last time, hoping he hadn't made a mistake by leaving

Jimmy and Cindy behind, no matter how foolhardy Jimmy was being.

Jimmy climbed over the snow drift separating him from the ghoul, kicking snow out of his way as he walked.

Glancing over his shoulder, he saw the others walking away, but also saw that Cindy was staying behind. He felt a well of love growing inside for her, one even greater than before; she was watching his back.

The ghoul slowed its shamble and turned to face Jimmy. As Jimmy moved closer to it, he saw it was in very bad shape. One arm was missing, only a jagged stump exposed to the weather, and one leg looked as if it was broken. As the zombie walked, the leg dragged behind it like a lifeless tree branch, leaving marks in the snow.

Its face was the worst of all. The skin had dried into a brown, leathery parchment, the lips pulled back to expose the gums beneath. Bits of flesh, now dried, still protruded from the yellow and brown teeth, and its nose hung askew, waiting for the right moment to fall off completely.

Its eyes were sunken, pools of white, and both ears were missing.

The actual body was so emaciated the ghoul resembled a walking skeleton and as Jimmy moved to within a few feet of it, he wondered how it was able to keep moving in such a decomposed state. But then he put such trivial thoughts from his mind, raised the panga, and lunged at the ghoul, slicing its head off in one meaty *thwack*.

The head fell into the snow to disappear in a snow drift and the body toppled over to twitch for a moment and remain still.

"Too fucking easy," he muttered to himself, his breath blowing out in a thick cloud. "That's one less of you bastards in the world."

Suddenly, Cindy shouted and he glanced over his shoulder to see what she wanted, and he spotted her waving to him from the road. But now her rifle was up and she was aiming it at him and he didn't understand why, when without warning, she fired at him.

Standing perfectly still, not comprehending why on earth she would want to shoot him, he felt the bullet whine by his ear and a second later his body reacted and he dropped to the snow-covered ground.

"What the fuck, Cindy! What's going on!"

She replied by firing again and again, the bullets flying over his head like angry hornets. Though he couldn't imagine what had gotten into her, he swung his shotgun from off his shoulder and was about to bring it to bare on her, for if she was trying to kill him he had no choice, when he heard footsteps crunching behind him in the snow crusted layer covering the forest floor.

He spun around quickly, and his eyes went wide when he saw five ghouls stumbling toward him, each in different stages of decomposition. No sooner did he spot them then two of their heads exploded, the faces dissolving in a glorious spray of brown, rotting brains and skull fragments.

As gobbets of flesh splattered the pristine snow, Jimmy realized Cindy wasn't shooting at him, but at the roamers that had appeared as if by magic in the woods, exactly at his position.

As the three remaining ghouls came at him, he rolled to the right and used his shotgun to devastating effect.

One blast took a ghoul in the midsection, sheering off the upper torso from the lower half, and the ghoul tumbled over like a fallen tree. The legs kicked for a few second as intestines painted the snow a dark color that once might have been the blood.

The last two zombies Jimmy shot in the head, the shotgun blasts ripping off the heads and blowing them into a hundred bloody fragments. As the headless bodies fell forward, a dark ichor seeping from the stumps, he rolled to his knees and waved to Cindy, who returned it and lowered her rifle, seeing that the threat was over.

Jimmy stood up, and he saw another four ghouls now very dead with headshots lying a few feet away from the first group. These were the targets Cindy was shooting at and he didn't want to think what might have happened if she hadn't been there to look out for him.

Turning, he jogged back to her, cresting a snow drift to practically have her fall into his arms.

"Oh, Christ, Jimmy, I thought you were a goner for sure," she said as she hugged him.

"I might have been if not for you," he replied as he hugged her. "You saved my ass yet again, baby."

"That ass is mine, lover, and I'll be damned if any old deader is gonna bite it off." She kissed him on the lips and he felt her warmth. "If anyone's gonna bite it off, it's gonna be me."

He laughed and pushed her aside, bringing up his shotgun at the sound of footsteps coming back up the road.

Cindy spun around and leveled her M-16, the two lovers ready to send the next attackers on the last train west, when Henry, followed by the others, rounded the bend, their weapons drawn and a look of concern on their faces.

Jimmy waved that there was no cause for alarm and he and Cindy began walking to meet the others.

"What the hell was all that shooting?" Henry called as he slowed and stopped in front of Jimmy and Cindy.

"Nothing, Henry, it was nothing," Jimmy said. "It looked like that deader wasn't alone after all. When I went to put it down, a few more popped up. Cindy took care of most of 'em and I got the rest with my baby here." Jimmy patted his shotgun lovingly. He loved the way the shotgun was a room sweeper, and he didn't have to particularly aim with the weapon. Just point in the general area and let loose, and nature would take its course, by shredding whatever was in front of him.

"No kidding?" Henry asked. "See, I told you to leave it be," he said, angry. "You could have gotten yourself killed, and for what?"

"Henry, leave it, it's over," Mary said by his side as behind them, Sue and Raven were just catching up.

"No, Mary, he should have listened to me. What would have happened if he had gotten bit or worse? And for what? To take down one more deader in a world that's full of 'em." Henry turned to face Jimmy. "You were reckless and you jeopardized us all."

"Hey, old man," Jimmy snapped, "just wait a fucking minute. It's my life and if I want to risk it, that's my business."

Henry shook his head, his eyes flaring with rage, but then, he caught himself and paused, as if he was counting from one to ten to calm down a little.

"No, Jimmy, it's not your life. When we agreed to travel together then all our lives belong to each other. I thought you'd learned that by now. I guess I was wrong." He turned away and began walking. "I'm done talking to someone that doesn't want to listen. Make sure my panga is clean and give it back to me later." He joined with Sue and Raven and headed back down the road.

"Henry, wait!" Jimmy called but Mary touched his arm and shook her head. "Don't, Jimmy, just let it go for now. When he calms down later you can talk to him some more. You know how he gets. In the end, he wasn't trying to control you, he just didn't want anything to happen to you, not for such a stupid reason."

"Maybe so, Mary, but it's my reason, and if I believe it's worth it then I have a right to do what I want," Jimmy said.

She shrugged. "Maybe, but Henry has a point. If you get hurt, it would be him and the rest of us that would have to take care of you. Hell, Henry would carry you on his back until we found help if he had to. You know that. So before you go 'head and say it's your right, just think about that one." She glanced at Cindy and winked, the two women sharing a nod, then she turned and began jogging after the others, leaving Jimmy and Cindy to stand alone once more.

Jimmy scratched his cheek, as he wiped away a small piece of bone fragment from his face.

"Shit, Cindy, what do think about this? Do you take their side, too?"

She shook her head. "I'm on your side, babe, that's all that matters. As for who's right or wrong…" she shrugged. "Come on, the others are getting quite a lead on us, we better get moving, too."

She took his left arm in hers as they began walking down the road, the snow now crushed and disturbed from the companions' boots.

"That was nice shootin', babe," Jimmy commented as they walked. "Ya know, for a brief moment there, I almost thought you were shooting at me."

She chuckled at his statement and pulled him closer, hugging him. "Aw, baby, you might make me want to kill you sometimes but I would never do it. I love you too much."

He opened his mouth for a rebuttal, but then closed it again. Thinking about it for a second, he didn't really know how to reply to her statement, so he decided for once in his life to just shut up.

The two walked on in silence, and upon turning the bend in the road, they soon spotted the others, each walking in pairs once more.

They picked up their pace to catch up.

It was Sue who spotted the small light through the trees.

The drizzle had slowed to the point it was nonexistent, and with night having descended, the road was hidden, only a dim outline to separate it from the tree line.

As they traversed the road, it opened up so that one side became nothing but a steep incline. If one of them accidentally wandered off the road in the dark, there would be no way for them to rescale the hill and return to the others.

So Henry had everyone stay as close to the opposite side as possible, and even then, with no light, they would wander away from the side only to be pulled back by one of the group.

The road wound downwards, twisting and turning constantly until the companions had no idea in what direction they were heading.

And then Sue spotted the light in the midst of the trees when she accidentally wandered too close to the edge of the incline, Henry pulling her back before she could slip off. At first she assumed it was a reflection, perhaps of some moonlight that had cut through the cloud cover, but then, as she continued walking, she saw it again and again. No matter where she moved, the light remained, and she finally told the others of her discovery.

"Could be trouble," Mary suggested as she looked out into the woods at the light, the others by her side.

Henry grunted an ascent. "True, but it's not like we have a lot of options here, people. We need shelter and food and that's our best chance at finding it."

"So, what?" Jimmy asked. "We just go over there and hope for the best?"

Henry shook his head, and then realizing Jimmy could see him, he said, "No, Jimmy. When we get closer, you all stay behind and I'll go find out what I can. If we all go to that light in the dark, we could end up blundering in on some cannie camp or who the hell knows what else. I'll go alone, and if it's safe, I'll signal for you to follow."

"What kind of a signal?" Cindy asked.

Henry gave it a quick thought and said, "I'll have whoever's out there douse the light. If it goes out for a few seconds and then comes back on, that means it's safe to follow me."

"And what if the light doesn't go out?" Sue asked with concern.

Henry didn't hesitate this time. "Then I'm dead, and you should move on, and try to find what I had no luck in finding …someplace safe."

"Oh, Henry," Sue said, but he stopped her.

"That's how it is, Sue, you know that. There's no use talking about it." He looked at the outlines of each of the group in the dark. "So, are we all onboard with this?"

No one disagreed, as it was the most prudent way to find out if it was safe. Better they lose one member than all of them.

"Yeah, Henry," Jimmy said. "But I've got one thing to say."

"Go 'head."

"If that light doesn't go out, and that means your dead, I know those bastards are gonna pay…in blood."

Henry reached out and touched Jimmy's shoulder so his friend would know he was reaching for him, then he lowered his hand so the two could shake. "Jimmy, I wouldn't have it any other way."

Henry made his way down a well used path, now covered in snow, and paused for a moment to glance over his shoulder. He could just make out the small glade where his friends were waiting for him.

Turning back around, he continued walking.

When he came to the light Sue had spotted from the road a few minutes later, he saw it was an oil lantern, hanging from a black, steel post.

The lantern signified the beginnings of a gravel driveway, most of it cleared of snow so a person could walk easily.

The driveway was lined on both sides with rhododendrons, their leaves dripping wet and in the darkness resembling green, protruding tongues with mouths hidden just behind them. Henry had the feeling he was walking into the lair of a giant monster, those mouths just waiting to devour him alive.

Though the bushes seemed to press in on him, he shrugged off his wild imagination, and continued walking up the driveway, his boots crunching on the crushed gravel.

The driveway was long, and as he followed it, he began catching glimpses though the gaps in the bushes and trees of a building, its framework made of stone and iron.

As he rounded a tight corner, he found himself looking up at a grand old house, two stories with ornate architecture, a pitched roof, a heavy wooden front door, and a foundation made of concrete blocks.

Though heavy curtains were drawn over the first floor windows, light seeped through the cracks, and when Henry turned around to look behind him, he saw nothing but wilderness. The house was tucked away so far into the woods that it couldn't be detected unless someone knew exactly where to search for it, which made him wonder why the occupants would want to have a light on a post advertising there location.

Looking up, silhouetted against the dark sky, he saw the brick chimney, and smoke rising from it, indicating a fire was going somewhere in the house. Just thinking about sitting in front of a roaring fire had Henry sighing with pleasure.

As he stood in the driveway, admiring the home and wondering who could be living inside it, the subtlest hint of music floated on the air, and as he listened more intently, he heard the distinctive sound of a piano playing.

He realized standing there would get him nothing, so with a deep breath, he walked up to the ornate porch with ten stone steps, climbed them, and stood in front of the large main door. It was made of oak or some other heavy wood, varnished with a dark stain, and there was a bronze doorknocker set at head height in the shape of an eagle, the round ring to use for knocking hanging out of the bird's beak.

He checked his Glock to make sure it was where it was supposed to be, then let his hand drop down to his panga. If there was trouble, he could only pray he would have time to draw his weapons.

He reached out and knocked three times, as if he was a salesman dropping by to see if the homeowner wanted to buy the latest vacuum cleaner, knife set or encyclopedia collection.

Then, he waited.

Immediately, the music stopped from inside the house and Henry heard nothing but silence.

He waited for almost a full minute, wondering what he should do next. Should he knock again? That seemed pointless as the homeowner obviously knew he was on the porch, or should he just leave, deciding it was all a mistake.

But when he felt how cold he was as well as knowing how bad off the others were, he knew that wasn't really an option.

It was while he wrestled with what to do next that he heard the door click as someone began to unlock it. It took a while, as the locks were many, and it didn't surprise Henry at all. This secluded in the forest, good locks would have been a necessity even before the world fell apart.

It was as he waited for the locks to stop clicking that the door was suddenly thrown open, and before he could so much as reach for his Glock, he found himself staring down the muzzle of a very large shotgun.

"You so much as move a muscle and you're dead," a voice said from within the shadows of the house.

Henry thought that was an excellent idea.

"Shit, it's been almost a half hour and the light still hasn't gone out," Jimmy said worriedly. "Something's happened to Henry, I just know it."

The five companions were standing around, cold and impatient as they waited for the signal from Henry that it was safe to approach whatever lay beyond the light.

"Relax, Jimmy," Mary said softly, calmly. "He's fine; we need to give him time. Whoever he meets, he's going to have to explain carefully that there are five more armed people in the woods. If he doesn't do it right, whoever's out there might think we're raiders, or worse."

"I don't know, Mary, maybe Jimmy's right," Cindy said. "It has been a while and if something's happened and all we did was sit here and wait..."

Mary shook her head. "No, we wait here like Henry said."

"But I'm freezing my ass off out here," Jimmy said as he slapped his gloved hands together."

"We all are, Jimmy," Sue added, sitting next to Raven on a fallen tree, as the teenage girl passed the time by honing her fingernails with a nail file. A few needed tending to after the fight with the zombies.

Sue happened to glance toward the light, and when she did, she saw it blink out. "Hey, the light's gone out."

All eyes went to the light far off in the woods and each waited, praying this was the signal from Henry. Mary was counting softly, her lips moving, and when she reached ten seconds, the light came back on.

"That's it, that's the signal, thank God he's okay," Mary said as she let out the breath she was holding.

Jimmy went to the front of the group and jumped up and down like a kid going to the circus. "So, come on, let's go already, what the hell are you all waiting for? Man, I can't wait to get warm."

"What makes you think there's a place there to get warm?" Cindy asked.

"Wishful thinking, babe, wishful thinking."

Cindy and Mary looked at one another in the gloom of the forest and both smiled at each other. "Think it's safe?" Cindy asked her.

Mary shrugged, a gesture she'd picked up from Henry. "Guess it has to be or else Henry would never have signaled us?"

"That's true," Cindy added, and with Sue and Raven by her and Mary's side, they headed off in the direction of the light, not knowing what was there, but knowing if Henry had signaled them, it must be safe.

Fifteen minutes earlier.

Henry swallowed the knot in his throat as he stared down the muzzle of the shotgun, a wisp of gray hair appearing out of the shadows behind the weapon.

"Who are you? What do you want?" a voice asked, and Henry immediately knew it was a woman, old if he was correct.

"My…" Henry began and then cleared his throat as he regained some of his composure. From his experience in the new world, he was fairly certain if the old woman had wanted him dead, then she would have fired upon opening the door.

"My name's Henry Watson. I'm a traveler. I saw your light at the end of the driveway and I was hoping you could spare some food, maybe a warm place to sleep for the night. My friends and I…"

"What friends?" the woman demanded. "Where are they?"

Henry decided all or nothing was what was needed here and he went for the former, so he continued. "My friends are waiting for me to signal them if it's safe to come here. We didn't know what was here and didn't want to arrive in a group." He tried to smile, despite the shotgun in his face. "Thought it would be better if I just came alone first and said hello."

The old woman leveled the shotgun for another moment and then abruptly lowered it. As she stepped closer to him, he could see her smiling.

"Why didn't you say so, dear. There always room for hungry mouths at my dinner table. We love guests. You'll have to forgive me, I thought you might have been from town."

"Town?" he asked, curious.

"Yes, dear. About twelve miles from here." She waved it away as if it meant nothing. "It doesn't matter, what does is that you're cold and hungry. Where are my manners? You go get your friends and have them come back; I'll put a pot of tea on while I'm waiting for your return."

Henry nodded. "Thank you, that's mighty generous of you. I'll be back in a few minutes."

"Take your time, dear, we'll be here."

He paused that time at her use of the term *we*. If there had been others in the house, he would have expected them to have shown themselves at the sound of him knocking. Deciding the old woman must be a little *off*, he ignored the term, and with a wave, went to signal the others that it was safe to come to the house.

Her name was Abigail Yorkshire and she was seventy-two years old. Her silver hair was done up in a bun and her cheeks were red, like small apples, her kind eyes always seeming to be looking at you when you looked the other way. She had a wide smile, too perfect, and Henry assumed they were dentures.

She wore a flowing black dress and a large silver necklace. On the end of it was a locket in which she told the companions there was a picture of her and her husband, Philmore. That was the *we* she referred to, her husband, who she said was always with her and thus why she referred to herself as *we*.

After washing up in simple basins of water taken from an underground well located at the rear of the house, the six companions were now sitting in the dining room of the old house, each waiting for Abigail to return with the main course of the meal she had offered them before they would retire to their bedrooms for the night. She had told them that the house was quite large and there was plenty of room for everyone.

All of the companions felt as if they had hit the lottery, back when such things still existed.

The meal had started out with a hearty salad of home grown lettuce, complete with ripe cherry tomatoes. Abigail had a greenhouse and grew her own vegetables. The dressing was a simple oil and vinegar, taken from the large pantry stockpiled with flour, sugar and other canned necessities for survival.

All eyes looked up when Abigail wheeled in a table, and on it was large steel tureen filled more than halfway with a rich stew. More vegetables were in ceramic side dishes; carrots, green beans and onions.

To the companions, after traveling for so long and only having their meager rations, it was a feast fit for a king and they dug in happily the instant Abigail ladled out a bowl full.

"Please, eat all you want, my friends. I imagine after your journey through the mountains you must be famished. There's plenty for all, so don't be shy."

"No worries, there, ma'am," Jimmy said and dove in, shoveling spoonful after spoonful into his mouth. It was so hot he burned his tongue but he didn't care, so pleased to be eating real food. The gravy was a dark brown with bits of flour still in it, reminding him of a homemade stew his mother used to make. Jimmy finished off his first bowl and quickly asked for more, receiving it without question.

"So, Abigail," Henry began as he swallowed a mouthful of stew. The spices were so strong he could barely taste the meat, but it was still hot and good, filling his stomach so he was already content after only a few mouthfuls. "How do you manage out here all alone? Especially with all the snow."

Abigail smiled at Henry and her eyes filled with sweetness. "Oh, my, Henry, that's so kind of you to ask, but this old house is made of stern stock. We've managed just fine out here."

Mary spoke up. "You do know what's happened out in the rest of the world, don't you?"

Abigail nodded, her smile vanishing as sadness filled her eyes. "Oh, my dear, of course I do. We have television and radio, well, we did before they stopped working. We've even seen a few of those dead people now and then. They wander in from the mountains. I suppose it's just luck that has them finding this house, but they're easy to put down." She shook her head. "It's so horrible, but we've learned to adapt to our new world, each in his own way, am I right?" She looked to Henry with her question.

"Yes, ma'am, I would have to agree with you on that one," Henry replied.

Jimmy finished off his second helping and picked up his bowl. "Can I have some more, please?"

"Jimmy, don't be a pig," Cindy said next to him. She was eating only some of the stew, not finding the spices to her liking, the vegetable side dishes were more her preferred taste. After eating some of the stew, the spices disagreed with her to the point she had only eaten a little, finding after all this time to not have much of an appetite.

"Oh, no, dear," Abigail said, "it's perfectly fine, as I said, there's plenty for all." She stood up from her seat at the head of the table and ladled Jimmy another heaping bowl full.

"It is good," Sue said as she took a bite. "Do you grow the spices as well?"

"Yes, dear, but some are dried, I will have to admit."

"Oh, of course," Sue added and continued eating. As she finished her bowl, she suddenly felt exhausted and Henry noticed this.

"Are you all right, Sue?" he asked.

She wiped her brow with her cloth napkin. "Yes, I'm fine, I just...I guess now that we finally have a safe place to rest and with food in me, I think it's all catching up to me."

Henry nodded. "You know, now that you mention it, I am feeling wiped out."

"Me, too," Raven said simply.

"Yeah, I could go for a nap right about now," Jimmy said and in fact his eyes looked as if he could barely keep them open.

Abigail glanced at Cindy and saw she hadn't eaten very much and said, "My dear, what's the matter, don't you like my cooking?"

"Huh? Oh, yes, it's fine, it's just...I'm not a fan of some of the spices and herbs you put in the stew. I don't think they're sitting too well with me."

For just a moment, Abigail's sweet look vanished, but then it quickly reappeared.

"Oh, well, I put ginger, fennel, some lemon balm, a pinch of oregano and basil to name a few. Perhaps some of the dried spices had gotten too old. They say that can happen." She stared at Cindy, as if her *will* alone could make her eat.

Cindy, feeling uncomfortable by the old woman's glare, picked up her spoon and took a small bite. She licked her lips and smiled, nodding her head as she went in for another spoonful.

Abigail, seeing Cindy was now eating, looked away and began talking to Henry once more.

Cindy saw that Jimmy was about done with his third bowl of stew so she quickly reached out and switched bowls with him. "Here, lover, you can have mine, too."

"Oh, thanks, babe, I was just gonna ask for more." He dug in, barely slowing down to chew. She shook her head at seeing him eat like a ten-year-old, his mouth and chin covered with gravy. She handed him a cloth napkin and told him to wipe his face.

"Shit, Cindy, lighten' up, enjoy the grub," he said as he finished off her bowl. With four bowls of stew in him, he finally felt full and he burped, a quick, "excuse me," following it.

"That's our Jimmy, always a gentleman," Mary said, the others chuckling.

"Ha, ha, Mary, you're hilarious," Jimmy said and looked to Abigail. "Man, that was awesome stew, what kind of meat was that? It tasted like pork but it was hard to tell with all the spices."

Abigail nodded. "You're right on the first try, my boy. We have a few pigs out back and we kill one now and then for the meat."

"Well, it was awesome," Jimmy replied and stretched. "Man, I'm ready to go to sleep," he yawned, setting off a domino effect as each of the others then yawned. "I could go to bed right now."

"I was hoping we could all adjourn to the sitting room and have a nightcap. I have a bottle of brandy I've been itching to crack open," Abigail suggested.

Stifling a yawn, Henry nodded, then looked at each of the others, seeing the same weariness in their faces that he felt in his own. "Okay, that would be fine, but I don't think any of us could go past that. Your cooking is just too good, Abigail."

She waved his compliment away. "Oh, please, it's passable at best." She stood up and led them into a sitting room after walking down a short hallway.

A fireplace was in the corner and behind the metal grating, a fire roared, filling the room with warmth. The walls were adorned with oil paintings and a rich, plush sofa lined another wall. Two more arm chairs completed the furniture and there was more than enough room for everyone. A small end table was in the corner, and Cindy went to it and looked at the framed photos set out on top of it. She saw Abigail in them and another person, a man.

"Is this your husband?" Cindy asked as she picked up one of the photos and studied it. The man in the picture was tall, over six feet, and he had a receding hairline and smile wrinkles around his mouth. He looked happy, they both did.

Abigail went to her and took the frame back, then set it back down in the same exact spot. "Yes, dear, that's my Philmore."

Abigail went to a waist high cabinet with bottles of liquor lined up on top of it, and picked one of the glass bottles, then opened the cabinet and took out seven glasses. The glasses were made of Waterford crystal. They were thin to the point they looked like if they were squeezed too hard by a hand, they would shatter.

She opened the bottle and poured an inch of gold liquid into each glass, then, with the glasses on a silver tray, she walked the room, each of the companions taking one.

"To your health," Abigail said as she raised her glass and each of the companions did the same. As she drank hers, the others did also, and soon a growing warmth filled their insides.

The alcohol went right to Henry's head, despite his full stomach. "Wow, that's strong, either that or I've become a lightweight," he said, his words slurred slightly.

"Ha, probably both," Jimmy said and smacked his lips.

Mary shook her head to clear it, the fogginess closing in. God she was tired. "Henry," she said. "I can't keep my eyes open anymore and I think the brandy was about it for me. I need to go lay down."

"Me, too," Sue added. "I didn't realize how truly tired I was until after eating."

"Yeah, I have to agree with you guys," Henry said.

Raven nodded as did Cindy.

Abigail set her empty glass down, picked up the silver tray, and collected everyone's glasses. An oil lamp sat on a nearby table and she picked it up, then moved to the wide archway leading back out to the hallway.

"Where are my manners. I'm so sorry. Of course you're all exhausted. I've just been so starved for company here that I'm being selfish. Truth be told, I also retire early as there isn't much to do after the sun goes down but read, and I try to save the fuel for the fires and there are only so many candles. Come, come, I'll show you to your rooms and in the morning, we can talk some more."

On unsteady legs, each of the companions rose from their seats and followed Abigail down a long hallway to a large, sweeping staircase leading to the second floor.

"Feel free to take any of the rooms upstairs with the exception of the very last room. That's mine," she said. "There is also a bathroom upstairs but of course there's no running water. A bucket in the tub can be used to flush, but only if absolutely necessary. We all have to rough it now, I'm afraid." She was on the first step, looking at each of the companions now gathered in a group. "Oh, by the way, would you like to leave your weapons with me for safe-keeping? I could store them until tomorrow, that way there won't be any *accidents* in the middle of the night." She eyed Henry's panga. "That is a handsome knife you have there, Henry. What is that, a machete?"

"Panga, and thank you, but we'd prefer to hold onto our weapons."

Abigail's face seemed to grow hard as if storm clouds had rolled in on a clear morning, but it was for less than a second, a smile quickly appearing like a summer's day. "Of course, of course, it was just an idea, don't worry about it. Well, off you go to your beds. There are twin beds and full ones depending on what room you take."

"We'll figure it out, thank you, Abigail. You've been very kind," Mary added as she yawned, covering her hand with her mouth. "Oh, wow, I can't stop yawning," she said as she saw Jimmy and Cindy doing the same after seeing her.

Henry nodded. "Tell me about it, I can barely keep my eyes open."

Abigail turned and walked down the stairs past Henry and the others. "Then go on, and sleep tight. I have a few things to clean up from dinner before I retire. It's not often we have so many guests staying here. I have to tell you this is quite a treat."

"We're just glad we found you," Henry said as he began to climb the stairs with Sue on his arm. "Goodnight."

"Goodnight, dear, sleep tight, all of you."

The companions climbed the stairs, Jimmy barely able to put one foot in front of the other, he was so tired. Cindy helped him along. She was tired too but not as much as the others seemed to be. She didn't give it much thought as she reached the landing and pointed to a door. "Me and Jimmy will take that one, Henry. If I have to carry him another three feet he's gonna fall over."

"Fine, Cindy, go 'head. Me and Sue will take that one and Raven and Mary can have the one next to us."

"Sounds good," Mary said and walked past him to the indicated door, swaying a little as if drunk with Raven by her side. Both went in without another word, the door clinking softly once more.

"Henry," Cindy called. "Are we gonna have someone on watch tonight?"

Henry yawned loudly, and shook his head to fight off the grogginess suffusing his body. "Nah, Cindy, we should be safe enough here. If Abigail wanted to do us harm, there's been ample opportunity, don't you think?"

"Yeah, I guess so, okay, I need to get Jimmy to bed." She opened her door and shoved Jimmy inside, then with a wave, she was in and closed the door.

Henry did the same, and soon he was closing the door to his room and looking at Sue.

"I hope you don't mind if I don't want to wash up some more before bed, Sue," Henry said as he stepped into the bedroom. A full-size bed greeted him, and it was as if it was screaming at him to fall into it.

She shook her head. "No, not tonight, you can skip it," she replied "I don't think I have the energy to wash up either." She was sitting in a chair near the window, bent over as she took off her boots, and she realized Henry hadn't replied to her. "Henry? Did you hear me? I said it's..." she stopped short and grinned widely. Henry was lying face down on the bed, his eyes closed, his mouth hanging open, sleeping soundly.

She went to him, took off his boots and took a spare blanket from a side chair, then after covering him up, she climbed into bed. She kissed him once on the cheek, the man not so much as stirring. Then she stretched out and closed her eyes.

She was out in seconds.

Cindy carried Jimmy across the bedroom and dropped him on the first twin bed. His body fell half on, half off, but he didn't stir; he was already sleeping. She went to him, wanting to get him on the bed better. As it was now, only his upper half was on the bed, his knees on the floor. For all purposes, he looked like a small boy praying at the side of his bed; only he had decided to rest his head.

She tried once but he was just dead weight and finally she gave up. Pulling the blanket off the bed, she draped it around him.

"Good enough," she breathed heavily as she kicked off her boots and went to the other bed.

Stretching out, she closed her eyes, but though she was exhausted, sleep wouldn't come. Her mouth was bone dry and she began to feel a headache, the steady throbbing just behind her eyes.

Jimmy began to snore and she let out a large sigh, not understanding why she couldn't fall asleep. She was definitely tired enough, she knew that, and by the way the others had looked, she figured they were probably all fast asleep by now, just like Jimmy.

She lay silently, her hands on her stomach, her headache pounding for almost a half hour when she began to hear an odd noise floating in from somewhere in the house.

It was a sound she couldn't put her finger on. A *thunk* sound.

At first she ignored it, as it wasn't her problem. Maybe Abigail was working in the kitchen?

But then she felt pressure on her bladder and realized she needed to pee.

But exhausted as she was, she still tried to ignore all the distractions and squeezed her eyes tighter, as if she could make sleep come.

The *thunk* sound repeated itself, steady, like a heartbeat every minute or so.

Cindy sat up, another heavy sigh escaping her lips. Between the thunks, Jimmy's snoring, her headache, and the need to pee, she knew there was no way she would be sleeping any time soon. Plus, she had a feeling she was now overtired, and that all she would be doing is wasting time if she didn't want to admit it to herself.

Figuring the bathroom should be first, she slid out of bed and padded to the door. She glanced at her boots, lying like two dead carcasses in the gloom at the foot of the bed, but decided to leave them. It wasn't like she was going outside, just to the end of the hallway.

With a brief look at Jimmy, she saw he was sleeping heavily, a thin line of drool now collecting under his mouth and saturating the sheet, and she opened the door and stepped into the hallway.

The hardwood was cold on her feet and she felt a chill go up her spine from the soles of her feet.

In the gloom of the hallway, she quietly walked to the bathroom, did her business and then returned to her bedroom door.

She was about to go inside when she heard the *thunk* sound again.

Her curiosity getting the better of her, she padded to the stairs and went down them, careful to stay on the outer edges of each step so as to avoid any creaking steps. She needn't have feared this, as the stairs were made from old world craftsmanship and were solid as the day they were built.

Walking through the house, she ended up in the back, and found a door cracked a few inches. As she studied the door, to her it looked like the door was supposed to be closed, because a cold breeze was blowing into the house through the opening. Peering into the doorway, she saw a set of stairs leading down to what had to be the basement, the darkness all but complete, a dull glow coming from somewhere at the bottom.

Another *thunk* sound came to her and Cindy bit her lip, wondering if she should go get Henry.

Whoever was down there had left the door open by accident and the noise of their work was filtering into the house. As she felt the edge of the door, she saw it was heavy, and if it had been closed, the noise would not have reached her upstairs.

This was a mystery and Cindy was a curious woman.

Deciding she would check out whatever was going on and if it was somehow serious, she would go get Henry, she began walking down the stairs. The third one down creaked and she paused, hoping she hadn't been heard, and when the *thunk* came to her again, she knew she was fine.

She continued downward.

At the bottom of the stairs she found herself in the basement, just as she'd figured and her eyes took in all the odds and ends. A small oil lantern hung on the far wall, lit but turned down low, and it gave off just enough light to see her surroundings easily.

Her eyes played over old boxes, a small workbench with tools, and other miscellaneous items one would expect to find in a cellar.

The *thunk* noise came to her again and she turned her head to the right, seeing the outline of an outer door.

Her feet were cold on the concrete floor but she ignored it, wanting to know what that damn noise was. There was a hammer on the workbench and she picked it up, wanting to have something as a weapon out of habit. She had seen too much in the past two years to travel unarmed, and regretted not taking her sidearm with her. Even her knife would have been better than nothing.

Reaching the door, she opened it slowly, the cold frigid air flowing over her and causing her to get the chills. She might have closed the door right then, not wanting to freeze, but the *thunk* sound came to her and prodded her onward.

There was a pair of old rubber boots at the foot of the two stairs leading to the door and she borrowed them, sliding them on. They were three sizes too big but they did the job of keeping her feet dry as she stepped out into a snow laden path.

As she closed the door behind her, careful not to accidentally lock herself out, she saw a small building about twenty feet away.

The window facing her in the building had a ragged curtain over it, but light still spilled through the cracks. The *thunk* came again, and she began walking down the path, her rubber boots crunching on ice crystals from where the snow had melted to then freeze over. She wished she had a jacket on but she knew she would only be a few minutes, so she gritted her teeth and walked up to the small building.

Reaching the window, she looked inside, not knowing what to expect, but as she rubbed some of the condensation from the glass and peered inside, her eyes went wide in shock at the tableau before her and everything she'd seen and heard that night at dinner came into focus.

Bending over, she promptly threw up, splashing the rubber boots with her dinner.

Cindy wiped her mouth, feeling better after vomiting.

She didn't know why, but she felt slightly better, less groggy than before.

Peering back into the building, she let her eyes take in the charnel house one more time.

There were three people inside. Two were male, and the older man she recognized from the photos; Abigail had said it was her husband, Philmore. So he wasn't dead.

The other man was at least thirty years younger, and by the family resemblance, Cindy knew the younger man had to be Philmore and Abigail's son. Abigail was also inside. She was working at a counter in the corner, chopping pink meat into cubes and setting them into a pan.

But that wasn't what had Cindy vomiting.

What had shocked her was what Philmore was doing. The man was standing in the center of a room at a large square table with his son beside him. The older man had a large cleaver in his right hand, and each time he brought it down, Cindy heard the *thunk* that had floated to her as she lay in bed.

The sound was what happened each time the cleaver chopped into the human torso lying on the table, the cleaver slicing through meat and bone to strike the table.

Male or female, she couldn't tell the gender of the torso, but it was definitely human. The arms were gone and the insides had been taken out, much like the cavity of a cleaned chicken, and Philmore was hard at work cutting up the rib cage into decent sized ribs. At the end of the table were the arms and legs of the torso, the meat waiting for its turn to be chopped up by Abigail.

From Cindy's perspective, it looked like the father was teaching the son the family business, the son nodding as the father made certain cuts, like a butcher teaching his son his trade.

Stumbling back in horror, Cindy now understood why the stew had tasted *off*. It wasn't spices that had made her dislike it, but something far, far worse. And now that she was feeling better, she had a feeling she knew why she had been so tired, but not as tired as the rest of her friends.

She hadn't partaken of the stew, only having eaten a few bites to be polite while the others had all eaten heartily, Jimmy the most with four servings.

The stew had been drugged, and the painful truth was obvious after seeing the torso being cut up.

The companions had been drugged so they would be easy pickings, so Abigail and her family could slaughter them in their sleep, thus having more meat to cut up and feed to the next unknowing travelers and so continue the cycle.

And then she saw movement in the corner of the building and her eyes went wide when she saw it was a zombie.

It was tied to the wall by its waist, the reason being it had no arms. Cindy watched as Abigail walked over to the ghoul, and with an axe, hacked off one of its legs. The ghoul fell to the floor to flail about and Abigail took the leg back to the counter and began chopping it up. Cindy could see where the other flesh had been pink, the zombies flesh was dark brown, and some portions had patches of rot on them. Abigail began trimming this away to toss into a discard bucket.

Abigail turned to her husband and said, "The outlanders should be asleep by now, are we going to kill them soon?"

Philmore nodded as he chopped off another piece of the torso. "We will, I just want to finish with this one first. With six more bodies it's going to be a long night. So I want to finish with what we have before we start on the new meat."

"I get to have two of the women before we kill them, though, right, Dad?" the younger man asked.

Philmore nodded. "I told you yes, you can take two of 'em, and have some fun, but only for a few days, then they need to be processed and packed away."

The younger man grinned. "That'll be more than enough time," he said with a lecherous grin. "The hard part is deciding which ones to keep for a while."

Backing away from the window, Cindy knew she needed to get back inside and wake the others, warn them of what was going on and what was soon to happen.

As she took a step away from the building, her eyes caught a flash of white where there should be only darkness.

Something told her she needed to investigate before returning to the others, so she quickly left the path and walked to the end of the building. Here, she found a wooden cart with a tarp over it. The wind blew the edge of the tarp where it had come undone, and when it was raised slightly, Cindy saw what had attracted her attention.

Pulling the tarp back and letting it fall to the snowy ground, she saw the clean white of bones picked clean.

And human skulls, more than two dozen, if not more.

She didn't have time to count, but there were enough bones to build a lot of skeletons.

The moonlight cast a pale light on the mound of dead souls and she saw not all the bones were clean. Many still had dried flesh and meat stuck to them and though it was cold, maggots still writhed about, feeding on the rotting meat.

Cindy felt a slight warmth when she had pulled the tarp off the charnel mound and she realized the decaying meat would build up heat. With it covered, it was warm enough for the maggots to prosper, though she doubted they would live long as the temperature continued to drop.

Still, the entire fetid pile crawled with white worms, sliding between open jaws and gaping eyes sockets.

The worst thing she found was that the bones on top of the pile, the ones that had just been added, looked very fresh, no rot had touched them yet and she felt another bout of revulsion fill her as she tasted bile at the back of her throat once more. With an iron will, she forced it down.

Fighting off a wave of nausea at what she and her friends had eaten unwillingly, she turned away to return to them, all the while visualizing the large pot filled with stew, the greasy meat swimming in the dark gravy, and seeing Jimmy eating bite after bite as the gravy coated his lips and ran down his chin.

"Henry, get up, damn it," Cindy whispered into his ear as she tried to wake him up.

He groaned and rolled over, then began snoring. Sue was out as well and hadn't stirred when Cindy entered the bedroom.

After discovering the bones, Cindy had crept back to the basement, slid off the boots, wanting to put them back where she'd found them so as not to be discovered, and had then taken the steps to the first floor as fast as she could. Once inside the house, she ignored stealth, knowing the only people who posed a threat were still outside.

She ran up the wide stairs to the second floor and right to Henry's bedroom door. Slipping in, she dropped to the side of the bed and began shaking him, but no matter how much she pulled and shook him, he refused to wake up.

She knew it was the drugged food that had him sleeping heavier than usual and she also knew that if she had eaten the stew like the rest of them, she would be asleep too, all of them easy game to the twisted family living in the house.

Now it was up to her to save them all or else they would be next in the stew pot.

She idly wondered if she should take the family on by herself, simply get her M-16, go back to the building they were in, and blow them all to hell, but she decided recklessness might not work.

For all she knew, they had guns, and if she was caught off guard, as she didn't know the entire layout of the house, she might end up getting shot or worse before she knew it had happened.

Or worse, she went to deal with the threat while the threat came for her friends. She could end up in an empty building while her friends were slaughtered in their sleep.

No, she needed to watch over them, and if the murderous family came for her friends, she would deal with them.

"Damn it, Henry, wake the fuck up," she hissed. Deciding she needed more drastic measures, she slapped Henry across the face. The loud crack filled the room and Henry grunted, but still he remained asleep.

She was panicking inside, though still holding it together, and she glanced around the bedroom, wondering what she could do to wake him up.

And then she saw the window and the snow piled on the outside edgework.

Coming to her feet, she went to the window, opened it, and scooped up a double-handful of snow, then took it back to Henry, and with a sigh as to what she was going to do, she pulled back the blankets and shoved the snow into Henry's shirt and pants. Then she stood back and waited.

Henry didn't move at first, but within a few seconds he began to groan, as if he was having a bad dream. His hands went to the spots the snow touched his skin and he began to rub it. Slowly at first, then more heavily.

Suddenly, his eyes snapped open and he sat up, unstable and off balance, but awake.

"Jesus, it's cold in here," he slurred as he began to twitch, the snow melting from his warm body and the cold water bringing him to a higher awareness.

His voice was groggy as he turned to see Cindy in his bedroom. "Cindy? What's wrong? What are you doing in my room? Why am I all wet and why the hell is it so damn cold in here?"

In quick, short sentences, Cindy filled him in on what she found and what she believed had happened to him and the others. When she was finished, Henry was standing and awake. His head was still full of fog, like he'd drunk way too much alcohol and it was the next morning, but with each passing second, adrenalin suffused his system, overriding the drug from the stew, his will to survive more powerful.

"Okay, we need to leave here right now." The room was spinning and he shook his head to clear it. "Look, normally I'd say we kill the cannie assholes and then leave, but I'm still pretty out of it. So we need to get everyone up and then we get the hell out of here."

"But what about Abigail and her crazy family?" Cindy asked. "They need to pay for what they've done. There were so many bones there. They've been doing this for a while."

"Maybe so," he replied and moved around the bed to rouse Sue who was still sleeping, "but it's not worth one of us getting killed. So we run. Let the next poor bastard deal with it."

"But, Henry…" she began.

He spun on her, and though he tried to snap at her, it didn't come off very forceful as he was still so groggy. "I said no, Cindy, damn it, listen to me when I give an order. Now, go get Raven and Mary, and then together we'll all get Jimmy. That damn fool ate more stew than all of us put together. He's probably so zonked out a bomb could go off and he wouldn't know it."

She looked as if she was going to protest but a hard look at Henry, in between trying to stir Sue, stopped her.

"Okay, but I don't like this one bit," Cindy said and went to the door to leave.

"Neither do I," Henry agreed and then he began gently slapping Sue on her cheeks to wake her.

Mary and Raven were easier to rouse as they hadn't eaten that much stew. Both groggy and unsteady on their feet, they listened to Cindy quickly and once they had heard the entire story, their eyes were more alert and adrenalin began to fill them.

Soon, all were up and dressed with the exception of Jimmy. Only a few minutes had passed since Cindy first woke Henry and now the five companions were in Cindy and Jimmy's room, each of them looking down on a sleeping Jimmy.

They had slapped him, poked him and sat him up, but Jimmy was still out cold, some drool sliding down his chin.

Finally, Henry had had enough of playing games and left the room, saying he would be right back.

When he returned, he carried the large bucket of water that was used in the bathroom for flushing the toilet.

With Jimmy sitting propped up on the bed, Henry walked over to him, raised the water bucket over the sleeping man's head, and poured the entire contents onto Jimmy. As the water sluiced over his head and soaked into his clothes and bed, he sputtered awake, his lips spraying water as he tried to figure out what was going on. He was about to let out a scream, but Henry placed his right hand over Jimmy's mouth, stifling him and causing him to only moan.

"Shut up, Jimmy, you'll let them know we're awake," Henry hissed as Jimmy's eyes went wide and he saw all his friends standing around him. His pupils were still dilated and he was tired, but he fought off the feeling, knowing instantly something was happening.

Henry took his hand away from Jimmy's mouth and took a step back, while Cindy handed Jimmy a towel.

"What the fuck, old man? Is this some kind of a damn joke? Why the hell would you dump a bucket of water on me?"

"Just get changed and we'll fill you in. And hurry up," Henry ordered as Cindy went to Jimmy and began unbuttoning his sodden shirt.

For a moment, Jimmy was worried when he didn't feel his .38 or see his shotgun, but Mary stepped up and showed him she was holding them. Mary had made sure to remove them and take the .38 out of its holster before Henry dumped the water on him.

Sue went to Jimmy's backpack and took out some fresh clothes, handing them to him, then once he was dressed and filled in on what was happening, he gritted his teeth and said, "Those no good fuckers, I'll kill them."

"No, you won't," Henry ordered. "Neither you or the rest of us are at peak condition. Look at you, I dumped a bucket of water on you and you can still barely stand up. Like I told the others, we leave this place and let the next bastard worry about it. I told you before, we can't save the damn world; we just need to save our-selves."

"Fine, Henry, I can't say I agree with you, but seems there's two of you in front of me, I guess I'm outnumbered," Jimmy said with a slight grin.

Henry looked at Mary and Sue who both shrugged.

"You said he's more doped up than the rest of us, he probably *does* see two of you," Sue said as she went to Jimmy to help him button his new shirt. "Come on, Jimmy, I'll help you."

Seconds later, Henry was at the bedroom door now and he looked over his shoulder at the others, each ready to leave.

"Okay, so no noise, we head to the front door and we leave, no stopping. Got it?"

As Henry made eye contact with each of them, they nodded in kind. "Okay, let's move."

Henry opened the bedroom door and stepped into the hallway, his Glock leading the way. Behind him, the rest of the group exited. Mary was behind Henry, followed by Raven and Sue who half-carried Jimmy between them, and Cindy took up the rear flank as she was the most alert.

Like children sneaking downstairs on Christmas morning to open presents before their parents were awake, the six warriors crept down the hallway and then to the wide stairs leading to the first floor.

"Go, I'll cover you," Henry whispered to Mary as he used the railing to steady his arm, pointing the Glock at the foyer below. "When you reach the bottom, wait for everyone to catch up."

"Okay, but pay attention," Mary said.

She climbed down the stairs one at a time, wincing with the expectation of a stair squeaking. When she made it to the bottom, she peered around the archway leading to the hallway that would take them back to the dining room, sitting room and the front door. She turned and waved to the others that it was safe.

One at a time, they each crept down the stairs, and when they were all together once more, Henry pointed to the opposite end of the hallway, to the rear of the house.

"Cindy, you take everyone out the back way. I want to gather some supplies before we head out, otherwise we're gonna be in the same shape we were in a day ago. Don't worry; I won't be taking any meat with me, no matter what it looks like."

Mary spoke up. "I'll come with you, there's no need to go alone."

He was going to say no when he saw the resolve in her eyes. "Fine, I could probably use the help, okay the rest of you, out the back way and we'll meet back where you were waiting for my signal with the light."

Cindy looked as if she was going to protest but Henry touched her on the shoulder, giving her his most sincere smile. "Hey, I'll be fine, and now I have Mary to watch my back. You guys get going, none of us are in any condition to fight right now, but we need food. And Jimmy's suffering by the look of him."

She nodded, not liking it but knowing he was right. All she had to do was look at Jimmy to see this was true. Though he had woken up initially, he was all but sleeping again. She frowned when she looked at him. Serves the idiot right for stuffing himself like a pig.

"Huh, some suffering," Raven said. "Me and Sue are the ones carrying him. He ain't light ya know."

"Try having him on top of you when we…" Cindy began but was stopped in mid-sentence.

Raven held up her hand. "Uh-uh, no thank you, that's an image I can live without."

"Okay, Henry, you and Mary be careful," Cindy said.

"Will do, now get going, our luck can't last all night," Henry replied as he winked at Sue who smiled back half-heartily.

Cindy turned and led the others to the rear of the house. Henry heard a door open and felt the cold air rush in. A second later the door clicked shut and he let out the breath he was holding. He looked to Mary and said, "Good, at least they're safe. Okay we get to the kitchen, take as much food as we can and then get the hell out of here, sound good?"

"Yes, let's do this; I want to be gone as soon as possible from this lunatic asylum." She shook her head. "I still find it hard to believe, Abigail seemed so nice. I should have known better, nothing's ever as it seems anymore."

"Tell me about it," Henry said and began walking down the hall. "Okay, stay close."

A minute later found them in the kitchen. With only the faintest amount of moonlight filtering in through the kitchen window, they could barely see, but in no time they were shoving their backpacks full of canned goods and packets of dried food. Five minutes later and they were ready to leave. It had taken longer than Henry would have liked, but there was no choice, they needed food if they were to survive in the wilderness of snow and ice.

"Okay, let's go, we've got enough," he said and Mary nodded, zipping her pack up.

Walking down the spacious hallway, Henry was beginning to feel more relaxed. The exit wasn't far and it looked like Abigail and her family was still outside in the meat shack or whatever they called it.

Perhaps it was the drugs still in his system that let Henry drop his guard more than he normally would have, but for whatever reason, he reached the end of the hallway, turned the corner that would lead to the front door, and bumped right into Abigail.

"And what do we have here?" Abigail asked as she glared at Henry and then shifted her gaze to Mary, who was standing behind him. "Were you perhaps stealing a midnight snack or were you leaving without saying goodbye? Now that's not very polite, whatever the reason you're about. Don't you know? All good *meat* should be in bed, waiting for the sandman to come up and slice your throats."

Henry's reflexes were slower than he would have preferred, and he only blinked at the woman in her odd clothing. For she wasn't wearing a standard dress like at dinner, now she wore a long, black rubber apron complete with rubber boots. A pair of plastic goggles covered her eyes and her gray hair was tied back into a pony tail, a shower cap on the top of her head. She looked like she was about to do some serious bloodletting and didn't want to get splattered with her victims' blood.

In her right hand, she held a wicked looking carving knife, the edge razor sharp.

"We found the footprints under the window, which one of you has been sneaking about past their bedtime, hmmm?" she asked nonchalantly. "And how in the world did you find out? It was supposed to be so simple. I drug you, you all fall asleep, and I come up and kill you one at a time. You never feel a thing. Now you've made it oh so difficult."

"Sorry to spoil your plans," Henry said.

"Indeed," Abigail replied.

As she stood perfectly still, looking at Henry, her expression remained impassive. So Henry never expected it when she brought up the carving knife, swinging it around with her right arm outstretched, the blade slicing the air and heading directly for Henry's throat.

With his nervous system impaired thanks to the drug still flowing in his blood, his reflexes were a fraction of what they might have been. Time seemed to stand still as he watched the blade coming at him.

Then something snapped inside him and he went into action, darting to the side as the knife whispered past his jugular with barely an inch of clearance. The attack put Abigail off-balance, and Henry used the opportunity to push her away from him, his Glock falling to the floor at the same time. He would have done more to keep her down for good but a bout of dizziness flooded his vision and he had to lean against the wall for support. The drug was still trying to do its job, but he was fighting off the effects with everything he had.

From behind, footsteps pounded the floor and Mary spun, holding her .38, to see Abigail's son coming at her, a long boning knife held tightly in his right hand. She never hesitated. She fired two rounds into his chest, blowing his heart apart and spraying blood onto the wall and furniture behind him as the exit wounds punched fist-sized holes out of his back. The young man was thrown back to trip over an ottoman, where he tumbled head first to the floor. His eyes were glazed over in death, dead before he landed.

Abigail saw Mary shoot her son and she let out a maniacal scream that almost had Henry clapping his hands over his ears to protect his eardrums.

"My boy! My beautiful boy!" she shrieked as she climbed to her feet and charged at Mary.

"Mary, look out!" Henry yelled and was about to grab Abigail and pull her back when he was stopped short and lifted six inches off the floor.

From behind him, two large hands had clasped around his neck like a vise and were now squeezing his throat. In the half-second since the hands wrapped around his neck, Henry had already begun to choke, white flashes of light dancing across his vision.

Through the haze of his faltering vision and lack of air, he saw Mary fighting with Abigail, the old woman a formidable opponent. Mary tried to shoot the old woman but her .38 was knocked from her hand by a swipe of the carving knife and Mary was now facing her hand-to-hand.

Then Henry had his own problems as he struggled to stay conscious.

"I'm going to snap your neck and suck your bones dry, little man," a low male voice growled, Henry's mouth opening and closing like a landed fish as he tried to suck in air.

For all of Henry's hardened muscles, he was like a child in the grip of the giant who had a hold of him.

Blackness was beginning to descend, and though dying, the massive adrenalin rush fueling his body was enough to override the drugs in his system and for just a moment Henry had total clarity.

Thinking fast, not wasting the moment he was given, he did the only thing possible under the circumstances. He kicked backward with his right boot, right where he prayed the groin was for the man who was holding him.

As the sole of Henry's boot crushed something soft and yielding, the hands around his throat immediately let up and he dropped to the floor to gag and gasp, spitting bile as he sucked in a precious breath of air.

But he knew there was no time to spare and he looked up to see Abigail's husband, Philmore, bent over and wheezing from his crushed testicles.

Taking the initiative, Henry could see the large man was already recovering and there was no time to do anything but lunge at him. Henry hit Philmore low with his head down like a linebacker. Though Philmore was larger than Henry, the deadlands warrior was no small man either and the hit sent Philmore crashing back into an end table.

An oil lamp glowing softly sat on the end table, and when the large man hit it, the lamp fell to the floor, smashing and spreading burning oil in all directions. Some landed on Philmore and the man's clothing caught immediately, the material burning like dried newspaper, the stench of burning meat quickly filling the air.

But Philmore wasn't down yet, and though his hair had burned off and his face was melting, he roared in pain and anger and charged at Henry, who had stumbled backwards after hitting Philmore.

Reaching down, Henry pulled his panga from its sheath, the sixteen inches of steel, razor honed blade reflecting the flames like a mirror.

Henry waited for just the right time, and as Philmore came at him, Henry rolled to the side, came up in a crouch and jumped back at the flaming man, the panga raised over his head to come down in a chopping motion.

The panga found the back of Philmore's neck and cut more than halfway through before stopping. The weight of the dead man pulled the body forward and Henry held on to the hilt of the panga as the body slid off the blade to hit the floor with blood spurting out of the neck stump. Wherever the blood landed in the fire, the odor of burnt copper filtered into the air and Henry had to breathe through his mouth, not wanting to gag on the stench.

The flames were out of control now, the curtains and furniture catching and spreading to the walls, the old wallpaper adorning them excellent kindling for the growing inferno.

Stumbling through the room and back into the hallway, Henry saw Abigail on the floor, and Mary was underneath her. Dread filled him, as it looked like Abigail had killed Mary and was now dead on top of her. But then he saw Mary's hand wave to him and he rushed to the both bodies, grabbing Abigail and pulling her off Mary.

Coughing and wheezing, Mary rolled to her feet as she reached out and picked up her .38.

"Thanks, Henry, she almost had me, but I got lucky."

Henry glanced down at the corpse of the old woman to see the carving knife was embedded in Abigail's chest. It looked to Henry that the woman had attacked Mary but Mary had managed to grasp Abigail's arm and twist the knife back on her. When Abigail fell onto Mary, the knife slid into her chest easily, the old woman a victim of her own razor-sharp blade.

The room Philmore was in was now burning out of control. The fire had reached the bottles of alcohol sitting on top of the cabinet, more than half of the bottles having exploded from the heat, thus fueling the fire even more. The house was filling with smoke to the point Henry was coughing and hacking, as was Mary.

"We need to go, right now!" he yelled as a piece of the ceiling came crashing down, timbers burning like cordwood. He spotted his Glock on the hallway floor and he lunged for it, burning his palm in the process but not caring. The Glock was more than just a sidearm to him, he'd taken possession of it since the outbreak first began and it was a piece of his history, a part of his past life that he didn't want to forget. Back when he had first found the Glock, he was his old self, someone who was now long gone as he adapted to the new world of the living dead.

"Lead the way!" Mary replied as the two tried to reach the back door, which was closest.

But as they took their first few steps, they were blocked by licking flames, the fire flowing through the walls to now encapsulate all the rooms around them.

As the flames seemed to reach out at them with a life of its own, Henry backed away. "Head to the front door, we can't get out this way!" he yelled.

"No shit!" she replied, cursing in the heat of the moment, something Mary rarely did.

They backtracked through the house, but found the front door was closed off for them as well, the fire burning through the wall as if it was nothing more than tissue paper. It was easy to see that the old home was nothing but a giant tinder box just waiting for a match, one Henry had accidentally supplied.

Trapped in the hallway, there was nowhere to go and Mary huddled next to Henry, as he shielded her as best he could with his arms. His neck was raw from where Philmore had grabbed it and he was sure if he had a chance to look in a mirror, he would see that his neck would look as if he'd almost been hanged.

"What do we do?" Mary cried out as flames licked at her face.

"I don't know, give me a second!" he yelled back over the roaring fire.

"We don't have a second!" she yelled back as more of the ceiling in the next room collapsed, spewing soot and flames in all directions.

He knelt down with her so they could be closer to the floor, the smoke not as bad there but still not very good, and he knew he had seconds to figure a way out or they were both dead. He coughed some more, the smoke filling his lungs, sucking the oxygen from his body.

In his mind, the seconds ticked by unabated.

At the end of the driveway, Jimmy and the others stopped running, deciding they had gone far enough.

Cindy and Sue were standing together, and Raven was next to Jimmy, helping him stand.

"Where the hell are they?" Jimmy asked as he looked back at the house.

Raven took a step forward, pointing at one of the first floor windows. "There's a light there but it's not from a lamp or a flashlight."

Sue took a step forward. "Wait, I smell smoke."

"Yeah, so do I. Oh, shit, did someone start a fire in there?" Cindy asked as she moved up next to Sue.

Jimmy looked at each of them, already making up his mind. "We need to go back, they might be hurt," he said and pushed Raven away, standing on his own. He looked at Sue as he began to head back to the house, Cindy and Raven with him. "You stay here, Sue. Without a gun you'll just be another worry."

"Okay," Sue said, knowing she would be a liability.

"Come on, let's go," Jimmy yelled as he took off back down the driveway, towards the waiting house.

He didn't get more than halfway there before three windows on the first floor blew out, glass flying out to land in the snow. Immediately, flames licked out the windows, orange and red tongues reaching for the night sky. The roar of the fire could be heard as the inferno grew.

Jimmy stopped, staring at the flames, the fire reflected in the pupils of his wide eyes.

"Henry! Mary!" he screamed, gripping his shotgun tightly, knowing raw force wouldn't help this time. "We need to get in there, save them!" He was about to run at the house, ignoring the flames, when another explosion ripped through the house, sending him falling backwards. "Jesus Christ!"

Cindy and Raven were by his side, both helping him to stand. The lower half of the house was now a raging conflagration, parts of the siding burning as the intense heat inside burned through the inner to the outer walls.

Jimmy heard footsteps on the gravel, and he turned around to see Sue running to the house with eyes wide and her mouth open in a silent scream.

Jimmy ran to her, grabbing her and halting her forward movement. "No, Sue, it's too late!"

"Let me go, Jimmy, Henry's in there!" Sue yelled as she looked at the house. "Henry, where are you? Henry!"

Raven shook her head, her eyes watering slightly. "If they're still alive, they gotta be dead by now."

"No!" Sue screamed. "Henry! No, oh, God no!" She crumpled to the driveway, tears flowing down her face as Raven knelt down to console her.

Cindy went to Jimmy and he wrapped his arms around her. "Oh, shit, Cindy. Mary, Henry, it can't be. They were right behind us. This shouldn't be happening. Fuck, this can't be happening." He squeezed his empty hand into a fist, the other wrapped around the shotgun so tight his knuckles were bone white. "Fuck!" he screamed into the night, the loss of his two best friends over-whelming.

Cindy was sobbing softly at the thought that both Mary and Henry were dead, but as another explosion rocked the house, she knew the reality had to be faced.

"Goodbye, Mary," she whispered, praying her friend didn't suffer before the flames found her. "Bye, Henry."

From the back of the house, one of the windows was still intact, the massive inferno not yet reaching that part of the home with its fury. As the four companions either stood or kneeled in silence while watching the giant funeral pyre of their two fallen friends, the intact window suddenly exploded outward, glass raining down to land in the snow, twinkling like ice crystals. As the window exploded, a chair flew out to fall onto the ground, rolling three times before coming to a stop on its side.

All eyes went to the window, not understanding what was going on, and no sooner did the chair come to a stop, then something human-shaped, and burning, was thrown through the window to land in the snow. As fast as the shape landed, it began to move, to kick off the burning material of the rug it was wrapped in.

As the figure rolled away from the burning rug, all eyes went wide to see it was Mary.

"Holy shit, I don't fucking believe it!" Jimmy yelled as he ran at top speed to Mary, who was coughing and stumbling away from the house. She was in a daze, the smoke she'd inhaled causing her to falter as she tried to clear her vision.

Behind Jimmy, the others ran with him, each reaching Mary in seconds. Just as she was about to fall over, Jimmy was there to catch her.

"Jesus, Mary, you're alive!" Jimmy said as he caught her and cradled her like a baby. "Take it easy, you'll be fine. Are you hurt, are you burned?"

She shook her head, coughing as mucus rolled from her nose, down her lip and over her chin, her nose running from the smoke she'd inhaled. "I'm...okay...Henry...he wrapped me...tossed me out...where is he?"

"Shit, Henry's still alive?" Jimmy gasped before turning back to the house. "Oh, shit, where the fuck is he?"

The window that Mary had come through was brighter now, the flames finally attacking that part of the house, and Jimmy's hopes, just raised, were quickly dashed once more when he saw nothing inside the window but flames.

Sue and Cindy were with Mary now and they helped her walk away from the house, Jimmy standing with Raven as they stared at the window.

"Maybe he didn't get out in time?" she said. "Saved Mary, then the fire got him."

"I..." Jimmy began and then, from in the midst of the flames, Jimmy saw another shape come running at the window. As the figure jumped through the opening, Jimmy saw it was on fire, resembling a giant matchstick. The shape fell to the snow-covered ground and lay still.

"Raven, with me!" Jimmy ordered as the two darted at the form now lying still in the snow. The flames were crackling and hissing, and as Jimmy crossed the few feet, he saw it was another rug, something inside it once more. He had to hope it was Henry.

"Raven, put out the fires, hurry; use the damn snow!" Jimmy yelled and began to use his feet to kick snow onto the flaming carpet. Raven went to her knees and used her hands, and in seconds the fires were out, the carpet still smoking.

Jimmy dropped to his knees and went to pull the rug off whatever was inside, but he burned his left hand, the corner of the material still smoldering.

"Shit," he cursed as he scooped some snow and with the ice in his hand, he used it to pull back the rug, the hiss of melting snow carrying to his ears.

As he pulled back the rug, Jimmy saw the ash-gray hair that was so familiar to him, and with Raven helping him, he tugged on the rug some more, to expose a face covered with black soot, a pair of eyes looking up at him.

"Hey, buddy, how's it going?" Henry asked, his voice hoarse from smoke inhalation. No sooner did he speak then he coughed loudly, choking on mucus as he placed his forehead in the snow until the bout had passed.

"Jesus Christ, old man, don't fucking scare me like that," Jimmy said and helped Henry to his feet.

"Mary, is she...?" Henry began.

"She's fine, Henry, we got her, she's doing fine," Jimmy said.

Henry coughed some more, having to lean on Jimmy for support as he let the spasm fill his entire body, but eventually it passed. Jimmy and Raven helped Henry walk away from the house to get some clearance from it, and when Henry reached Sue, she ran into his arms, hugging and kissing him.

Cindy was with Mary, talking to her and both went to Henry, hugging him as Sue stayed glued to him. She wasn't about to let him go, not now, not after almost losing him.

Hocking a large ball of mucus, Henry spit into the snow. The mucus was black, more soot. He wondered if he'd be spitting up soot for the next week, his lungs were burning so much.

"Come on, let's get the hell out of here," Henry said as he began to walk down the gravel driveway, Sue helping him and carrying his full backpack, both he and Mary still carrying them when they jumped through the window.

The others followed, and by the time Henry reached the end of the driveway, he was walking by himself, his vitality and indomitable will taking over.

They didn't speak for the next fifteen minutes, each walking silently after the outpouring of emotion at the thought of losing two of their group, but when Henry, on point once more, crested a hill that overlooked the house, he stopped and leaned against a tree. The others gathered around him, each now gazing out to the burning house, a beacon of light in the middle of complete darkness.

Through the crackling of the flames, each of them heard the single scream.

No one was able to see where it came from, but as the fire touched the night sky, it seemed to come from the heart of the conflagration, gathering power and volume with each roar of the inferno. The scream rose higher and higher until it petered out, the last second of it filled with agony and despair.

And then it was gone, lost on the wind.

Each of the group looked at the other, wondering if what they had heard was real or just an effect of the fire.

"Maybe one of them was still alive," Mary surmised as she hugged herself, the scream still in her mind, haunting her despite the evil intentions of the owner.

"Doesn't matter," Henry said. "They're dead now and they got what they deserved. In the end, that's what counts." He turned and began walking away, in the direction of the road they had found previously. It had to lead somewhere and that would be their next destination. "Come on, people, we need to make camp for the night before we set out in the morning."

The others shifted their packs of food salvaged from the house and followed Henry, single file through the pitch black woods, while behind them, the house continued to burn, the inferno resembling a small piece of Hell that had found a home on Earth.

LOVE IS DEAD: A RAGE VIRUS STORY

"I love you," Mark said with a wide smile.

"No, I love you," Susan replied as she reached out and took his hand.

Mark leaned over the table slightly and Susan did the same, the two kissing tenderly and passionately over the salt and pepper shakers. Both had their eyes closed, no one else in the restaurant but them, tongues entwining as heartbeats raced.

Eventually the young couple came up for air and sat back in their seats. Mark glanced around the restaurant to see a few eyes on him and his date and he blushed, not wanting to make a public spectacle of him and Susan, but he just couldn't help it. He loved her so damn much.

"We have an audience," he said while grinning slyly.

Susan cast a glance to the other restaurant patrons also and she chuckled, placing her hand over her mouth.

"I can see that. Well, what do we expect? PDA's always do that."

"PDA? What's that?" he asked.

"Public displays of affection, silly. Don't you know anything?"

"I know that I love you. That's enough for me," he said as he stared into her beautiful eyes.

"Oh, stop it, you're embarrassing me."

The waiter came up to the table and cleared his throat. Mark looked up at him to see the man wasn't at all happy.

"If you're finally ready to order..." the waiter began and Mark realized he'd been waiting for a chance to approach their table without wanting to barge in on their tender kiss.

"Sorry, about that," Mark said with another bashful look. "You see, this is our one year anniversary."

"That's right, we've been dating for an entire year," Susan added with a grin.

"How wonderful for you," the waiter said drolly. "Are you ready to order?"

Mark looked down at the menu and realized he had been so busy kissing Susan that he hadn't bothered to read the menu, Susan's was also still on the table before her.

"Ah, uhm, actually, no. We haven't looked at the menu yet."

The waiter frowned, as if Mark was wasting his time, but then his face lightened as he realized if he wanted a good tip, he needed to be nice. "No problem, sir, I'll come back in a few minutes. Is that okay?"

Mark nodded and the waiter walked away to another table.

Susan giggled slightly. "I don't think he likes you," she said as she picked up her menu, the lower part of her face now hidden behind it. Mark could see her eyes darting back and forth as she looked at the colorful dinner specials.

"Yeah, well, I think I can live with him not sending me a Christmas card this year," Mark rebutted as he began to scan his own menu. As he scanned it, he couldn't help but let his eyes roam back up and over to hers. Her eyes were the deepest brown he had ever seen and he loved looking at them.

As if she knew she was being watched, she stopped perusing her menu and looked over the top at him.

"What are you doing?" she asked.

He shrugged and looked back down. "Huh? Oh, nothing, I was just staring at your beautiful eyes."

She lowered her menu. "Oh, you, that's so sweet. Come here," she purred and leaned forward. He did the same and then they were kissing again, the two becoming one.

The waiter was suddenly at the table again and he cleared his throat in an annoyed fashion. Mark pulled his lips from Susan's to look up at the waiter's face.

"Are you ready to order now, sir?"

"Oh, uhm, gees," Mark scratched the back of his head, feeling like he had been caught talking in class at school when he was ten.

The waiter then lowered the facade of politeness, deciding he didn't have time for this.

"Look, pal, I get it, your girlfriend's hot. So if you can wait half an hour before touching her, why don't I just get you tonight's house specials and get this over with. There's a line waiting to get in here and I would love to keep my tables moving."

Mark looked up at him and felt his anger rising. He was about to open his mouth and tell the waiter where he could go take a flying leap, when Susan spoke up, her smile wide and genuine.

"You know what? That's sounds wonderful. And could you get us two more beers, too?"

The waiter blinked, and as he looked at Susan, a beautiful twenty-one-year-old with a body any man would kill to touch, his visage softened.

"Of course, miss, I'd be happy to do that." He reached over, took the menus, and was lost in the back of the restaurant on his way to the kitchen.

Mark stared at Susan, his eyes still full of fire. Now he was revved up and had no one to yell at. "I had that, Susan. I didn't need your help."

"I know that, baby, but I felt bad for the guy. We were taking forever." She batted her eyes, puffed out her chest, and pursed her lips. "Forgive me?"

Mark melted in her gaze. "How could I not?" he reached for her hand and she did the same, the two caressing fingers and palms as the other patrons concentrated on their food, and not each other. "How did I ever get so lucky to find a woman like you?" he sighed.

"I should say the same thing about you," she added. "You treat me so well. You never argue and you always try to make me happy."

"I love you," he said as he raised her hand to his lips and kissed it.

"No, I love you more," she sighed.

As the two love birds stared into each other's eyes, at the next table over sat a man and woman, both in their mid-forties. They had been married for well over twenty years, and despite their differences, were still together.

"My God, Martha," the man said as he overheard the two lovers. "I think I'm gonna get diabetes from those two."

"Oh, John, you hush. They're sweet. I remember when you were like that."

He rolled his eyes in embarrassment. "Please, don't remind me. All that lovey-dovey crap. What a load of bull. Give it a few more years. Wait till they're married and she puts on a few pounds, then we'll see how much he loves her." He gestured to his wife's plate of food.

Martha frowned deeply as she looked down at her plate of pasta, and thought back to when she was three sizes smaller. Since then she had given John two healthy boys, and once the baby fat had been added, she had never gotten rid of it, even now, after all these years. Though he had a point, it was still easier for her to attack than defend.

"Before you go throwing rocks at glass houses, John, take a good look in the mirror. When I married you, I don't remember a beer belly or no hair on that dome you call a head."

He sipped his beer and frowned deeply. "Ha, ha, always with the hair, will you never give it a rest?"

"And what about my weight? You always start in, day after day, why I ought to…"

Back at Mark and Susan's table, the two love birds paused for a moment of making googily eyes at one another to listen to the older couple bicker. When it didn't seem like it was going to stop, Susan looked Mark directly in the eyes and said, "Promise me we won't ever get like that."

"I promise," he said. "I love you way too much to ever let something like your weight make me stop. Though I hope you always stay as thin and trim as you are now."

She nodded, agreeing. "I would. If not for you than for myself."

"And I'll try not to lose my hair, but it's kinda out of my control," he joked.

"Just don't get a beer belly and we'll call it even," she replied. Then she gave him a quizzical look as she studied him harder.

"What?" he asked.

"Oh, nothing. I was just trying to picture you with no hair."

He growled playfully and she giggled.

The waiter arrived with the meals, and once the food was spread before them and the waiter had left, they dug in, concentrating on their meals while chatting politely about their day.

Meanwhile, behind them, the older couple continued to bicker, like two estranged friends who knew way too much about one another.

"Check please!" Mark called to the waiter as he leaned back and patted his stomach. "Man that was good," he sighed as he pushed the remnant of his steak dinner aside, only a gnarled bone and some fat left on the plate.

"You always eat too much, you know. That beer belly is right around the corner," Susan said with a sly grin as she finished off her Ceasar salad.

"Well, maybe but I..." he began but was cut off by a cacophony of noise that filled the restaurant. It was coming from the front of the dining hall, near the main entrance. Screams, shouts and angered voices were the beginning, but soon the sound of crashing glass and dishes shattering on the floor filled the air, sounding like World War Three was erupting in the restaurant.

"What in the world is going on up there?" Susan asked as she tried to see to the front, but was blocked by the other tables of patrons.

"I don't know, but seems we're done anyway, why don't we go see?"

She nodded and they stood up, Mark grinning as he looked around. "Hey, maybe we could dine and dash. Serves that jerk of a waiter right if we stiffed him with the check."

Susan frowned. "We'll do no such thing, Mark, and shame on you for saying something so immoral."

He held his hands up in surrender. "Okay, okay, don't get so worked up, I was only joking." Though deep down there was a kernel of truth to his words.

Other patrons were now rising from their chairs to see what the commotion was at the front of the restaurant.

Mark pushed a few people aside, muttering apologies, and when he reached the front of the small crowd and was looking into the small foyer where the hostess' desk was located, he saw something he never would have believed possible if not for witnessing it with his own eyes.

The glass doors leading to the street were shattered and a police officer was on the floor, along with the hostess. Mark had remembered her easily from entering the restaurant. Though he loved

Susan to death, he was still a red-blooded man and the hostess was attractive in a dress that showed a lot of leg and a low neckline.

Both of the beleaguered people were fighting for their lives as two other people were on top of them, looking for all purposes like they were trying to eat them!

As Mark watched, surrounded by gasps and cries of shock from the other patrons, the policeman pulled his revolver from his holster and jammed the barrel against his attacker's stomach. There were the muffled reports when the gun went off and the attacker's lower back exploded outward to spray nearby people with gore and blood.

Mark jumped where he stood, still in shock at the violence before him and he expected to see the policeman's attacker fall off him but the figure barely seemed to notice his now missing insides. Mark could tell the figure was male but that was where any identification ceased for the man's face was lathered in a generous helping of gore, the eyes peering out as if the head had been dipped in ketchup.

The hostess was doing no better. Her attacker was female, and as Mark stared in horror, the attacking female sank her teeth into the hostess' neck and tore it out like it was a giant piece of taffy.

Blood shot straight up toward the ceiling, and as the hostess rolled on the floor, her position shifted and blood spray splattered across the closest patrons, who screamed as they were doused with a generous layer of blood.

Then a few patrons snapped out of their stupor and dove in to help the two hapless people.

The policeman was first to be helped and his attacker was torn from him. The cop rolled to his knees, his training helping him stay focused in the heat of the chaos and he raised his gun again, wanting to put the madman down once and for all. But as the gun came up and he fired, the madman kicked out with his foot, sending the gun flying across the foyer as the expelled bullet went off in the wrong direction, hitting a watching young man who had been out for his twenty-first birthday with his friends, right between the eyes and killing him instantly.

The gun was soon lost in the myriad of feet moving about as the madman reached down and bit into the arm of one of his captors.

The man screamed and let go as the madman chewed the flesh, swallowing the pieces whole. The second man saw what had happened to the first and decided this wasn't any of his business, so he let the madman go, and before he could take a step back, the madman spun about and sank his blood-red teeth into his right cheek, tearing the flesh off and exposing bone as blood poured down the victim's face. The eye seemed to swim in the gaping eye socket and the screaming man spun and ran into the crowd, cradling his torn face.

Then, at the shattered glass door, more figures appeared out of the darkness. Each face was twisted into a visage of pure hatred, rage-filled eyes boring into the horrified restaurant patrons. For a moment in time, all voices ceased inside the restaurant as each of the patrons looked at the killer crowd staring back at them.

Then, like a light switch had been flicked, the first of the killers in the crowd lunged into the restaurant, followed by the others.

In seconds, killers and victims were intertwined as throats were torn out and eyes were gouged from their sockets. In the middle of the melee, Mark struggled to hold onto Susan as she cried out in fear.

Mark's foot stepped on something and he glanced down to see it was the policeman's lost handgun. Bending down, he grabbed it, then was shoved to the side by the shifting crowd.

"We need to get out of here!" Mark yelled as he fought to remain on his feet.

Susan yelled back but her words were lost in the maelstrom of fighting, dying humanity.

An opening appeared before Mark and he had a clear view of the door leading into the kitchen, and he pointed with the gun, pulling Susan with him.

"The kitchen! We can get out the back way?" He tugged her along and she went meekly, tears of fear rolling down her cheeks.

A feral man with blood coating him from head to toe jumped in front of Mark, snarling loudly. Mark, panicking, raised the gun and squeezed the trigger, his eyes closing as he did so. He didn't see when the bullet struck the raging man in the forehead and blew out the back of his head in a glorious spray of skull fragments and brain matter. Then Mark was moving again.

Susan was yanked back when a wild woman with dark red hair lathered in blood grabbed her free hand and tried to pull her back into the tidal wave of killers. Mark, feeling Susan stop, turned to see the glaring madwoman and he raised the gun again, shooting her in the face. The bullet went into her mouth, ricocheted off her teeth and shot straight up, blowing off the top of her head. Her scalp flew into the air to flip over and plop back down on her open head wound, the glistening skin seeming to sparkle under the lights of the restaurant. Then she toppled over, dead.

"Come on, this way!" Mark screamed as he shoved a wounded patron out of his way. The wounded man went head first into a cart of desserts, knocking the puddings and pies to the floor in a cascade of sugary treats. He heard Susan scream and he spun around, ready to shoot any who were threatening them, when he saw what had made Susan cry out.

Ten feet away, in the foyer, the hostess was now in pieces, her organs strewn about the floor. A young woman, no more than fifteen, was jumping into the main dining room, a severed hand between her teeth, blood dripping out the sides of her mouth. The woman's teeth, though they were sunk into the flesh of the hand, could still be seen as they gleamed in the wan lighting. Mark and Susan watched horrified as the woman tore off a piece of the hand, chewing on the flesh like she had nothing more than a chicken leg in her grip. Then more people blocked the view and the woman was lost from sight.

"Jesus Christ, what the fuck is going on around here?" Mark gasped as the visceral image stayed with him.

Another killer jumped at Susan and Mark raised the gun and fired. The bullet struck the man in the center of the chest, blowing a fist-sized hole out of his back. As the man stood immobile, Mark could have sworn he was able to peer through the hole like it was a telescope. Then the man fell to the floor where he twitched and spasmed in his death throes.

"Come on, before more get in here!" Mark yelled and pulled Susan after him. They ran like demons from Hell were after them because that was how it felt. Mark kicked open the swinging door leading to the kitchen and looked around desperately for the back door.

Then he spotted the glowing **EXIT** sign to the right and he dashed for it, pulling Susan behind him like a small child. As he hit the horizontal bar across the middle of the door, and it popped open, he halted in his tracks to see an alley full of people, all covered in blood and more than one holding a severed body part. The entire crowd looked up from their feast and Mark let out a soft squeak.

Then Susan was yanking him back inside the kitchen as the first of the gore-covered crowd ran at the door.

As the door slammed shut, bodies bounced off it, the metal door easily up to the challenge. But no sooner did Mark let out a sigh of relief, then he turned to see more people spilling into the kitchen via the way Susan and he had entered.

He looked left and right, not knowing where to go, and he spotted the freezer and the vegetable walk-in.

"Here, follow me!" he yelled and shot at the first killer to come at them. The bullet caught the attacker in the shoulder and spun him around. As blood seeped from his wound, the howling man ignored it and was soon up and charging forward with the others.

The vegetable walk-in was too far away, the extra few feet would spell their doom, so Mark reached out for the handle to the freezer. Throwing it open, he pushed Susan inside and spun around to close the door. As he did, three sets of hands became wedged in the door between the frame, and try as he might, the metal door wouldn't close.

"Help me Susan!" he yelled as his breath plumed out of his mouth like gray smoke.

She got to her feet, wiping her hands on her slacks, and went to his aid, the two now pulling on the handle as hard as they could. The hands were still wedged in the door, the fingers spasming as more fingers tried to get a grip. Mark knew if that happened, the killers would force the door open and then he and Susan were done for.

"Come on! Harder! We need to pull harder!" he screamed as he let out a yell to rival that of the murderous, hungry crowd outside. He used one hand to punch at the hands, causing them to retreat slightly, so now only the fingers were exposed.

Susan mimicked his groaning and together they used every ounce of energy to close the door.

Like the door was a giant pair of scissors, the edge began to slice into the fingers. Blood shot out to hit the walls, freezing on contact. A few sprays hit Mark in the face, some getting into his mouth. He spit out the coppery fluid, and let out a laugh of victory as the doors slammed closed and more than a dozen fingers fell to the floor.

The digits rolled back and forth like worms severed from the main body, the first joint twitching. Then as seconds passed, the fingers became still. With a disgusted mumble, Mark kicked them away from the door. Most of them rolled across the frozen floor to end up under a metal rack holding frozen tenderloins and T-bone steaks, while a few stayed behind like soldiers late for the battle. Susan let out a cry of anguish as she stared at the severed digits, almost throwing up but forcing it back down by sheer willpower.

The door handle jumped and Mark grabbed a four inch pin—similar to a cotter pin—that hung from a chain and slid it into the handle. The handle still moved, but with the pin jammed inside it, the door couldn't be opened.

Mark let out a loud sigh as his body slumped to the floor.

"We're safe...for now," he said as he stared at the door.

"It's cold in here," Susan said softly.

"No shit, Susan, we're in a fucking freezer. What do you expect? Eighty with the sun shining?"

"Well, you don't have to be mean about it," she said and began crying. Mark felt like an ass and he pulled her to him, the two sharing body heat. Neither was dressed for the frigid temperature inside the freezer as it had been a balmy seventy-five degrees outside.

A beautiful night to go out for their anniversary, he'd thought.

Oh, man, if he'd only known how the night was going to end.

As the two hugged each other, the pounding continued on the freezer door.

"I'm cold," Susan said for the hundredth time in an hour.

"Christ, Susan, so am I. But you don't see me saying it every five goddamn minutes."

She pouted but didn't reply.

The two had been in the freezer for hours. Their eyebrows and noses now had little icicles on them and no matter how many times Mark knocked them away, they were back again in what seemed no time flat.

The pounding on the freezer door never ceased, a constant reminder that not only were they trapped inside, but there was absolutely no way to escape without being ripped to shreds. He knew this beyond a doubt because about an hour ago, the banging had stopped for a while and Mark had risked sneaking a peek into the kitchen. When he had pulled on the handle to the door, it had sounded like a gunshot to his frozen ears, and when he cracked the door an inch, his hopes were dashed when he saw the entire kitchen was filled with blood-soaked, raving maniacs.

The reason the banging on the freezer door had stopped was because a large group of killers had taken down a middle-aged couple and had dragged them into the kitchen. Unknown to Mark, the couples' names were John and Martha, and as the two had been ripped apart, Martha had cursed John for bringing her out on this fateful night. As John had his throat torn out, he had told her to *go fuck herself* and that at least he wouldn't have to listen to her nagging anymore and that he would see her in Hell.

In fact, the two were probably in Hell right now, both arguing over what torture they would suffer next as they spent eternity at each other's throats.

"What are we going to do?" she asked as she shivered from the cold.

"I don't know," he said. "Wait them out I guess."

"What if they don't leave?"

He opened his mouth to snap at her, to say that if they didn't leave then it was very possible they could die inside the freezer. Finally he just said, "I don't know."

Mark played with the gun taken from the police officer. He had never been proficient in firearms and had only fired a gun once before in his life. He had been sixteen at the time and he and his buddies had gone into the woods to mess around. Then, James, his friend since kindergarten, had pulled out a .45. He had taken it from his father's nightstand and had suggested they shoot it at targets.

Each kid had taken turns and when Mark's turn came, he had sighted on a crumpled soda can placed on a log. When he'd squeezed the trigger, the gun had jerked in his hand but other than that nothing had happened.

A spray of dirt had erupted near the can and his friends had laughed at him for missing. He had stared at the gun then, trying to imagine how that simple act he'd committed could take someone's life if they had stood before him.

A feeling of power had suffused him but then it had been taken away when James had plucked the gun from his hand, wanting a turn.

James was a much better shot and he proved it, when after a few minutes of talking to the others, a squirrel, unafraid of the gunshots and talking of the boys, had wandered into view. It scuttled across the ground, searching for possible leftovers left by the boys such as discarded chip bags or candy wrappers filled with bits of chocolate.

James had nudged Mark and pointed to the squirrel; then with practiced ease, had shot the small animal.

Mark had been amazed at the way the small, furry creature had simply exploded from the force of the bullet. Blood and viscera had splattered in every direction and when he felt a drop on his cheek, at first Mark thought it was raining. But when he touched the spot with his finger, it came away red.

He had the squirrel's blood on him!

When he looked back to the tiny carcass, it was in pieces, the head now blown off from the torso. The mouth still moved slowly and the eyes were like two small marbles, and James felt sick and awed by the power of the gun at the same time.

As if it was nothing, as if killing another of God's creatures was barely worth mentioning, James clapped his hands to get the boys' attention, put the gun away, and said it was time for them to go home.

Banging on the freezer door brought him back to his dire reality and Mark thought about the people he'd shot before reaching the safety of the freezer and he found he didn't feel too bad about it. If there was supposed to be guilt for taking another life, he was still waiting for it to come.

Now he understood why James had felt no compassion for the squirrel he'd killed.

He played with the gun, figuring out how to pop the clip, and he inspected it. There was a thin line of missing metal molded into the side of the clip so he could count how many bullets remained. Whatever he'd thought might have been left, he was shocked to see there was only one single bullet at the top of the clip, the spring holding it ready to be fired.

One bullet.

Something came to him then, a thought he hadn't entertained until that moment.

Stuck inside the freezer, there were two possible ways to die. One would be freezing to death, but the other was far worse. As he looked around the freezer, at the frozen food lining the shelves, he saw nothing that could be eaten. Frozen roasts and other assorted meats were everywhere as this was storage for meat, but when he stood up and went to one of the roasts, it was as hard as the proverbial rock. He opened a box of chicken and scraped at the frozen flesh but nothing came off. This meat was frozen to the point it couldn't be eaten, no matter how hungry he or Susan might be.

The young couple was literally surrounded by food but they could quite possibly starve to death.

He looked at the gun once more.

If it came to it, a bullet in the head would be preferable to starvation.

But there was only one bullet left and there were two of them.

He forced the gruesome thoughts from his mind. They'd only been inside the freezer for a few hours, certainly not a death sentence. Susan was falling asleep and he grabbed her, shaking to wake her up.

"Hey, wake up, we need to stay warm. Come on, let's exercise," he prodded.

"No, I just want to sleep, leave me alone," she slurred her words.

"No, you can't sleep, come on, let's jog in place." He began doing just that, forcing her to join him. At first she hesitated, her eyes still droopy, but after a few minutes she became more alert.

"Okay, okay, I feel better now," she said as she slowed her exercising. Her cheeks were less flushed and her eyes were now bright.

Four more hours passed terribly slowly with the two of them trying to keep from freezing to death. They had just finished another bout of exercises when Mark checked his watch, frowning at the time that had passed. By his watch, it was morning. They had spent the entire night inside the freezer.

"Look, Susan, we can't keep doing that forever. We need to get out of here," he said.

"I'm all ears," she replied. She was already rubbing her arms again, the chill quickly creeping back into her body. She was tired and had been so cold for so long she wondered if she would ever feel warm again.

"Okay, look, here's the deal. It's very possible help won't come in time to save us so we need to try and get out of here. I have an idea but it's pretty risky," he said.

"Yeah, and…" she prodded.

"Well, if we open the freezer door and one of us runs to the left, the other might make it to the walk-in that's for the vegetables. Once there, it won't be as cold and there'll be food to eat. Someone could last for along time in there until help arrived."

"Why can't we both run to the walk-in?"

"Because the second we open the door they'll be on us. We need a distraction. So one of us has to sacrifice herself so the other can make it to safety."

She raised her hands to stop him from talking further. "Whoa there, hot shot. What do you mean by *sacrifice herself?* Why isn't it *himself?*

"I didn't mean anything by it," he said. I simply mean that one of us will have to be the decoy if the other one wants to make it to freedom."

"So then that's you, right?" she asked. "I mean, you love me, right? You'd sacrifice yourself so that I could live, wouldn't you?"

Mark bit his lip, not replying immediately.

"Hey, what's wrong with you? Why didn't you tell me 'yes' the second I asked? What's to think about?"

"Huh, oh, uhm, nothing I guess, it's just, well, I don't think I want to die for you is all. I mean, shit, we've only been together for a year. That's really not that long when you…uhm…think about it."

She stared at him open mouthed. "Why you no good bastard." She reached for the gun in his waistband and he jumped back.

"Hey, what's the deal?" he snapped.

"The deal is; I want that gun so I can shoot you with it. You said earlier there was only one bullet left, right?"

He nodded. Hours ago he'd informed her of the lack of ammunition for the gun.

"Well then, I want to shoot you with it."

He stared at her eyes, seeing the venom their, and he shook his head. "Shit, you're serious, aren't you?"

"Fucking A, I'm serious. You just said you wouldn't give your life for me. You prick, some man you are. I could have been with Tim Johnson but I chose you instead. Now I see I made the wrong choice."

"Tim Johnson? That asshole?" Mark snapped back, angry now. "Look, Susan, I think you have a pretty fucking high opinion of yourself. I mean, shit, a lot of women would kill to be going out with me but I picked you."

She rolled her eyes, the red in her face now from anger instead of being cold.

"Oh, really? Do you mean like Tina Smithers?" Mark blinked at the name and she nodded. "That's right, I know all about her."

"Hey, that was a one time thing. I was drunk with the guys."

"Uh-huh. And that's why I let it go, but now, well, it's all pretty clear to me what that was about."

Mark was flush now as well. "Well, maybe you're right. I have to admit she was better in the sack than you ever were. At least she moved around once in a while. With you it's like I'm fucking a corpse!"

"Well, maybe if it was bigger and I actually felt like it was in me I might actually move around a bit. Here's something to think about, not only do I fake it, but I have to go into the bathroom to finish off 'cause you can never get me there!"

"Oh, you bitch, that's so much horseshit and you know it!"

"I don't think so, I have to try and stay awake till you finish so I don't hurt that precious ego of yours. 'Oh, baby, give it to me. Oh, baby, you're the best.' Shit, I should get an Oscar for my performance!"

"That's it, you little bitch, you're so fucking dead!" Mark screamed as he pulled the gun from his waistband, but Susan was quicker and she jumped him, the two falling to the freezer floor as they fought for possession of the gun.

Outside in the kitchen, a dozen raving killers stood by the freezer door, listening to the muffled voices of the two 'lovebirds'. Though their minds were filled with killing and hunger, there was a part of them that recalled their old lives and they found it amusing to listen to the trapped couple fighting.

Then, suddenly, there was one muffled *pop* of a gunshot, the sound barely heard through the metal of the freezer door. The killers all stood around, looking at one another, more than one of them chewing on a body part like it was a buffalo wing at happy hour.

As time went by and there was no more noise, no voices, they became uninterested in the freezer and they wandered to other parts of the kitchen to feed on the remains of the middle-aged couple, while others left the kitchen and went back into the dining room.

More than two hours passed without incident until most of the killers didn't remember there were people in the freezer, but for some reason they still stuck around, perhaps a hint of remembrance still in their heads.

Then, more than a day after being chased into the freezer, the door was opened. Slowly at first, a single eye peered out into the kitchen. The eye could see the killers moving about, most sitting down, a few sleeping, and without warning, the freezer door was thrown open and Susan lunged out and to the left at the same time Mark jumped out and ran to the right.

But Susan must have tripped on her own feet because no sooner did she come out of the freezer then she was falling to the floor, her limbs limp, her head striking the floor painfully.

Mark didn't see this as he was running for the walk-in like a marathon sprinter; his eyes taking in the scene of the kitchen in an instant. There would be no other escape but the walk-in. The killers were blocking the rear exit to the alley as well as the swinging doors to the dining room, and beyond it Mark could see the figures of more killers moving about.

Immediately upon Susan falling, the killers turned to face her, others moving close and growling menacingly. Like a pack of wild animals they jumped on her, teeth and nails sinking into her flesh. Some had knives but most were barehanded.

The entire time they attacked Susan, she said nothing, not so much as a gasp, as her limbs were torn from her torso and her throat was ripped open. No blood shot forth from her wounds, but simply spilled out to pool on the tile floor, a congealed mass of red.

Mark dashed the few feet to the walk-in, opened the door and closed it at the same time five killers bounced off the door. There was a similar pin for the handle and he slid it in place, locking it. He sucked in a breath and laughed loudly, knowing he had made it. His plan had worked perfectly.

Falling back onto a pile of produce boxes, he looked around at the shelves of vegetables, mayonnaise, cheese and salad dressings. There was enough food lining the shelves to last for weeks, months even.

Outside in the kitchen, Susan's head was pulled from her neck to be held aloft like a trophy. As her hair was brushed from her forehead by being waved about, the single, clean, bullet hole stood out against her pale skin. The edges were black, the flesh puckered, and under her hair on the back of her head the skull was a ghastly mess of bone fragments; bits of her brain slid out of the cavity like overflowing pudding.

She had been dead long before her 'sacrifice' to escape the freezer.

Inside the walk-in, Mark laughed louder, thinking back to when he and Susan had battled over the gun. It may have been an accident, but in the end there was really no choice. Sure he had loved her, but in the face of certain death, he hadn't loved her *that* much.

It was as he sank his teeth into a ripe tomato that he realized that though he had cared for her, *love* might have been a bit much.

In fact, in his eyes, when it came to who would live and who would die, well, love was dead, and would always be so, for he was still alive and would remain that way until help finally arrived.

Outside, the streets of Chicago burned as society collapsed upon itself. The city was in flames and more than ninety-nine percent of the population was either dead or *changed*.

Mark was still laughing when the power went out and he was thrown into darkness.

Months later, with a corner of the walk-in filled to knee height with his feces and urine, and still no hope of a rescue, and the killers still waiting outside in the kitchen for him to finally come out, he was still laughing, only now it was tainted with madness.

LAST ONE STANDING

The water slapped the side of the lifeboat, the gentle motion almost soothing if not for the harsh rays of the sun. The sky was cloudless, only a deep blue that, if inverted, reflected the ocean below.

Kyle Summers squinted at the bright sun, his eyelids closing on instinct.

Glancing down, he let the blinking spots leave his vision and he looked at his fellow survivors for the thousandth time.

There were seven people in the lifeboat with him, all refugees from the cruise ship when it had gone down.

Like the infamous Titanic, the cruise ship had struck an unmarked, massive coral reef and had cracked in half like an eggshell.

For those hours as the ship sank beneath the waves, it was absolute Hell on Earth. People fought and even killed to get on a lifeboat. Kyle witnessed mankind at his best and worst, unfortunately it was usually the worst. Now, the cruise ship would become a new coral reef, only this one would have thousands of dead bodies trapped within its cracked and dented hull.

He took stock of the other survivors, thinking of their names as his eyes settled on each of them.

There was Seth McCall, a thirty something business man from Detroit and his wife, Lisa. The two had been enjoying their five year anniversary before the ship went down.

There was George and Martha McConnell, both now retired and living in Key West, the cruise a way to get out of the house for a bit and see the world. The next one was Michelle, a buxom cruise director whose job it was to see that the passengers had fun. Kyle almost wanted to snap at her, tell her he wasn't having much fun, but in the end he kept his mouth shut. Frankly, he was so thirsty he didn't know if he could talk anyway.

The next unlucky soul, or lucky as he was still alive, was Brian, a forty-seven year old man with a balding pate and eye glasses with the left lens cracked. He hugged a bag to him like it was a life preserver and when asked, wouldn't say what was in it. No one really cared that much so he was left alone.

The last person in the lifeboat was a woman in her seventies who went by Elle. If she had a last name she wouldn't share. She was morose to the point of suicide. Her husband had been lost in the abandoning of the ship and she was still contemplating whether she wanted to live or not without him.

As Kyle looked at Elle, she returned his gaze with one of her own, though it was less enthusiastic and hollow.

"We need to do something," Seth said to the group.

Brian chuckled, though it was forced. "Oh, yeah? And what would you like to do exactly? We're in the middle of the damn ocean with no food and very little water. We have no way to signal for help and the sun is cooking us like game hens in an oven." Brian glared at Seth. "So I ask you again, just what should we do that we aren't doing? Which is to sit, wait and hope we don't die before we're found."

"That's not what my husband meant," Lisa said, sticking up for Seth.

"Then what did he mean?" George asked Lisa, as his wife, Martha, leaned against him, asleep. They were all dehydrated and exhausted, sleep the only way to pass the time and conserve their strength.

Seth leaned forward, making fists of his hands. "I simply mean we need to do something or we're gonna die out here."

Kyle decided to speak up then before the conversation grew more heated. It had in the past, the survivors all of different personalities and therefore always arguing. One of them would want to go left while another would want to go right, while another wouldn't want to go at all. They had been down this road before, ever since winding up in the lifeboat together.

That was four days ago. The lifeboat had been caught in a current shift and had been pulled far away from the cruise ship's last known coordinates. No one was looking for them because there was no reason to be searching this part of the ocean.

"There's nothing we can do but wait and pray," Kyle said from the bow of the lifeboat.

"That's bullshit, there has to be something we can do," Seth reiterated.

Kyle held his hand out to the ocean, nothing on the horizon in all four points of the compass.

"Then get swimming, Seth," Kyle said. "And maybe you might get lucky and somehow get found. But we both know it would be suicide. There's nothing to do but wait and hope we're found. You may not like it, but it's the truth."

Seth opened his mouth for a rebuttal, but George shook his right hand at him to silence him. "That's enough out of you, Seth, you need to be quiet," George commanded.

Knowing he was outnumbered, Seth closed his mouth, crossed his arms over his chest, and sulked like a child told there would be no cookies before dinner. All the while Lisa was giving everyone the evil eye, wanting to defend her husband.

Kyle couldn't blame her as her husband was right. They needed to do something. But the question was: Just what could they do?

A small beeping began and Michelle touched her wristwatch, silencing the beep.

"It's time to drink," she said as she looked at everyone and reached down for one of the few bottles of water they had left.

"Finally, I'm so thirsty," Martha said.

"Tell me about it, my tongue feels like sandpaper," Brian added, reaching out for the bottle.

"Now remember, I know we're all thirsty, but please, take little sips. We need to make this last. Rationing is our only chance."

A low grumbling was her answer, but she knew they all understood. Seth and Lisa were talking softly together, but no one knew what they were saying.

The water bottle was passed around and each passenger took a few sips. Then it reached Seth. Before he could be stopped, he began to drink in great gulps, then he handed it to Lisa who did the same.

"Hey, stop that! Don't drink it all!" George cried out and everyone turned to look at Seth and Lisa.

"Get her, get the bottle from her!" Brian yelled and Michelle leaned over and yanked the bottle from Lisa's grip.

"Hey, you bitch!" Lisa snapped.

"I'm a bitch? You and your husband just finished off a whole bottle. What the hell's wrong with you?" Michelle yelled back, her eyes filled with anger.

Lisa didn't reply, but when she glanced at Seth and he nodded, the answer was there for all to see. They had said to hell with everyone else and were only worrying about themselves.

"Why would you do that, dear?" Martha asked, hoping to be diplomatic. "I know you're thirsty, but we all are."

"Screw you, you old bat, it's obvious we're all not gonna make it so it comes down to who is gonna survive and who isn't," Lisa said. "For some of us to live, some of you are gonna have to be sacrificed."

George spoke up. "So you just thought it should be you and Seth that get to live, is that it?"

Lisa shrugged. "Sure, why not? We're young and have our entire lives ahead of us. You and your wife and the old bat there," she pointed to Elle, "are on the end of the line. How many years you got left anyway?"

Seth spoke up. "Seems to me it's pretty obvious who gets the short straw."

"You two are terrible people," Martha said.

Lisa snickered at that. "Oh, please, why don't you take those knitting needles and shove 'em where the sun doesn't shine. What the hell are you gonna knit out here in the middle of nowhere, seaweed?"

Martha leaned back and touched the pair of knitting needles in her shirt pocket. She was an avid knitter and at the moment she had no yarn, but the two needles were a part of her. She had knitted all the blankets her children and grandchildren slept on with those exact needles.

"You leave my wife alone, dammit!" George snapped. "I'm not too old to take down a wise ass like you."

Seth laughed. "Bring it on, old man. I'll send your ass over the side and let the sharks eat you."

"Stop it, all of you!" Michelle snapped, getting everyone's attention. "This has gone on long enough. Look, Seth and Lisa drank too much but they won't get anymore tomorrow, that's all. Now arguing about it any longer is just a waste of energy."

"She's right," Kyle said. "I know we're all mad, but we just need to let it go." And he was mad. He stared at Seth and Lisa with anger in his eyes. They could have risked all their lives by guzzling that water. Though he had never considered himself an evil man, as he stared at the couple, he wished they were dead.

Eventually everyone settled down as there was no choice. The hot sun sucked any energy from them and all anyone wanted to do was sleep. A small tent was made of spare clothing at the aft end of the boat and each of them would take turns using it. Even getting out of the sun for an hour was a joyous respite.

So when the sun finally began to set, it was greeted with at first, welcome sighs, but then curses, for on the ocean, with no sun, the temperature dropped fast.

Kyle was fast asleep, dreaming of a swimming pool where the water was pure and fresh. All he had to do is open his mouth and drink...all he wanted until it felt like he would explode like a water balloon.

So when he first heard the screaming, he thought it was in his dream, but as the high-pitched screams and yells of multiple voices came to him, he opened his eyes. The moon was high, the moonlight reflecting off the surface of the ocean to bathe every-thing in a pale, anemic light.

At first, groggy from sleep and exhaustion, he didn't under-stand what was going on, but as he shook off his fugue state, he saw everyone gathered at the aft end of the boat.

"What...what's going on?" he asked anyone who would listen.

Then Michelle was at his side and she looked scared to death. "Oh, Kyle, it's horrible. Someone killed Seth and Lisa while we were sleeping."

"What?" Kyle asked, incredulously. "How?"

Before Michelle could reply, Brian and George were fighting, Brian pointing an accusing finger at Martha.

"She did it!" Brian yelled. "It had to be her!"

George defended his wife. "It wasn't her you idiot, she could never kill someone."

Brian wasn't hearing it. "Bullshit! That's utter bullshit. If she didn't do it then how do you explain those?"

Kyle was on his feet and moving to the aft end of the lifeboat to see what was going on. He had just reached Brian as the man pointed behind him.

"Holy Shit," Kyle gasped as he stared at the bodies of Seth and Lisa. They were inside the tent, both half naked. If Kyle had to guess it looked like they had tried to make love, perhaps wanting to comfort one another in the simple act. But that wasn't what was so disconcerting. It was the knitting needle each of them had jammed into their left and right eyes.

Seth had the needle protruding out of his left eye, while Lisa had one in her right. The needle had about three inches of the shaft sticking out, the rest buried in the brain's of the victim. A clear ooze mixed with spots of red dripped down the face of each victim, the eyes punctured like hardboiled eggs. Both had mouths open wide in silent screams, as if they had seen it coming and had been helpless to stop it.

Behind Kyle, the rest of the survivors argued as George fought off Brian.

Off to the side, Elle, the old woman, did nothing but stare at the deck, lost in a world of her own.

Kyle snapped out of the shock of seeing two dead people and he went to George's aid.

"Brian!" Kyle yelled. "Stop it, will ya? We don't know it was Martha who did this. For Christ's sake, she's an old woman. How could she take out two young adults? And one of them a man in his prime?"

Brian turned to Kyle. "How the hell should I know? Christ, it looks like they were screwing and Martha just snuck up on them and, bam, right in the eye. It was easy."

"And I'm telling you she didn't do it," George demanded.

Martha added her voice in her defense. "He's right, I didn't. I could never do something so heinous. I woke up when I heard screaming and my knitting needles were gone from my pocket. Someone stole them from me."

"Oh, how convenient," Brian said in a disgusted voice. "Someone simply stole them from you."

"That's right, yes, they were gone when I woke up."

George spoke up again. "Besides, if my wife did what you said there'd be blood on her hands, there's not."

Brian scoffed. "What?" he waved his arms around them. "We're surrounded by water, for Christ's sake. All she had to do was lean over and wash her hands."

Michelle shoved her way to Brian. "Look, no one's gonna get lynched while I'm here. Now when we get back to land, the authorities can deal with it, but till then no one is going to do anything." She creased her eyes and set her jaw. She was a formable woman when she wanted to be. "You got me?"

Brian backed down slightly, not wanting to fight with Michelle. She and Brian had become casual friends and Kyle thought Brian was attracted to her. And why not? Michelle was a beautiful woman and Kyle knew Brian must like her as he did, as well.

Finally, Brian threw up his hands in surrender. "Fine, fine, but we need to dump the bodies, there's not enough room in this boat for corpses. They gotta go."

He waited for objections, but for once everyone was on his side.

"Good, let's do it now then, no time like the present." Brian looked down at Lisa and Seth. "I guess someone wasn't too happy about you drinking their water, huh?" Brian turned to Kyle and George. "Come on, you big strong men; help me with these two stiffs."

Kyle glanced to George who only shrugged. Kyle moved in to help and he grabbed Lisa by the legs. Though she was dead, she was still soft and looked like she was sleeping, and he couldn't help but feel slightly aroused by the two perfect breasts and the soft, shaven juncture where her thighs met. He felt dirty for thinking such detestable thoughts considering the circumstances, but he couldn't help himself. As he picked her up and felt her bare left breast brush his right arm, he felt himself growing hard. Shifting position to hide his growing body part, embarrassed and ashamed, he let George help him and they picked her up and set her on the edge of the boat.

"Should we say something before we drop her in?" Kyle asked.

Brian was struggling with Seth's body and he sighed and set the corpse back down. He moved closer to Kyle and George and then looked down on Lisa.

"Ashes to ashes, dust to dust. She was a bitch and her and her asshole of a husband got what was coming to them. Now toss her."

With nothing else to do or say, Kyle shoved the body and Lisa dropped into the water with barely a splash. She sank immediately and was lost from sight.

Seth was next and he didn't get a eulogy. They picked him up and tossed him over, his pants still down by his ankles. Kyle thought it was disrespectful, but then he didn't want to be the one to try and dress the dead man either.

As the body floated down and away, Kyle turned to look at the others. Michelle was sitting with Martha, and George and Brian were to his right. Elle was mumbling something in a litany, a prayer if Kyle was correct.

"You all realize that one of us killed those two, right?" Kyle asked as he made eye contact with each one of them. In the moonlight, each face looked jaundiced.

"The question is, which one of us did it?" Michelle asked as, she too, eyed each of them.

"Maybe two of us should stay awake from now on. One to keep watch while the other watches the first," George suggested.

"That's a great idea. And it's the only way I'll close my eyes and feel safe," Michelle added as she looked to Kyle. "What do you think, Kyle?"

"Yeah, I agree." He looked at George, Martha and Michelle, while Brian messed around inside the small, makeshift tent.

"I still can't believe one of you killed Lisa and Seth," Kyle said. "It has to be Brian. You heard what he said. He said he was glad they were dead."

George looked at Brian's back as he rummaged in the tent and then back to Kyle. "Yes, son, I have to agree with you on that one. I suggest one of us keeps an eye on him at all times."

They all agreed to do just that, and though the excitement of the night thanks to two of their own being murdered had them all wired, their dehydration and exhaustion was more than enough to make them all want to rest.

Martha sat with George and Michelle went with Kyle. Brian saw this and he wasn't pleased, but he didn't say anything. Elle hadn't shown any sign she knew what was going on and Brian sat across from the old woman, complaining about how she was a nutcase and a waste of their resources.

Michelle wouldn't let him complain for long though. "You leave her alone, Brian. She's just a poor old woman who lost her husband. She has as much right to be here as you do."

Brian scowled deeply, but he didn't reply and soon they were all resting quietly as the water lapped against the wooden hull of the lifeboat. George and Michelle took first watch while the others tried to get some rest.

Though Kyle wanted to stay awake, too, not wanting to take chances, he soon found himself drifting off to sleep again.

Suddenly he was snapped awake yet again, this time a scream followed by a splash. His eyes popped open immediately and he used his will power to focus his eyes. Glancing up at the moon, he saw it hadn't traversed the night sky very far and was roughly where it had been before he'd fallen asleep. If he had to guess, only an hour or so had passed.

Looking around, he saw Michelle looking about like she had just woken up and he knew then she had drifted off to sleep while on watch.

Another yell called his attention to the opposite end of the lifeboat and he saw George and Brian fighting. It looked like George was trying to jump into the water, but Brian was stopping him.

"Stop it, you old fool, if you go in the water you're dead!" Brian yelled.

"Let me go, you little bastard," George snapped. "Martha fell in. I have to save her."

Kyle and Michelle were on their feet in an instant, though they had to be careful as the boat was rocking thanks to Brian and George.

Both moved to the two struggling men.

That was when Kyle realized Martha was gone, and when he got close to George, he saw a red spot on the edge of the boat, like a head had been whacked before going into the water.

Michelle moved in and tried to calm George. "Stop it, if you go after her you'll get lost in the darkness. You'll never find us again."

"I don't care, she's my wife, I have to save her," George spit. Then he managed to push Brian away. "I don't have a choice."

Before anyone could talk him out of it, he jumped over the side and into the water. He began to swim away as he called out to Martha. Kyle moved next to Michelle and Brian leaned over the side. Elle hadn't moved, sleeping the sleep of the innocent or insane.

"You dumb bastard!" Brian yelled. "Get back here before it's too late!"

George either wasn't listening or didn't care as he swam away from the lifeboat, calling Martha's name the entire time.

As the seconds passed, his calls began to grow faint until they were swallowed by the sound of the ocean itself.

"Jesus, how's he moving so fast?" Kyle asked.

Brian shrugged. "We're caught in a strong current and he's going the opposite way. With each foot he swims, we're moving two feet away from him. Even if he wanted to come back now we're too far away. He just committed suicide."

Kyle stared at the blood spot on the edge of the boat. "What the hell happened? I thought you were supposed to be on watch?" Kyle asked Michelle.

She looked down and then up, glaring at him. "So I fell asleep, sue me. Shit, I'm tired, hell, we all are."

Kyle pointed to the blood. "I don't think Martha went over by accident. Someone shoved her over. Look here, she must have whacked her head as she tumbled into the water."

Brian and Michelle both looked and nodded. Then Michelle backed away from Brian, going to Kyle for protection.

"You did it," Michelle said. "You were the one fighting with George. Was that because he saw you toss his wife over the side?"

Brian looked hurt. "What? That's crazy. I didn't do anything." He pointed to Kyle. "It was probably your boyfriend there. Sure, he acts all innocent, but so do most serial killers. They always say later, *he was always so quiet.*"

"Fuck you, Brian, I didn't kill anyone, I was asleep," Kyle defended himself.

Brian reached into his back pocket and pulled out a small knife. It was four and a half inches long and was tapered to a wicked edge. It was the kind of knife one might use for filleting a fresh caught fish.

"Well, you two stay away from me or I swear I'll cut you good."

Michelle looked angry, not scared, as she said, "Where'd you get that knife? Have you had it all along?"

Brian shook his head. "Not that it's any of your business, but I found it in the bottom of the boat. My guess is the crew must have taken the boat out to go fishing when in dock. Good thing, too, it'll make sure no one fucks with me."

He turned and went to the small tent at the aft end. "Just stay the hell away from me and you'll live to see tomorrow." Then he went into the tent, but made sure to turn so he could keep his eye on them.

Michelle turned to Kyle and rubbed against him. He felt himself slightly aroused from her touch. He couldn't help it, she was so damn pretty.

"Sorry I fell asleep, I don't even know when I drifted off," she said ruefully.

Kyle nodded. "Hey, I planned on staying awake, too, and I fell asleep. It's okay, we're all too damn tired to stay awake. Especially when there's nothing to do but stare at the ocean." He gazed off into the darkness. "I can't believe this shit, Michelle. It's bad enough the ship sank and I was glad to be alive, but now...Christ, Brian is a serial killer."

She picked up a bottle of water and held it tight. "I can't see straight, I have to sit down before I fall over the side. This is all too much for me. Join me?"

He nodded and the two went to the bow. On the way, Michelle gave Elle some water. The old woman had to be force fed the water and most of it dribbled out of her mouth. Kyle had to admit Brian was right, it was a waste of their water. The old woman was catatonic, mumbling some kind of chant. A prayer of some kind, but he couldn't understand her.

"That's enough, don't waste too much on her," Kyle said softly.

Michelle turned and glared at him angrily. "Not you, too, now. She's a person just like us, we need to help her."

Kyle shrugged. "Still, there's only so much to go around and you and me are young and healthy. We stand a better chance with what we have left."

Michelle shook her head. "No, I won't be that way. Either we all get saved or none of us do. I can't control what Brian did and when we get back to shore he'll have to answer for his actions, but as long as I have a say in it, we all share the water."

Kyle sighed deeply, understanding her sentiment. He thought it was naive of her, but still, he respected her opinion.

"Fine, whatever, I'm gonna go sit down, my legs are weak."

She stood up and followed, the two of them careful to crab walk to the bow. The boat tipped and bucked as they moved and both were relieved when they could sit down.

The darkened sky cast an ominous mood over both of them, the shroud of death ever present.

Kyle felt only slightly guilty actually. People had died, been murdered, and though he knew he should feel something more, in truth, he didn't really care. He didn't really know the people who'd died, not personally. They were strangers to him. Was that callous of him? Maybe.

He was just worried about himself, and Michelle, too.

He hadn't wanted anyone to die, but he had to admit their deaths gave him more drinking water to survive this ordeal.

Michelle curled up next to him and placed her head on his shoulder. Though he could barely see straight from exhaustion, he had to admit it was nice.

If events were different, if they lived to be rescued, maybe they could have something together.

"Uhm, Michelle?" Kyle asked.

"Hmmm?" she replied.

"You don't think it was me, do you?"

She snorted, it was really supposed to be a chuckle. "No, silly. If I did, I wouldn't be sitting here next to you. Look, I saw your face when you woke up. Your reaction wasn't that of a person who'd just committed murder and then was pretending. If so, then you should get an Oscar."

"Okay, that's good to know. And if it matters, I don't think it was you either."

She snuggled closer, already on the verge of sleeping. "That's good to know."

"Go 'head and sleep, I'll watch over you," he said. "If Brian takes a step closer to us I'll wake you and we can deal with him together."

But she was already asleep again, the lack of food and water causing her mind to crash as soon as it had the chance.

Kyle held her, his eyes boring into the small tent at the opposite end of the lifeboat. All he could see was Brian's feet, the man lying prone. Ten minutes later, Kyle began to hear snoring. Brian was out cold. Kyle knew the man was sleeping for the same reason Michelle was. They were all exhausted and could barely stand, let alone stay awake.

But he resolved to stay awake and watch over Michelle, protecting her from Brian.

Of course, his spirit was stronger than his body, and though he stayed awake for almost two hours, eventually his head drooped and he passed out.

The four survivors all slept fitfully as the boat drifted deeper into the ocean.

As he slept, there was a sound Kyle can't quite put his finger on.

It reminded him of the noise women make as they stomp grapes in Italy.

Squish, squish, squish.

In his dream, he imagined auburn haired beauties, stepping on the grapes, crushing them to make wine. As they stepped out of the large barrel, their feet were stained dark red...like blood.

The sound was voracious, attacking his unconscious mind until finally, he opened his eyes, coming back to the land of the living.

And as he did this, his first instinct was to check on Michelle. Her head was still resting on his shoulder, but this time something was wrong. There was a wetness there that he hadn't notice while he slept the sleep of the fatigued.

Reaching out to touch her face, his hand brushed her chin, and when it came away, he saw it was coated with something red, his fingers sticking together.

It was blood!

Sitting up, he shifted position, Michelle falling to the deck like a rag doll. As she fell, her head lolled to the side and Kyle gasped in horror to see her neck was sliced from ear to ear. The jagged mouth still seeped blood and Michelle's eyes were wide open, showing the horror she'd felt as her life's blood poured from her body. Her shirt was covered in blood, looking like she had been dipped in ketchup.

Scurrying away in shock, Kyle looked about the sun-kissed boat. It was just after dawn and the sun was already getting ready to cook the survivors in the small lifeboat.

Then Kyle spotted Brian across from him. He wasn't in the tent anymore, but was now draped with his back against the side of the boat, like he was lounging on the edge of a swimming pool. Kyle screamed when he saw the condition of Brian. The man had been gutted like a fish, the incision starting just below his chin and then drawn down to his groin. He had been peeled open like a two-tail lobster; his insides pulled out and tossed over the side. Around the boat, the water churned red as sharks feasted on the chum.

Brian's visage was one of complete shock, as if while he had been killed he refused to believe it. Kyle had no choice but to wonder if it had been him who had somehow done it in his sleep. Had his subconscious somehow made him a killer, as it was the only way to survive with the limited water remaining?

No, it was impossible. Kyle saw Brian's tongue was missing, the jagged meat stump protruding out of his mouth. Whoever had killed him had cut out his tongue to silence him.

Kyle crawled to his feet, not knowing what to do.

Then he spotted Elle slumped in the corner of the lifeboat. The old woman's head was sagging to the left and she wasn't moving.

"Oh, God, not you, too," Kyle gasped as he crawled to her after touching Michelle's face with loss. He would mourn her later, but right now he was trying to take it all in.

Reaching Elle, he knelt down beside her, and no sooner did he do this, then the old woman's head snapped up and her eyes flared hatred. She kicked out with her right foot, sending Kyle sprawling on the deck. With what seemed to be superhuman strength, she jumped to her feet. Kyle knew it was the strength of madness.

Elle straddled him, looking like she wanted to make love to him, but that was the farthest thing from the truth. Kyle, still too shocked to react, gazed up at the old woman as she produced a knife.

The same one Brian had shown him the night before.

"No, Elle, please. I looked out for you, I tried to help you," Kyle pleaded. But Elle wasn't listening. She raised the knife high over her head, the rays of the morning sun glistening off the tip where it wasn't covered in Brian's and Michelle's blood. With a growl of anger, she brought the blade down and into Kyle's chest, directly over his heart.

Kyle gasped as the knife slid into his chest, past his ribcage, and into his heart, slicing it in twain in an instant as Elle twisted it to the left and right, cutting deeper with each slice.

As the wound grew larger, spilling blood onto the deck by the quart, it began to resemble an autopsy incision; Kyle losing consciousness.

As he slumped into eternal death, he could hear Elle chanting again, and he realized she wasn't chanting some lost prayer to give her comfort.

She was chanting, "*Last one standing, last one standing, last one standing.*"

Then, like a television screen turned off by the remote control, Kyle's vision went dark and he was no more.

BOOK BY ITS COVER

"Open number nine!" the guard yelled.

"Opening number nine," came back from the end of the long hallway. On each side were the bars of cells, the bars of Clermont State Prison. Here, the worst of the worst were tossed in, the key not only thrown away, but it was melted into molten metal beforehand.

Here, killers, rapists and some crimes committed by men that were too horrible to discuss in most circles were kept like caged animals.

No one was innocent here, all were guilty.

And among them all, was Mad Dog Hanes. He stood six feet three in his bare feet and a single one of his hands could grab a normal man by the head and lift that hapless figure up and shake him like a wet tree branch till the neck snapped.

He could break a man in two and had done so not once, but on two occasions. He was serving three consecutive life sentences without so much as a whisper of parole and despite it all, Mad Dog still smiled.

Why?

Because he liked to kill, he liked to maim and he liked to distribute harm whenever possible.

It didn't matter whether he did it on the outside world or here in the prison. As long as he could see the eyes of his victim's as he squeezed the life out of them, he was happy.

Mad Dog was in his bunk, the top one of course, as he looked up at the guard and saw a small man standing next to him.

The small man was wearing the colors of the prison and he looked so thin that if there had been a breeze, even a gentle one, he might just blow away.

The thin man stood no taller than five six and his blonde hair was cut close to his scalp. He wore a pair of wire-rimmed glasses that were so thin, that from a distance it would look as if he wasn't wearing anything.

The man's eyes were a deep blue.

Mad Dog could see, even from across the seven foot cell, that those blue eyes appeared calm. He couldn't help but wonder why, as every prisoner in the system knew about Mad Dog and would have been petrified to be placed in the same cell with him.

Mad Dog sat up, let his feet fall over the side of the bunk, and he grinned as he looked at the thin man.

Though it had never been spoken aloud, both he and the warden had an agreement. If the warden needed to get rid of an inmate, then he would send that inmate to Mad Dog's cell.

Usually within a day, sometimes hours, that inmate would have an *accident*.

Those accidents ranged from falling down so many times that they died of a massive head injury, to tripping and falling so hard that they somehow would manage to get their heads stuck between the bars, despite this being physically impossible.

No inmate could ever be questioned about how this happened as they were all too dead to talk. And now here he was with another poor bastard, basically sent to death row via Mad Dog himself.

"Get in there, asshole," the guard said as she shoved the small man into the cell.

The man fell face first, his hands letting go of his folded blanket and toiletries so he could catch himself and not break his nose on the floor.

As he fell, the guard called out once more.

"Close number nine!"

"Closing number nine," came back.

The cell door rattled on its track as it closed with a hydraulic hiss.

The guard leaned into to the bars and used his club to push up his baseball cap.

"You all play nice now, here?" he chuckled as he walked away, whistling and slapping a few cells with his club when voices barked at him.

"Lights out, you no good pieces of shit!" the guard yelled and then there was a loud *thunk* as the overhead hallway and cell lights were doused. Only a few glowing red lamps in the corners of the hallway cast any luminance into the cells. The light was enough to get up and find the toilet, but not enough to read by.

Mad Dog jumped down to the floor as the small man picked himself up. He didn't seem afraid of his coming future and Mad Dog didn't understand this.

Normally, no matter how tough or hard a man might be in the rest of the prison, once a man got to his cell, they were cowering fools, begging for him not to kill them.

So far he had never listened, as there was no fun in letting them live.

Besides, he liked getting his steady ration of porn mags and cigarettes the warden let him receive.

And once in a while, he was even allowed a conjugal visit, something a lifer such as he should never have been allowed to enjoy.

The small man straightened his eyeglasses and he looked up into Mad Dog's eyes, though with only the one red light outside the cell, the two men could barely see each other.

"So, another one for me to get rid of, huh?" Mad Dog said with a growl. "You pissed off the warden somehow. What did a little runt like you do to piss off the big guy, anyway?"

The man didn't say anything at first, he merely bent over, picked up his blanket and assorted items, and set them on the lower bunk.

The man turned to look up at Mad Dog and slowly, as if there was all the time in the world, as if the man wasn't about to suffer unbelievable pain as Mad Dog tortured him long into the night to then kill him, the man smiled slightly, only with lips, no teeth.

"What the fuck are you smiling about, you little shit? Don't you realize the warden sent you here to die? No one comes into my cell and lives through the night." He slapped his right fist into his open left palm, the noise of the impact loud in the small cell. "You and me are gonna have a lot of fun tonight. You're a pretty one, ain't ya. I like 'em pretty."

The man looked away from Mad Dog, took off his glasses, and carefully placed them into the pocket on his shirt, then he looked back up at Mad Dog.

Though the light was almost nonexistent, and perhaps this was why, but Mad Dog saw that the man's eyes seemed to glow slightly—a red glow to match the crimson lamps in the hall.

"Mad Dog, Mad Dog, Mad Dog," the small man said in a whisper. "You have it all wrong. It's not me the warden wants killed." The man smiled again now but this time he showed his teeth, and as Mad Dog looked down at his face, he saw the whites of two very sharp incisors on either side of the man's smile, such as one would find on a wolf —or a vampire.

But that was ridiculous because vampires didn't exist, Mad Dog told himself as he stared at the man's glowing eyes.

"What the fuck are you talking about, asshole?"

"You screwed up," the man said. "That last inmate the warden sent you was still alive when he left your cell. You got lazy and didn't check. He talked about what he knew. What the warden didn't want him to talk about. That means you screwed up and are no longer any use to him. A killer who can't kill is pretty damn worthless, don't you agree?"

Mad Dog chuckled but it was hollow. The little man's confidence was so great that Mad Dog couldn't help but be intimidated, if only a little.

"And what the fuck are you gonna do to me, you little shit. Christ, I could snap your neck like I was making a wish," Mad Dog blustered and was preparing to reach out and do just that. He would show the warden he was still useful by ripping this guy into bloody pieces

But before Mad Dog realized what was happening, the little man opened his mouth wide and he lunged at him, slamming him against the back wall of the cell as if he was nothing but a child.

Mad Dog found himself with his feet dangling two inches off the floor, the small man's arm extended, his hand wrapped around his neck like Mad Dog had done to so many victims.

"You've been replaced, Mad Dog, you're not needed anymore."

Mad Dog was thrown across the cell like he weighed nothing. He bounced off the bars and then dropped to the floor where he landed hard. His eyes closed as he fell and he opened them fast, no more than a second could have passed, but as he looked up, in the wan light of the red hallway lamp, he saw the unmistakable flash of fangs coming toward him, the once blue eyes now glowing dimly in the gloom.

He tried to fight, but for some reason the little man overpowered him, his mouth clamping onto Mad Dog's neck as he began to slurp and suck like something out of a horror movie.

Mad Dog managed to land a few punches into the man's side as his life's blood was sucked out of him, but they did nothing to halt the attack.

As his vision began to dim from blood loss, he realized he was the predator no longer.

Now he was the prey

ADRIFT: A WEREWOLF TALE

The small, one man row boat rocked to and fro in the middle of the choppy Atlantic ocean, the sun baking the contents. The small waves slapped its sides, and every now and then a larger wave would strike, threatening to tip the small craft over.

It was when a particularly rough wave struck that something inside the boat shifted and a dark hand appeared to drape over the side.

The hand was an adult male's, and with the exception of the index finger twitching slightly, the hand was still.

The waves continued lapping the side, uncaring of the fate of the small boat's occupant.

* * *

The U.S.S. Miller cut through the water like a dagger, the white froth churning the dark blue water to mist as it sprayed up and splashed the face of Petty Officer Simmons. He was in the bow of the frigate, right where the port and starboard sides met at the tip of the ship, and to him it was the best place on earth or anywhere else to be.

When he was standing at the junction, he was able to gaze down into the water and pretend he was flying. It was a lot like that *Titanic* movie where the couple stands at the bow, only he'd been doing it without ever knowing about that particular scene in the movie. Not that he could blame the movie. If anyone had the opportunity to stand where he was, they too would feel the same exhilaration as the ship chopped through the water at 25 knots.

So it was not surprising that he would be the person to spot the small boat floating a thousand yards off the port side. His keen eye spotted it immediately as the ship crested the next wave and there it was. He had probably beaten the lookout on the bridge, as well.

He was about to leave the bow and get to a radio to call the bridge when he felt the ship begin turning hard to port, the bow now aimed directly at the small boat.

So he wasn't the first to spot the dingy or whatever it was floating all alone in the middle of nowhere.

He stayed put, watching the small boat, and as the frigate grew closer, an alarm sounded across the main deck and a bell rang from somewhere inside the ship, followed by the arrival of a few more crewmen. Simmons turned and watched as the crewmen went to the port side and took off the handrails, then waited with harnesses and ropes for the frigate to get close enough to the small boat to manage to secure it.

When this happened, a man climbed down a small rope ladder to reach the boat and then used a pole with a hook to pull it close. Others helped, and in no time the boat was tied to the frigate as men climbed down, found the unconscious man, got a stretcher, and then winched it back up.

This took time, and two hours later the lone occupant of the small boat was on the main deck and the Doc was quickly looking him over to judge his condition.

Simmons walked over to get a better view of the man who appeared to be barely alive. He was black, with dark curly hair and a small beard adorned his chin, a thin mustache riding his upper lip. His clothes were nothing but rags, and the material had what looked like dried blood covering it. But it was while Simmons watched that the most unusual thing on this man showed itself. As the Doc opened the button down shirt of the man, it was clear he had what was obviously bite marks on his upper shoulder and torso. The radius was large, more than six inches wide and Simmons' mind raced with what could do that kind of damage. Images of large dogs came to mind.

The edges of the wound were crusted with blood and the Doc immediately got to work, adding an IV and checking blood pressure as he pressed the edges of the wound. When he was satisfied the man was as stable as he could be, the Doc had two crewmen carry the stretcher belowdecks to his small closet of a sickbay.

After the ailing man was gone, the excitement over, Simmons hung around on the deck for another ten minutes, listening to others talk about what they had found today.

The small boat was brought up and then secured in the small helicopter hangar and the frigate got underway once more.

After chatting with a few buddies about this and that, Simmons went below decks. He had watch in a few minutes and knew if he was late again, he'd be scrubbing the bilges for the next week.

After his six hour watch, he went to the mess hall to grab some dinner and then headed back up to the main deck for a quick smoke. A few others were there already, each only a dark shape in the night, only their cigarettes giving away their position. The moon was just visible in the sky, having popped up as the sun went down, and its circular face looked down on the ship as it cut through the water.

Simmons loved the way the moonlight reflected the spray as the bow pierced the waves. Small bits of glowing algae could be seen in the spray as they bounced off the hull of the ship. It was magical, staring out into the utter darkness of the ocean, the lone frigate the only thing in sight for miles.

After finishing his smoke, and feeling more relaxed, Simmons went below to get some sleep, knowing the next day would be the same as today and the day after, but then, that was the life of a Navy man.

A few hours later, with the moon full in the night sky, down belowdecks, deep inside the ship in sickbay, the unconscious black man began to stir. The full moon had awoken the curse within him, and as he lay perspiring on the small, thin mat on the examination table, the IV now hanging from the wall behind him, he began to moan, his skin rippling as unnatural forces took hold.

The man's closed eyelids suddenly snapped open and they were filled with fear and pain. The eyes seemed to bulge out of their sockets and the man's body began to twist in unimaginable agony. Limbs began to contort and skin split, the man now shedding his skin like a giant snake. Underneath the lost skin, new flesh was growing, and on this flesh were dark brown hair follicles. As the man bellowed in agony, his leg bones shifted inward and his hips became extended as he went from humanoid to animalistic. His face took on a mask of agony as his jaw began to extend, the human teeth falling out as new ones grew in, these sharp and pointed. The nose receded to be replaced by a dark black one, the moisture on the tip making him look like a dog. His old, human ears fell off, now discarded, and fresh ones grew in, these with pointy tips and covered with coarse hair. As the head morphed into one resembling a wolf, a howl left the man's suffering mouth. Large claws grew out of the tips of his fingers, the fingernails already fallen off to lie on the deck, forgotten.

There were straps holding the man down to the bed, but they weren't there to hold him captive, but only to prevent the man from falling off the bed if a bad wave hit. The straps were ripped apart as the man who was not a man any longer howled to the ceiling, wanting nothing more than to escape his metal prison.

The dark skin of the man lay discarded on the floor like a pile of old clothes and the beast stepped over it, moving towards the hatch leading to the outer corridor.

At the exact moment the beast reached the dogged hatch, it was opened by a sailor coming in to see what the commotion was about. The man wore the blue jumpsuit most crewmen wore when the ship was underway, and he stepped inside in a rush, assuming the man they'd found was hurt and suffering.

So as the metal hatch swung open, and he gazed up at something from fairytales and legends, his mouth fell open and he didn't move an inch.

The werewolf looked down on the sailor from its seven foot height, its teeth flashing in the overhead light, as drool slid from the corner of its mouth.

And then, lightning fast, the werewolf struck, bringing its claws up and down, slicing the man practically in half from throat to groin. The sailor's ribcage was sliced in twain and his entrails spilled out as he gasped in shock, the one scream locked in his throat, never to escape.

The sailor, his hands cupping his intestines as he tried to keep them inside his body, fell to his knees as tears of pain and terror filled his mind and body.

The beast didn't care and only wanted to kill, and as the sailor knelt in front of the beast, like a man praying to his God, the creature swiped its claws across the sailor's neck, slicing the throat and setting free a warm geyser of blood. As the man's head flopped to the side, all but a thin amount of skin still holding it to his shoulders, the beast stepped over the fallen man and continued on.

It was time to go on the hunt, and though not in the woods or on an austere plain, this new, metal world filled with trapped prey would suffice for a hunting ground.

Stepping into the hallway, the beast galloped down the deck in search of the men hiding within.

* * *

On the lower deck, in the berthing area, the beds, or *racks*, were lined up in rows of three, stacked three high as well. There was no more than three feet of height between the bed and ceiling of each bunk and the men were crammed in like sardines.

Well past midnight, the phosphorescent lights were out, only the soft glow of the painted red *night light* bulbs at each end of the section being the only illumination. The berthing units were split into separate rooms around the ship. There were beds in the bow and the rear as well as on the upper deck for the officers' quarters. Each room could be closed off to create an airtight seal with the heavy metal hatches with rubber seals in the metal frames. But on top of protecting each area from water, when the hatches were *dogged*, they also blocked out almost all sound.

The werewolf wasn't just a dumb beast. It still retained the memories of the man it once was and now used that intelligence while hunting.

Stepping into the first berthing area, it closed the hatch behind it, dogging the hatch on all four corners.

The sound of snoring called to it and it went to the first bunk. A short, skinny man lay sleeping, a Penthouse still on his chest as he dreamed of women who wouldn't touch him if he was the last man on Earth.

Raising his right, clawed paw high, the beast brought it down, slicing into the man's abdomen and then dragging the claws up the torso, slicing the magazine in half, until finally stopping at the neck. The man woke up immediately, screaming, as unbelievable pain filled his system, but he was already dying even as he shrieked his last. Rolling to the side, his entrails spilled out to splash onto the deck as they then slithered down the aisle, following the slight slant to the deck.

Pandemonium ensued as the dying man's howls snapped every sailor in this section awake. Men jumped up and out of bed, looking around in the gloom of the red bulbs, searching for the reason for the screaming. But no sooner did they awake, then they were slaughtered like chickens in a hen house where the fox had free reign.

One sailor looked around, standing in the aisle with only boxers on, and he shrieked in pain when a set of claws appeared in his chest. Behind him, the werewolf stood silently, the man now impaled on the werewolf's limb. The beast's strength was so great it had shoved its claws through the back of the sailor and then out the chest, now holding the man's heart in its dagger-like fingers.

The sailor had enough time for the one screech, and then he died, the beast shaking the body off its paw as it turned for another target.

And there was plenty more. Fifteen men were in this berthing section at the time of the beast's arrival and each man was systematically slaughtered. Entrails were exposed, heads were ripped from shoulders, limbs pulled from torsos, and disembowelings were the common thread as the werewolf charged in with gusto, its bloodlust knowing no bounds. When every man was dead, the creature licked its claws clean, relishing the taste of the warm human blood, then it went to the next hatch, opened it, and moved deeper into the ship for the next berthing section of sleeping humans.

Though some of his kind may have found the hunting of the humans in this ship too easy, this particular beast had no problem with it.

As long as it could kill, it was happy.

And from the looks of it, the beast would be very happy this night.

*   *   *

Simmons was dreaming about running on the beach with the sun beating down on his head. As his feet squished through the warm sand, he could hear the water crashing against the shore. The steady crash of the water continued until he felt his bladder screaming for attention.

Snapping awake, he realized he needed to pee...immediately.

Climbing out of his rack, he padded through his berth, the snoring of the other men carrying to his ears, sounding like a strange symphony. One man's snoring was high, while another's was low. One was drawn out, while another was like a snorting bull. All very amusing, but it still didn't solve his bladder problem, so off to the *head* he went.

There was a problem however once he arrived. It seemed this particular head was closed for maintenance. On the door was a sign, and on that sign was the name of the department who authorized its *secured* status.

"Damn ship, lucky it floats at all," he commented as he moved away wincing. He had to go real bad.

The U.S.S. Miller was over thirty years old and needed constant maintenance. Something was always breaking and the main deck and hull had to be scraped and painted on a monthly basis. The salt water did a lot of damage to the old girl and only the hard work of her crew kept her floating.

The next closest head was a deck up, but it wasn't like he had a choice. So, though he didn't want to go for a walk, up the closest *ladder* he went until he was inside the head and peeing into the urinal.

As he went to the bathroom, a few times he thought he heard someone cry out, but when he stopped peeing to listen, it was gone. The vent near the door was clicking with each spin of the blade and it seemed to drown out any other noises of the ship very well. Just one more item to fix on this old ship, he thought.

Besides, he figured what he'd heard were either a few guys somewhere shooting the shit, as voices tended to carry and bounce off the metal bulkheads of the ship, or he was imagining it. Sometimes, when the waves were choppy, the sounds the water made as the hull cut through the ocean sounded a little like talking.

No sooner did he finish and was about to go back to bed then his stomach began to growl and he felt a sharp pain in his abdomen. Knowing he now needed to take a dump, he cursed the mess specialist who had prepared last night's dinner.

Shit on a shingle was what he'd had and he knew as he ate each bite that the food would come back to haunt him, and so here he was. At least he hadn't walked all the way back to his rack only to now have to come back. So thanking God for small favors, he grabbed a leftover newspaper from the sink and picked a toilet.

As he let himself go, he read the paper and tried not to fall asleep, knowing in a few minutes he would be able to do just that.

Thirty minutes later, Simmons was finally finished. He was like a volcano; every time he thought he was done, his stomach would rumble and he'd fill the toilet yet again. By the time he was actually through, he felt as light as a feather.

Flushing and cursing the cook's name yet again, he tossed the newspaper back on the sink for the next poor soul who had run afoul of the cook's cuisine and headed back to his rack.

Just before he reached the hatch that would let him into the section where his rack was, he detected an odd smell. Coppery mixed in with offal. He wondered if someone had shit themselves or maybe were farting their butt off, but as he stepped through the hatch and the small aisle that would lead to his rack, his jaw fell open in utter shock and disbelief and he felt his world fall out from under him.

His feet were submerged in something warm and he glanced down to see it was an inch deep in some viscous, dark fluid. With only the red night light bulbs for illumination, he couldn't tell if he was standing in water or not, but as he stared at the room, he knew water would have been a Godsend.

When he had left his rack a half hour ago, the other men had been sleeping fitfully, snores filling the air, but now, the room looked like something out of a slasher movie.

Body parts were everywhere; arms and legs were draped on every surface as well as internal organs, which were strewn about like garland. Stepping forward, he stopped at the rack to his right. It was the middle one, about shoulder height, and as he looked into the small cubby, a severed head stared back at him. It was Rollins, an eighteen-year-old who had joined the ship less than three weeks ago. Rollins tongue hung out and his eyes were wide open, the death mask now frozen on the face, the mouth open wide in a silent scream.

Simmons felt himself growing dizzy and he leaned against the rack to steady himself and his palm came away covered with blood.

On the next bunk to his left was Petty Officer First Class Watson. The man's torso was now ripped in half, his arms and legs nowhere to be seen. His eyes were missing, only large grooves where some kind of knife had clawed them out remaining.

Simmons stared at the charnel house of death for almost thirty seconds since entering the room, and then he felt his stomach explode and he vomited into the aisle, spraying the eyeless head with his dinner as he heaved for all he was worth.

When he'd recovered, he knew this had to be reported immediately.

Moving to the end of the aisle, careful not slip on a stray kidney or liver, he picked up the phone and dialed the bridge.

There was no answer.

Panicking, he then dialed the engineering department. There was always someone there, there had to be. The engines needed to be monitored twenty-four hours a day. But when he called, the squawking box alerting someone in the aft section that they had a call, no one answered.

Simmons began to panic even more, his breath coming hard and fast, the taste of bile on his tongue. He was already going to hyperventilate but now...

And then, if it was possible after what he'd already seen, he saw something that turned his world upside down and made everything he knew and believed nothing but fog in a heavy wind.

From the opposite end of the room, at the same hatch he'd used a minute ago, a large shape entered and gazed at him from the entryway.

It was tall, so tall its head brushed the ceiling, and the creature had to move slowly so it would fit through the hatchway. It was covered in hair and looked like a dog, but when the creature leaned forward and went to all fours, Simmons saw it resembled a wolf more than a canine.

And then all those fairytales and movies as a kid flooded into his head and he saw it wasn't a wolf exactly, for it walked like a man, as well.

With absolute clarity he accepted what was before his eyes.

It was a werewolf.

The phone slid from his numb hand, forgotten, as he stared at this creature of myth. As for the werewolf, it raised it hackles, its haunches wiggling, and Simmons knew it was about to jump for him.

Though frozen in fear, he knew he needed to leave now or he was going to end up as wolf chow, so just before the beast lunged at him, Simmons spun and jumped through the hatchway behind him, just as the werewolf landed where he'd been a second ago.

Simmons tried to slam the hatch closed, but a long claw became jammed in the frame. As he pushed on the door, the hatch bounced and wiggled beneath him as the werewolf tried to break through, snarling the entire time.

Simmons knew if he couldn't hold the hatch closed he was a dead man so he cried out in exertion and pressed harder. The claw began to bend and then, like a magic trick, the hatch cut the claw off like a giant fingernail clipper, the hatch seating, but still not dogged.

But no sooner did this happen then the hatch bounced under him again, sending him flying backwards to bounce off the far bulkhead. His head struck the metal plating and he saw stars, but he knew if he lost consciousness now he would never wake up.

The hatch, now a few feet from him was kicked in, the massive *clang* when it struck the bulkhead behind it vibrating through the ship, and Simmons saw the beast standing in the hatchway.

Sliding to the left, Simmons made it to the open passageway, and as the beast snarled at him, sharp teeth gleaming in the pallid light of the overhead lights, Simmons turned and ran.

He ran as if his life was at stake because it was, and as he reached the far ladder that led to the upper deck and the bridge, he took the thin metal steps three at a time.

Upon reaching the landing he spun around, expecting to see a hairy face coming for him, but the beast wasn't there.

Not complaining, he turned and ran for the bridge, wanting to let the duty officer know what was happening on the ship.

The duty officer was also armed and what he needed now was a gun.

* * *

Stepping onto the bridge, he gasped in horror and fell to his knees.

There would be no help here, he found out, as the five men who had had the graveyard watch were now nothing but bloody chunks and a few pieces of crimson rags that were once their uniforms.

Simmons crawled into the middle of the bridge, staring at the horror surrounding him.

His hands splashed in blood, but he ignored it, his mind racing with his predicament. Maybe he was dreaming, maybe this was all a product of the cook's shit on a shingle and he would wake up restless but fine.

He spotted the corpse of the duty officer in the corner and he crawled to it. When he reached the body, the man's gun wasn't in its holster. Looking around, he didn't see it anywhere and didn't know if there was time to search for it.

As he moved away, trying to find the gun, his hand came down in the open torso of what was once the ship's navigator and he pulled it free with disgust, a viscous slime still attached, like red and black snot. Shaking his hand clean, he climbed to his feet, and as he looked out through the large windows of the bridge and down the main deck of the bow below, he saw no one. Usually at least a few crewmen were up and about, no matter what time it was, having a smoke or taking a break, but the main deck was empty.

No, wait, there was something. As he stepped closer and peered harder, his eyes picked up shapes on the deck.

And then, as the ship cut through the darkness, the moonlight filtered down and pushed the shadows away for one brief second. And Simmons saw those shapes were people, men, and they weren't all together. Like a child's jigsaw puzzle, the deck was strewn with body parts. A head was here, an arm there, a puzzle to try to figure out which went with which torso.

It was all so surreal and he had a feeling the only reason he could still function at all, the only reason he wasn't curled into a ball and losing his mind, was the simple fact his brain wouldn't let him take all this in as real. It was like when someone dies close to you and at first it doesn't sink in. Sure they're dead, but you can't see them, it seems like its untrue and everything around you still moves on, the same as before. It's only later that reality sets in and you discover you'll never be able to call that person on the phone, never talk to them again, never see them smile or hug you. Then, usually in the middle of the night, it hits you like a ton of bricks, burying you under the weight of loss.

Simmons knew if that happened to him now he was a goner, so he wracked his mind to figure out what to do next.

And then it hit him.

The radio room! He could contact Newport, RI, and let them know he needed help. Big time help.

Shaking from fear and shock, he turned and was about to head for the radio room when the werewolf appeared in the far doorway. The overhead fluorescents lights were on in the bridge ceiling and Simmons could now see the werewolf in all its terrifying glory.

Muscles rippled under its fur and the teeth in that muzzle looked like they could tear him in half. And after seeing its handiwork from earlier, he knew this to be an absolute fact.

The paws of the beast were raised in front of it, the extended claws long and sharp and covered in congealing human blood. Only one claw was missing on its left paw, the missing claw seeming strangely out of place, as if the beast wasn't symmetrical now.

Simmons never hesitated this time, he just turned and ran, the werewolf bounding after him, now on the hunt for his hide.

He ran off the bridge and down the connecting hallway, only his knowledge of the ship's passageways allowing him to stay ahead of the beast, but he could hear it slavering behind him. As he passed by other rooms, he caught glimpses of mutilated bodies and internal organs splashed about the rooms, and he realized he just might be the last man alive on board the ship.

As he had sat in the head, cursing the cook, the werewolf had gone from section to section, disemboweling and slaughtering every man on the ship. And with him in the head, the fan blocking out all sound outside, he'd heard none of it and had luckily gone undiscovered by the beast.

But his luck had run out and now it was his turn.

He bounced off a bulkhead as the passageway doglegged to the left and he found himself now in officer's land. But if their higher ranking as members of the crew had made them think they were immune to death at the hands of the beast, they were sorely mistaken.

Officers were sprawled in their bunks; their chests ripped open, throats sliced nearly in half. Blood pooled on the deck like dark syrup, splashing as Simmons charged through the passageways.

He reached the door for the wardroom, a flimsy wooden construct that wasn't meant for anything but privacy, and he jumped inside, slamming the door behind him.

No sooner did the door latch then the beast was on the other side, raking its claws at the wood, shredding it like it was nothing but cardboard.

Simmons held the door for less than ten seconds and then had to jump away as claws slid through the facade, narrowly slicing his fingers off.

Falling away, his back hit the dinner table as dishes and silverware were knocked to the deck. As he turned to look around the wardroom, he saw the same scarlet decor on the walls and on the bench seat to his left was the captain of the ship. Only his head was there, the rest of his body was somewhere else on the ship and Simmons felt himself totally losing it.

That was it then; the door was giving way and everyone else was dead. And so would he in matter of seconds.

The door seemed to explode of its small hinges and the wooden facade hit Simmons in the face and chest, knocking him onto the table. As if he was setting himself up for the slaughter, he was now lying on the table, his legs hanging off the edge to swing back and forth.

The beast bounded in, only the low ceiling slowing it down, and Simmons stared into the eyes of death incarnate.

The werewolf raised it right paw, claws extended ready to rend his chest into bloody ribbons, but at the same time it prepared to strike, a large wave crashed against the hull. With no one piloting the ship, it had turned into the current, causing some mild upset of its stabilizers.

The werewolf was off balance for just a heartbeat, Simmons seeing this all in slow motion. As the beast reared back and recovered, it then prepared to rend him in half.

Simmons right hand was reaching, stretching across the table, wanting desperately to grasp a lifeline that wasn't there, but then his hand found something under a cloth napkin.

A dinner knife, one of many that had been set on the table for the officer's coming breakfast.

Grabbing the knife, Simmons swung it upwards, and as the werewolf came down, slicing him, the shiny blade slid deep into its chest, piercing the ribcage and puncturing the heart within. Though the beast's creation was the stuff of legends, the heart was all too mortal.

The werewolf fell on top of him as it spasmed, its jaws snapping at his face. He jerked his head to the side, but the teeth came down on his right bicep, the razor-sharp teeth sinking deep in to his flesh before the beast huffed out its last breath and sagged on top of him.

He lay there, on the table in the wardroom of the ship as the beast sagged over him like a spent lover. He was too afraid to move, not believing the creature was truly dead. But the blood seeping from the knife wound stuck in the creature's chest and onto his stomach was proof of that.

It was hard to extricate himself. First he had to pry the jaws open to free his arm, then he had to sort of slide out from under the hairy body as he pushed up at the thick chest. No sooner did he free himself than something amazing happened.

The beast began to shift, the flesh twist, and as he watched in stunned silence, only the cracking of bones and the sound of meat pressed against meat, the werewolf began to change; to revert back to the black man it had been before the transmutation.

The body moved on its own as this change occurred and soon the werewolf was gone, only the corpse of the man they had found in the small rowboat remaining.

After what had happened, Simmons felt vulnerable unarmed so he leaned forward and withdrew the steak knife from the corpse's chest, a sucking sound following as dark red blood dribbled out of the wound.

The shiny blade seemed to repel the blood on it, the metallic coating like rainwater to a waxed car, and as the blood receded and dripped down the hilt and over his fingers, he saw two words etched on the blade. ***Sterling Silver***.

Simmons actually smiled then. He smiled for the simple reason he was still alive, for the reason that he'd beaten the odds when no one else had. It was as he turned to leave the wardroom, heading back to the bridge to try and figure out what to do next, that he glanced at the knife yet again, reading the words one more time.

"Well I'll be, so it is true," he mumbled as he entered the passageway.

As he walked, he absently touched the bite mark on his arm, the impression of the werewolf's teeth a dark, bloody outline on his skin.

He wasn't worried, though.

He could get it bandaged later as it wasn't life threatening, and in fact the blood was already congealing in the wound.

After all, he was alive and well, and he had all the time in the world.

Or at least, unknown to him, until the next full moon.

ESCAPE

"You runnin'," Richard asked the big man standing next to him. He lit a cigarette and snapped his Zippo closed. He took a pull and let it out, the smoke drifting lazily into the dingy basement air. In the background, gunshots could be heard and screams for help as the rest of the SWAT team cleared out the tenement building.

For some unknown reason, the occupants had kept their dead with them, and now there was chaos in the rundown building.

The tall man with the dark face shrugged slightly, not replying to Richard's question. Truth was, he didn't know where the smaller man was going with it. To run would be to abandon his post; to take the coward's way out, and for all he knew Richard was trying to set him up. He didn't know Richard, the two troopers assigned to different units, and he'd just met the man. And though he'd sized Richard up as okay, he could be wrong.

Plus, Richard had seen him shoot Willy.

As if Richard sensed Paul's internal thoughts, he spoke up.

"I don't mean because of what happened to Willy. Shit, you had no choice, he'd gone apeshit." Richard shrugged then as he looked up into Paul's face. This large black man was an intimidating soldier. He had almost a foot on Richard and he exuded strength and confidence. Richard felt drawn to the man immediately. He already knew he would be honored to fight by Paul's side. And he had a feeling if he did run tonight; this man would be good to have with him to watch his back.

"Yeah, well, it's done so..." Paul trailed off.

"I could run, I could run tonight. A friend of mine does the weather for WGON. He flies the weather copter and he said I could come along when he leaves the city tonight."

Paul said nothing, only stared with hard eyes at Richard.

Swallowing, Richard continued. "You think it's right to run? To get the hell out of Dodge?"

Paul said nothing. Instead he swung his rifle over his shoulder and headed for the door leading out of the basement. Richard dropped his cigarette to the floor, stepped on it out of habit, and padded after the bigger man.

The two had an encounter with an old priest from the local Puerto Rican parish and after being informed the dead were in another part of the basement, and had been given their last rights, the two SWAT officers headed for the makeshift tomb to deal with the ghouls.

Once there, they found horrors only seen in nightmares. Paul took over with the distasteful chore of shooting the ghouls in the head, and when one zombie began to crawl towards him, Paul calmly began to reload. Tears slid down his cheeks as he slid fresh bullets into the cylinder. Most of the zombies still looked human and it sickened him to have to put them down. But they weren't human anymore, and though he told himself that again and again, it was still hard to face.

As the ghoul reached out for Paul's boot, Richard stepped up and aimed his revolver at the zombie's head. The gunshot filled the air, all the more deafening because of the close confines of the stone walls. The head exploded from the point blank impact of the round and the ghoul dropped to the floor in a spray of blood and brains.

Paul snapped his cylinder closed and began firing again. When he was finished, he turned to Richard, his cheeks still wet. He showed no embarrassment for showing this other man who he barely knew his emotions. He felt no shame for feeling how he did.

"You asked me a question, earlier," Paul said flatly.

"Yeah, I did...and?"

"And count me in," Paul said.

As more police and riot troops moved in behind them to begin with the final cleanup, Paul and Richard left, heading for the outside.

Just like that the decision was made. They were going to run. But first they would need to steal a squad car and make it free of the blockade surrounding the tenement building.

And that could prove easier said than done.

* * *

The side fire door to the tenement was locked, but a good kick by Paul had it flying open to smack the brick wall of the building with a loud clang.

Behind them, in the stairwell, three zombies lay twitching with their chests and heads demolished by gunfire.

When Paul and Richard had descended the stairs, the three zombies had been waiting, almost as if they were setting up an ambush. But the ghouls were no match for the two well armed troopers, and in seconds the bodies were riddled with lead as they dropped to the bottom of the stairwell.

As the two men stepped outside into the dark night, the blockade was still in full swing. More than a dozen squad cars were scattered around the tenement building, yellow saw horses set up to keep the small crowd of onlookers at bay. Both Paul and Richard moved away from the building and into the heart of the blockade.

Chaos reigned as men and women were escorted from the scene while off to the left the first body bags were being taken out of the building. More than one bag had dark stains on its surface, signifying the occupant hadn't gone down easy.

Richard paused to watch as a specially assigned group of troopers was making a funeral pyre with the bodies in the parking lot. Whatever was happening to Philly was at the point there was no time to bring the bodies in for burial, instead they would be burned right there in the rear parking lot of the building. Nearby, but not too close, sat a wood-paneled station wagon, a Datsun, a Dodge Dart and a white Charger, their owners probably dead or zombies.

The bodies were tossed one on top of the other like cordwood, the black body bags sliding against one another. More than one hadn't been bothered to be zipped up, and as the bags landed and slid; arms and upper torsos fell out.

Paul stopped walking when he saw Richard wasn't with him, and as he turned and went to him, he too paused to watch the pyre being lit.

A man wearing a white protective suit was tossing gasoline onto the bodies and then he stepped back and nodded to another man who lit a road flare, then tossed it onto the corpses.

Like a match being struck, the pile of arms and legs began to burn, a dark black smoke drifting up into the night sky to be lost in the darkness.

As the fire burned, more bodies were added, some merely dead, not zombies. These were the men who had tried to take on the SWAT team but had lost miserably. Richard watched as a man in a denim jacket and head band was tossed in the flames like he was trash. Richard had tried to save that man by warning him not to go out onto the roof, but the man hadn't listened. He'd been gunned down to then topple off the roof to fall to his death.

It was all such a terrible waste, Richard thought as he felt Paul's hand on his shoulder.

"Come on, brother, we need to blow this scene," Paul said in a low voice, not wanting any of their fellow officers to hear him.

"Huh? Oh, yeah, sorry, Paul, I was just..."

"Yeah, man, I know. It's cool, let's get moving. You said we need to be at the police dock by nine, right?"

Richard checked his watch. It was almost eight.

"Yeah, that's right. A little after nine. He said he's picking up his girlfriend first at nine sharp, then he'd meet me at the police dock. But it wouldn't take him long to get there from the television station."

"Okay then," Paul said as he turned and walked away, this time Richard was with him.

"What's the plan?" Richard asked as he plodded askance of Paul.

"We need to snag one of these cars without anyone gettin' wise on what we're gonna do with it."

"Why, you think we'll be stopped?" Richard asked as he lit a cigarette with his lighter.

Paul shrugged his large shoulders. He nodded to a few fellow cops as he glided through the crowd of police and other men of authority. Everywhere one looked, the spotlights set up to face the building showed men yelling and arguing, no one really having a handle on the situation.

"Maybe, I just want to be prepared for everything," Paul said.

From behind them, a side door to the tenement opened and a cry went up as more than a dozen zombies spilled out. Clouds from the tear gas drifted out of the top of the doorway and at first the zombies were hidden, their true appearance unseen by the nearby police. Each man assumed the zombies were just more of the occupants escaping, the tear gas driving them out of their homes, but when the first ghoul reached a cop and sank his teeth into the man's arm, chaos exploded as the police found themselves becoming inundated with the undead.

The zombies quickly were inside the ranks of the officers and a cacophony of yells, screams and gunshots filled the air as the men tried to defend themselves. A trooper turned when a black man, dead for more than a day, tried to take a bite out of his shoulder. Spinning, the cop fired wildly, his bullets spraying not only the ghoul, but three of his fellow troopers. The hapless men soaked up the gunfire as they dropped to the pavement, bleeding out from a dozen bullet wounds. Of course they didn't get the chance to bleed out, as no sooner did they hit the ground then the ghouls were on them, tearing at their black, SWAT uniforms for the warm flesh beneath.

Another SWAT trooper used the butt of his rifle to crack a female zombie in the face, the butt flattening her nose and pulping her features into a bloody gruel. As the woman stumbled away, the man flipped his rifle over and shot her five times in the chest. He knew the head was where he needed to aim to take her down for good, but in his panic he wasn't thinking, falling back on old rules of shooting human beings in the chest to take them down.

The dead woman stumbled backward and was tripped by another ghoul. As she fell to the ground, she attempted to roll over, and as she tried to get up, her head was suddenly flattened as a large boot flattened it like a melon.

Paul pulled his now, gore and brain covered boot out of the fetid mess and looked for another target. Next to him, Richard's rifle was searching for a target of his own, but with his fellow officers so closely packed together, he was wont to risk a shot.

"What do we do?" Richard asked Paul, deferring to the larger man.

"Our jobs," Paul replied and punched a Puerto Rican ghoul in the head when it came for him. As the ghoul fell back, Paul shot it point blank in the head, the skull exploding into a dozen fragments as brain matter rained down.

Richard, taking Paul's lead, began moving closer to the ghouls, shooting them from so close they received powder burns on their pale and blue flesh, the dark holes showing the scorch marks.

A moaning old man with an afro came for him and Paul kicked out with the sole of his black boot, catching the ghoul in the chest. As the zombie stumbled backwards, he let off a round that took the ghoul between the eyes. The slack-jawed face was destroyed and the back of the skull disintegrated as the body toppled backwards.

Paul was now moving in and out of the shifting bodies like a wraith, his revolver drawn in his right hand, his rifle in his left. Each time a figure popped up out of the shifting shadows of tear gas clouds and white light of the spotlights, he took it down without mercy.

Richard swung to his right and shot a ghoul coming at him from out of the darkness. The round caught the ghoul in the neck, and a second later another round followed the first. Both bullets tore through the muscle and tendons, taking the head almost completely off like a knife through butter. As the ghoul stumbled around with its head hanging on by a few scraps of flesh, its feet tripped and it tumbled chest first to the pavement, where blood seeped from the open cavity to pool across the ground.

All around Richard, his fellow cops were doing the same, and when the smoke finally cleared, more than two dozen bodies were sprawled on the pavement, more than one still twitching.

Stepping through the carnage, Paul stopped walking as he leered over a ghoul with a bad perm who was feeding on a now, very dead cop.

Without hesitation, Paul shot the ghoul in the head, and as the body dropped to the ground, the dead cop's eyes snapped open.

"Damn it," Paul muttered as he turned and shot the cop dead once more, a black hole appearing in the cop's forehead. Paul had known this man personally, had met his wife and kids, and now he'd been the one to put the man down for good. He wondered who would tell his family he was dead, first devoured by a zombie and then put down when he rose from the dead himself.

All around Paul, the battle was dwindling as the SWAT troopers finished off the remaining ghouls. As the dust settled, more than a half dozen troopers and cops were dead, their bodies twitching as they slowly began to revive.

Sporadic gunfire carried on the wind as the remaining ghouls were put down for good. Richard walked up to Paul, his eyes wide from the carnage. He knew almost every man now sprawled on the ground, their throats ripped out, faces peeled back like old bananas.

"How the hell did this happen?" Richard said more to himself than to Paul.

Paul didn't reply, but instead spit into the blood pooling at his feet, raised his revolver, and shot another good cop in the head just as the man slowly rose to a sitting position.

"Come on, Richard, we still have work to do," Paul said in a gruff voice.

Richard nodded curtly, and with five more troopers by their side, the two men strode through the death and gore to put down the reanimating cops once and for all.

* * *

"Okay, let's get these poor bastards to the fire at the other end of the building!" an authoritative voice cried out. He wore a brown sport coat, a red shirt underneath, and had a dark mustache riding his upper lip. He was the commander in charge of this little shindig and he took it very seriously.

Another man with a fedora and large eye glasses was standing next him. This man, a sergeant, had been with the commander when the gas had been applied, and he now added his voice to the proceedings, much as he had commented before on how Martinez and his people inside the tenement were going to fight the police.

"Wait, you're not going to place our fallen men in that fire, too, are you?" the sergeant asked.

The commander sighed and shook his head, the decision he'd made weighing heavily on him.

"What choice do I have, Sal? We don't have time to gather the bodies, you know that. Headquarters said to just add the bodies to the fire and be done with it. The times for niceties is over, hell, this shit is out of control as it is."

"But the families..." Sal said.

The commander chopped his hand in front of the sergeant's face, ending the conversation.

"Dammit, Sal, I know this, and you telling me isn't going to change a damn thing but make me feel worse. There's no time for proper burials and autopsies. You know that as well as I do. It sucks, but that's the way it is. Now how about helping instead of commenting, huh?"

"Yes, sir," the sergeant said and moved off to help coordinate the cleanup. More of Martinez' people were being herded out of the building as well as the tenants who had refused to leave voluntarily. Screaming children, women, and old men over sixty were the majority, all the younger men gunned down when SWAT had attacked the building. The tear gas had been the deciding victory, none of the tenants able to fend off the eye and throat clogging gas.

As the bodies of the zombies and dead cops alike were gathered, Paul and Richard lent a hand. Neither man could just turn and leave their brothers behind, not like this. As the bodies were tossed into the back of a SWAT truck, both men felt their hearts fill with lead. The dead faces of their fellow brothers gazed back at them accusingly, many having only the bullet holes in their foreheads to tell of their violent deaths, though many had bloody wounds suffered by the hands and teeth of the zombies' violent attack.

As Paul set another corpse down, he turned as two riot troopers carried another cop between them. As Paul stepped aside, he saw it was the dead body of Willy. The man's back was peppered from gunfire. Gunfire he had inflicted when the cop had gone apeshit and began killing people indiscriminately.

As Paul watched the two troopers toss Willy's corpse into the back of the truck, Richard stepped up next to him, lighting another cigarette as he joined him.

Paul had pulled out a cigarette of his own, a dark brown cigarette that smelt of cloves. As he popped it into his mouth, he found Richard's lighter below his nose, the flame flickering in the night air. Without saying a word, Paul bent forward, lit his cigarette, and nodded curtly to Richard. The smaller man said nothing, only snapped the Zippo closed with a flick of his wrist and made it disappear into his black jumpsuit. His turtle neck was high on his neck and only his face and hands stood out in the shadows, the truck blocking most of the spotlights.

"It wasn't your fault," Richard said as he thought back to fifteen minutes ago when he'd been hanging onto the back of Willy, trying to subdue him, as the wild man tossed him off his shoulders like a bucking bronco. Richard's gas mask had gone flying and he'd found himself sucking tear gas. Luckily, the effects were minimal, most of it already dissipated on the level he'd been on.

"Yeah, I know, it still sucks. He was a brother, but he went too far. Someone had to do it," Paul said more to himself than to Richard.

Richard exhaled a plume of smoke and stepped in front of Paul. He had to raise himself on his tip toes so Paul had to look at him, not over him.

"Look, it's already past eight. I told Stewart if I was gonna go with him I'd be there by nine. If I'm not there, if we're not there, he's gonna leave without us."

Paul seemed to snap out of it then and he looked into Richard's eyes.

The far away look he'd had was gone, like a light switch had been flicked, and the cold eyes of a warrior returned.

"Okay, let's get moving," Paul replied.

Richard stepped aside and the two headed off towards the squad cars lining the blockade.

They had done all they could for their fellow troopers and the city itself. Now it was time to worry about themselves.

* * *

Paul and Richard worked their way through the crowd, their destination, the squad cars at the outer perimeter. As they passed by a line of ambulances, Paul slowed to watch two paramedics working on a black woman wearing a bloody housedress. Her neck was a torn mess and the two men were struggling to get the bleeding under control, though it didn't look good.

He recognized her immediately. She'd been the woman who had been attacked by the tall, dark zombie inside the tenement. He remembered her scream the zombie's name. "Miguel…Miguelito," she'd uttered.

That is before her former husband sank his teeth first into her shoulder and then into the meaty part of her left arm. He was shot down then, while still chewing her flesh in his mouth, as the woman was carried away for medical assistance.

But as Paul watched, the woman, now prone on a gurney with wheels, didn't look like she was going to make it.

And that was what he was waiting for.

Richard, not understanding what Paul was doing, waited beside his new friend anxiously, his eyes flicking about nervously as he waited for someone of authority to call out and ask what they were doing and where they thought they were going.

"I'm losing her," the first paramedic said. "Give her a shot of adrenalin."

The second paramedic complied, but the woman didn't respond. Paul saw her chest rise one last time as she inhaled her death breath, then she exhaled it, her eyelids fluttering once, her mouth going slack.

On a monitor in the ambulance, the white line went from a jumping beat to a flat line.

"That's it, she's gone," the first paramedic said calmly. He'd done all he could and death was a part of his job…as much as life was.

"Paul, what the hell are we waiting for? We need to go," Richard urged as he lit another smoke and stuffed his lighter away.

"In a minute, brother, just a minute more," Paul replied smoothly as his hand calmly went to the revolver on his hip. All around the two troopers, screams, yells and sporadic gunfire could be heard, and so far no one was paying Paul or Richard the slightest bit of attention.

Richard was about to ask yet again, knowing to hang around was madness if they were truly going to leave, when the woman on the gurney suddenly opened her eyes and uttered a guttural moan.

The two paramedics, still not used to their dead patients reviving, were totally caught off guard, and the first man screamed as the dead woman reached out with her left hand and grabbed his arm, pulling his wrist towards her mouth so she could feed much like her husband had done less than an hour ago.

A sharp crack of Paul's revolver filled the area surrounding the ambulance and the dead woman's forehead blossomed a red hole, half her skull blowing out to splatter onto the pillow on the gurney. The body was slammed back down from the force of the heavy round and the hand let go of the paramedic.

Jumping away, the paramedic stared at the dead woman and her brains now dripping over the side of the gurney as Paul turned to casually look at Richard.

"Now we can go, Richard."

Richard smirked slightly and the two troopers walked away, the pair of paramedics still staring at the dead woman as their eyes then went to follow Paul. The paramedic who'd been saved didn't even get the chance to tell Paul thank you before the two troopers were lost in the chaos of the blockade.

* * *

"Which one do we take?" Richard asked as he studied the five black and white squad cars lined up one next to the other at the edge of the blockade. The gumball lights on the car roofs were on, the red and blue strobes casting shadows in every direction. The street lights were out in this section and only the vehicles lights pushed back the night.

There were seven troopers on patrol here, each moving about as they managed the crowd gathered nearby.

Though most citizens were smart enough to stay indoors, not wanting to risk meeting one of the walking dead, there were still more than enough who feared nothing. Hookers, drug dealers and homeless stood at the edge of the barricade, numbering more than thirty strong, all watching the tenement building be assaulted. They sent catcalls and derivatives at the police, taunting them with each word and insult.

The tenement building wasn't in the best part of town and the police normally were never seen around here unless someone was getting rousted. But this time the damn cops were rousting an entire apartment building.

"Doesn't matter, one is as good as another," Paul replied.

Richard was about to add a retort when he felt a hand fall onto his shoulder. Turning, he found himself looking into the face of the sergeant, the man doing rounds to see how the rest of the troopers were doing.

"DeMarco, what the hell are you doing over here?" the sergeant asked in an angry voice. "You're supposed to be inside sweeping the building with Cataldo's unit."

Then the gruff man turned to see Paul standing behind him. "And you, I sure as hell know you're not supposed to be back here."

"Oh, uh, yeah, Sarge, about that," Richard replied. "The commander told us to head over here and make sure there's no trouble on the police line. He figured maybe with everything going on that some of the bystanders might get antsy and try something. He said we should take a car and drive around the perimeter. You know, show a police presence."

"He did, huh? That don't sound right. Especially as we need more men on body duty." He shook his head in disgust. "Christ, we have to burn our own damn men with those *things*, it ain't right I tell ya." He reached down to his two-way radio on his belt. "I'm gonna check with the commander to make sure what you say is true."

Richard and Paul looked at one another, their gazes locked. They knew what would happen if the Sarge got through to the commander. He'd find out Paul and Richard had abandoned their posts sweeping the inside of the building and were probably looking to desert. It was happening more and more as time passed and the situation grew worse. If a trooper was found deserting, they now received a lot more than a reprimand and a slap on the wrist.

The sergeant began calling the commander, but the man wasn't answering. The sergeant tried twice more and finally gave up.

"Look, you two, I don't care what the commander said. Get your asses back to the building and help with disposal, that's an order." Without waiting for a reply he turned and moved away to check on the rest of the men. Everyone was uneasy and the veteran of over twenty years knew one itchy trigger finger aimed at the unsettled crowd surrounding the barricade could cause a riot they could never contain.

Richard looked to Paul again as the sergeant receded into the night.

"Damn that was close."

"Too close," Paul added.

"Once he catches up to the commander and asks him about us…" Richard let the rest hang.

"Yeah, so we better get moving," Paul said as he moved towards the line of black and whites cars. Richard followed, having to pick up his steps as Paul's longer gait covered more distance faster.

The other cops ignored Paul and Richard, not knowing or caring what they might be doing on the edge of the barricade. There were so many people doing so many things no one person knew what everyone else was doing. This would be good for Paul and Richard, who were able to find a squad car with the keys still in the ignition that wasn't blocked in too badly. Many of the cops had been in a rush to arrive at the tenement, and so had left the keys in the ignitions. This now served Richard and Paul well. It took only a few minutes to find a squad car with the keys dangling from the steering column, and as they climbed in and the doors slammed shut, the cacophony of screams and gunshots dwindled. Paul was in the driver's seat and he turned over the engine, then hit the siren.

As he slowly backed out of his spot, bystanders had to move out of his way. He hit the horn a few times as well to get them to move faster, and a minute later he was free of the crowd.

As Richard stared at the faces of the hookers and drug dealers who yelled at him and called him derogatory names through the window, the crowd parted. That was when he saw the sergeant running towards the squad car, waving a fist at him and Paul.

"Paul, the Sergeant…" Richard said, trailing off.

"Yeah, man, I see him," Paul replied, but instead of stopping and waiting for the man to catch up, Paul swung the wheel and floored the gas pedal, the cruiser shooting into the street.

"He looks pissed. He must've found out the commander doesn't know a thing about us," Richard said as the black and white shot down the dark street. A few shadowy forms lined the sidewalks, but it was mostly deserted. This area of town was full of rundown, dilapidated buildings, many in the same state of repair as the tenement they were leaving behind

"Why, you plan on comin' back here?" Paul asked.

"No, guess not."

"Exactly, so what he thinks he knows doesn't mean squat. We pretty much just gave our resignations and this car is our severance package."

Richard grinned and Paul pulled out his pack of smokes, sliding one out with his teeth. As he went to put the pack away and reach for the cigarette lighter, Richard's lighter was there. Paul leaned forward and took the light, and Richard flicked it away with a twist of his wrist. The two were already getting into a groove and they had only known each other for an hour.

As the cruiser drove deeper into the city, Philadelphia, the city of Brotherly Love began to burn.

*　*　*

As the squad car cut through the heart of the city to get to the north side and the waiting police dock at the marina, the moonlight cast its pallid glow on an embattled city. Destruction was everywhere, more than one dark shadow sprawled on the street being a corpse, and more than a few were walking around, like drunks after last call. Automatic gunfire and explosions filled the air as the squad car weaved through the stalled traffic.

It seemed like overnight, the city had collapsed and chaos reigned supreme.

Stalled and abandoned cars and trucks littered the road as Paul swerved around and through the obstructions. Once the front tire ran over a severed hand and the sound of brittle bones carried into the interior.

Neither Paul nor Richard commented on it, both wanting to pretend it didn't happen.

As they drove deeper into downtown, signs of looting were more apparent. Storefronts and convenience stores had shattered windows and sparking overhead lights, more than one showing telltale signs of violence.

And there were more people, pedestrians running to or from something.

Richard checked his watch to see it was coming on 8:30. Good, they still had plenty of time to reach the police dock and the waiting helicopter. Of course there was always the possibility Stewart wouldn't be there, but he had been friends with Stewart for years and if the pilot told him he would be there, then Richard was confident the man would do everything in his power to do so.

It was as Paul was slowing to a crawl to go around a particularly nasty accident, the three cars now just crushed metal with blood on the safety glass, that a shrieking woman came running out of a side alley, bounced off the driver's door, and began to pound on Paul's window. She was half naked, her clothing looking like it had been torn off her body and there were large scratches on her face and neck.

Richard's immediate instinct was that the woman had run afoul of a few of the walking dead, but no sooner did she begin crying for help, than five men came charging out of the alley, the one in the lead carrying what was obviously the woman's panties.

"Get back here, you bitch! We're not done with you yet!" the first man screamed. When he saw the black and white squad car he swore angrily.

"Shit, cops!" But then he realized there were only two cops and there were five of them and they were all armed. If he seemed intimidated by the two policemen, he showed none of it.

Inside the patrol car, Paul looked past the woman banging on his window, leaving red streaks on the glass, and took in the five men who had come out of the alley. They wore the colors of a gang proudly on the right sleeve of their jackets, all leather except for a man in the rear who wore a denim one.

All five were armed; three holding handguns and two had what looked like sawed-off shotguns. Paul knew in the confines of an alley or the inside of a building, the sawed-offs would be devastating to anyone unfortunate enough to be standing in front of the blast.

It was as Paul was watching the men that he saw the leader, the one with the panties, bring up his shotgun and level it at the woman and also the squad car.

"Get down!" Paul yelled, reaching out to Richard and pushing the smaller man lower in the seat just as the massive boom of the weapon was fired.

Both Paul and Richard felt the impact of the blast against the driver's side of the squad car, but nothing happened other than a muffled thump.

Neither man understood this until Paul risked a peek to see what was happening.

The woman was still feebly banging on the side of the squad car, but as Paul stared at her, he saw her lower half was now gone, severed by the barrage from the shotgun.

As her intestines slid out of her body to splash onto the pavement, her legs lying in the road like two spent logs, her mouth opened and closed and her one free hand slapped the window. The other hand was holding the top edge of the roof, keeping her attached to the side. Paul could only stare in horror as the woman's grip grew weak and her grasp failed her, the body falling away to twitch next to the squad car and lower half.

Paul had less than a second to take in the brutality of her death before more gunshots filled the street, and he knew he needed to act fast.

"What the hell's going on?" Richard yelled as bullets slapped the side of the squad car.

"Looks like a gang was raping her! Damn it, we need to get out of here!" Paul snapped as he tried to steer around the three car crash blocking the road.

Paul slammed the transmission into reverse, but no sooner did he do this than the right rear tire was blown out by a stray bullet. Paul ignored this, not worried about driving on the rim, but as he tried to back up, he found he couldn't. With the tire flat, he couldn't get the traction he needed as that was the driver side of the vehicle.

As bullets pounded the car, Paul pushed Richard against the passenger door.

"Get out! We need to return fire or we're both dead!" Paul yelled.

Richard, a trained warrior, never argued, never even thought about questioning Paul's assessment. Reaching out, he pulled the handle on the door and it flew open as Richard jumped out and went to his knees, Paul following suit.

Both men went to either side of the car, Richard going to the hood and Paul the trunk, and like a well oiled team, they began to return fire, giving back a little of what they'd received.

The worst part was they both knew they couldn't call for backup. By now, the sergeant would have put the word out on the two-way that two of his men had stolen a squad car and were deserting the force, and he'd be damned if he would let them get away with it.

Paul had his rifle in his hands, while Richard favored his revolver. Paul was the first to return fire, and as he lined up and fired over the trunk, one of the gang members went flying backwards, the piece of lead shredding his heart.

Richard was next to lay a gang member out.

He lined up a shot, but the first one went wild.

"Dammit," Richard spit as he realigned his target.

The second round caught a bearded man with a bandanna in the upper right shoulder. The man was sent backwards to fall onto the sidewalk where Paul put him down for good with a shot to the chest.

That left three and Richard was next to score a hit. As bullets whined around his head, he calmly shot a man in the stomach, the gut shot gang member dropping face first to the pavement with a ragged, bloody wound where his belly button should be.

Paul had to duck behind the squad car as a barrage of shotgun blasts soared over his head, the pellets scarring the paint of the black and white. The trunk looked like it had been through a sandstorm and been buried for years before driving back into the city. When the barrage finally stopped, the man trying to reload, Paul stood up and shot him in the neck, severing his jugular and sending the gang member flying backwards. As he landed on the pavement, his blood spread out in a growing pool of dark liquid as he gasped for breath, but only managed to suck in blood. Drowning, the fourth man spasmed as his eyes fluttered their last.

That left the leader, a burly man with a hairy chest, muscular arms, and a large bushy mustache. He yelled in anger to see his crew gunned down so easily and he shot at Paul and Richard, spraying the entire squad car with buckshot.

But he was a little too far away and the sawed-off lost much of its punch by the time the blast reached the car.

Paul, waiting for the right moment, popped up and shot the man in the shoulder. The gang leader was knocked backwards where his back met the building that made up the wall of the left side of the alley. Cursing a blue streak, the wounded man turned and fled down the alleyway, his running form swallowed by the darkness.

Paul never hesitated when he saw the man turn and flee. He jumped up and dashed for the alley, his rifle in his hands, as he ran as fast as his long legs would allow.

"Paul! Where the hell are you going?" Richard called out, not understanding where his partner was off to.

"To finish this!" he yelled back, his voice hard and cold.

Where Richard had been sitting in the squad car, he didn't see the woman cut in half by the shotgun blast, but Paul had, and though he knew they needed to get to the police dock, his honor wouldn't let this piece of shit get away with cold-blooded murder, especially when he was a witness to it. He was still a cop and he took the oath to serve and protect seriously.

"Goddammit!" Richard yelled, but he took off after his partner. He may not agree with the choice Paul made, but he wouldn't leave him alone.

As Richard charged across the street and into the dark alleyway, jumping over the prone bodies, he glanced down at the dead gang members, the four corpses still leaking plasma onto the ground.

As he ran, he checked his watch, the dials glowing softly, and he saw it was twenty to nine.

Shaking his head, he put on a burst of speed.

Man, they were cutting it close, he thought as his eyes searched every shadow of the alley.

There was a muzzle flash up ahead at the far end of the alley and Richard ducked behind a dumpster, the smell of urine and decay filtering into his sinuses. Philly was a beautiful city, but it had its hidden underbelly, where crime and disease was rampant.

Unfortunately, the alleyways and hidden doorways were where a lot of that seediness was prevalent.

He heard Paul's rifle fire twice and then another blast of the shotgun from the gang leader, and he waited until it looked safe, then began moving from trashcan to dumpster to pile of wooden pallets.

His partner was somewhere at the end of the alley and he needed to get to him.

* * *

Paul ducked down behind a dumpster as a barrage of buckshot flew by him, the patter of the pellets so strong it felt like the dumpster actually moved an inch on its wheels when the blast struck it. When the gang leader fired, the alley lit up like a car's high beams had been turned on, and Paul made sure to look away or risk losing his night sight. It was almost pitch black in the alley, the dull moonlight not able to penetrate past the buildings on either side. Gritting his teeth and setting his jaw taut, he waited for his chance to end this.

"Come on, mocha man! I'll take your ass down! You bastard, you killed my whole damn crew!" the gang leader screamed as he cracked open the housing to his shotgun, slid two more shells into the chamber, then flicked the short barrel up and closed the breach.

Paul didn't move and the gang leader continued screaming curses. Paul knew the man's shoulder was bleeding profusely, but either the man was on something or he was so full of rage he didn't feel pain.

The gang leader fired again, the lead pellets flying down the middle of the alleyway.

Paul waited for the initial blast and light and then jumped out, rolled across the filthy ground, and came up a few feet closer to his target. If he was correct, the gang leader hadn't seen him change position.

Slowly, praying he wasn't about to get his head shot off, Paul poked his right eye around the new dumpster he was hiding behind.

144

This one had the redolence of Chinese food, while the other had smelled like rotting lettuce.

When he had a clear view of the alley, he could see the gang leader's body silhouetted at the opposite end of the alley. The fool didn't realize he was making himself a perfect target, as he wasn't thinking of defense, only offense.

Paul waited for the man to fire again and ducked back slightly as the barrage peppered the dumpster he'd been behind a second ago.

Seeing that the gang leader didn't know where he was, he brought up his rifle and set it on the dumpster, placing his eye to the scope. He was a crack shot and all he needed was a few seconds to line up his target.

As the scope moved slightly, the gang leader's head came into focus, though it was a darker blob amongst others. Paul let out his breath slowly and as he gently inhaled, then exhaled, he squeezed the trigger.

Through the scope, he saw the gang leader throw his hands up as he went toppling backwards.

As the man fell over, Paul stepped out, his rifle now leveled at waist height, his finger still on the trigger.

He heard footsteps behind him, and when he turned, he saw Richard materialize out of the darkness.

"You okay?"

"Yeah, I got him. What took you so long?" Paul joked, smiling wanly.

"Took me a second to catch up, what with those big legs of yours," Richard replied.

"I'm gonna check it out, watch my back," Paul told Richard and then headed up the alley. Richard, his revolver in hand, nodded once, then slowly followed while his eyes still searched the shadows. He spotted movement once, and when he swiveled at the hip, finger a quarter ounce from firing, he stopped at the last instant, seeing two furry rats crawl out from under some dirty cardboard as they made their way to the next pile of refuse. Feeling silly, he moved further down the alleyway to catch up with Paul.

The large trooper was standing over the supine gang leader, half the dead man's skull splattered behind him, bits of brain matter looking like pink, shell-less snails in the moonlight.

When Richard reached Paul, he too gazed down on the dead gang leader. Richard saw the dead man's left eye was gone, a large open wound now replacing the orb. This was the entry point of Paul's bullet, an excellent shot considering the lighting and distance, not to mention the time he had to line up the shot.

"Nice shot," was all Richard said.

"Yeah. The bastard got what he deserved."

Richard checked his watch again to see it was now a quarter to nine.

"Paul, we're running out of time. Stewart said he wouldn't wait around for me and I told him that was fine. I said if I wasn't there at nine sharp then I wasn't coming. Granted we probably have a few extra minutes, but if he's ahead of schedule then we're sunk."

There was movement down the street as the two troopers glanced left and right at the end of the alley. They both looked at the same time to see what looked like ten people coming down the street. At first they looked ordinary, though they were all moving rather slow. But when the first few wandered under a working streetlight, it was clear to both men these weren't people any longer.

Then the first ghouls in line spotted Paul and Richard and began walking in their direction. They were still at the end of the street and it would take them a while to reach the two SWAT troopers.

"Looks like more of 'em?" Richard said solemnly.

"Probably, they can't contain this, that's for sure. It's getting worse by the hour," Paul said. "Let's get out of here. I did what needed to be done."

Richard said nothing, only turned and began walking back into the alleyway.

Paul looked over his shoulder one last time at the approaching ghouls and then, he too, followed his new partner.

*　*　*

Minutes later, the first ghouls reached the dead gang leader. Like children fighting over a fallen piñata, they went to their knees and began tearing at the still warm corpse. Clawed hands dug into the soft flesh of the gang leader's stomach, tearing and pulling until the skin was flayed from the bone. The rib cage was soon cracked and hands dug deep, pulling out the warm insides, feeding on the spleen, kidney and liver. Intestines were pulled out like a magician's magic trick, one ghoul taking a greasy rope and walking away, the multiple feet of entrails dragging out behind it until another zombie stepped on the crimson rope and caused it to rip.

The ghoul was yanked back like a dog that had reached the end of its leash, but the zombie only yanked harder and the intestine came free. Ignorant on what had happened, the zombie stumbled onward; chewing on the intestine like it was a massive, raw, sausage link. Congealing blood spilled out to coat the cement red as greedy mouths dropped to the ground to lap it up like puppies to milk.

In less time than it took to kill the man, the zombies had torn him apart and there was nothing left but a bloody carcass that vaguely resembled a human torso, all the limbs and the head now gone. With their chunks of flesh and entrails, the ghouls moved off, eating on the move as they stuffed their mouths and filled their stomachs with human flesh.

When the last ghoul was gone, the rats in the alley appeared, and soon were covering the corpse, feeding on what little remained.

The zombies had been thorough and anything worth eating was now long gone. But the rats wouldn't complain; they would find what was left, ignorant of the origin of the meat, but only glad to have sustenance.

*　*　*

At a steady jog, Paul and Richard reached the opposite end of the alley where the squad car waited, the run taking them less than fifteen seconds.

But in the time they had been gone, the situation had changed drastically.

The gang members were no longer on the ground surrounded by pools of blood.

Now, they were standing again, and were feeding on the bifurcated woman who had been shot in half by the gang leader.

There were also three more zombies added to the four gang members, to make a total of seven. They'd heard the sounds of the gun battle and had stumbled towards the alley and the squad car, arriving just as Paul and Richard had disappeared into the alley in pursuit of the gang leader.

As Paul and Richard slowed to a stop, gripping their weapons tightly, they stared at the feeding zombies as they chowed down on the dead woman's entrails and internal organs.

But no sooner had the ghouls begun, then the dead woman's eyes snapped opened. Vacant eyes looked around and she slapped a nearby ghoul in the face, her hand waving around as if it had a mind of its own.

As the zombies lost interest in her reanimated flesh, she used her arms to try and crawl away, dragging herself across the road as her intestines splayed out behind her. She ended up pulling herself under the squad car, her sense of direction off. But the rest of the zombies still had meat and they tore at her separated waist and severed legs, tearing the fatty meat off the thighs and calves.

The two troopers stared in disgust, fascination, and just a little fear, though it festered deep in their guts like acid.

"When there's no room in Hell…" Paul whispered softly; so low Richard didn't hear what he said over the feeding frenzy and moaning twenty feet away.

"What's that, Paul?" Richard asked.

"Huh? Nothing, Richard, just thought of something I heard once. I'll tell you later if I get a chance."

They had no choice, they had to take the zombies down so they could get to the squad car, it was too risky to just try and run for it. The time it would take to open the doors could spell their deaths.

Paul aimed his rifle at the seven ghouls then slapped Richard on the shoulder. "Come, on, baby, let's get this done and get goin'."

Richard nodded and raised his revolver. His rifle was still in the squad car. In all the excitement of escaping the vehicle he wasn't able to grab it.

He flicked open the cylinder of his gun to see he had three rounds left.

"I'm low on ammo and my extra bullets are in my belt on the front seat," he told Paul.

Paul checked his ammunition and then shook his head.

"Damn, I'm low, too. Okay, let me take point and you bat cleanup. There's only seven of 'em. We can do this easy."

Richard blinked his reply, his visage saying he was on board.

The zombies had now turned to face the two warriors, having lost interest in the severed woman's lower half and they began to shuffle towards the two men.

Though it would have been quite easy to turn and run away, outdistancing the ghouls, the two troopers needed to get back to the squad car as fast as possible so they only had the one option, and there was no time for games such as leading them away to double back later.

Around or through, those were the choices.

But as the zombies spread out, the only way was through.

Paul raised his rifle to his shoulder, lining up the first pale and blue face in his sights.

No sooner had he done this then he fired, blowing out the rear skull of the bearded gang member. The body was thrown backwards to strike another ghoul who was knocked off balance, but soon it righted itself and was on the move again

Paul shifted his aim and shot another ghoul, this one the gang member who had been shot in the throat. Bright arterial blood glistened in the moonlight, the entire front of the ghoul's body covered in scarlet from bleeding out.

This time Paul's shot hit the ghoul in the nose, shattering cartilage as the round continued into the brain to then take out the rear skull plate.

Two down, five to go, he thought as he shifted his aim.

Richard took a shot despite being low on ammo and another gang member went down with an exploded eye and half a head.

The body flopped to the pavement like a landed fish as the arms spasmed in death.

"Nice shot, brother," Paul commented as he lined up another target.

Richard beamed with pride. He already felt a kinship with Paul, his quiet strength an admirable quality, and he found himself wanting to impress this large, dark man of few words.

Paul's next target was a mailman by the uniform, the ghoul's throat all but ripped out right where the Adam's apple should have been. The mailman opened his mouth wide and moaned as he stumbled toward Paul, and when the man was no more than eight feet away, Paul fired, the round going into the mailman's mouth. Front teeth were blown away, shards of enamel flying up into the brain and out the sides of the pale cheeks. The bullet continued on to sever the brainstem, the mailman flopping forward onto his face to twitch and spasm. The head was still active but the brain wasn't connected to the body any longer. The ghoul was out of action for good.

The gang member was moving to the side of Paul and the big trooper hadn't noticed this, the shadows on the street causing forms to blend together.

As the dead gang member came up and prepared to sink his teeth into Paul's arm, another gunshot rang out and the ghoul was thrown to the side, a large hole appearing in its side. It wasn't a killing shot, but it saved Paul and the man swiveled at the waist and shot the gang member at point blank range. The head didn't just explode; it disintegrated from the high impact of the bullet, sending skull fragments skittering across the road like a flat rock on the smooth surface of a lake.

Paul turned to Richard and gave him a curt nod in thanks.

"Thanks, brother, I missed that one."

"Anytime," Richard grinned then turned and shot a waitress in the throat. His aim was off, however, and though the left side of her neck erupted in blood, she only paused before continuing on.

Richard lined up another shot to finish off the woman, but the hammer clicked on a dead cylinder.

"Shit, I'm out," he grunted as Paul swiveled and took out the waitress.

"I got her," Paul said as if he was casually shooting cans with some buddies in the middle of a glade in the woods.

The rifle's retort reverberated throughout the street and the waitress dropped with half her face missing.

Low moans carried on the wind and both troopers looked to their right, behind the squad car, to see more shuffling figures approaching.

"Damn it, more of 'em," Richard stated.

"Doesn't matter, we're out of here, come on," Paul said as he strode toward the last ghoul and the waiting squad car beyond.

The zombie had once been a business man, complete with expensive suit and shoes. Now the suit was covered in gore, the dark-maroon stain on his chest showing where his blood had seeped out of his wounds on his face and neck to slather him in blood. On his right wrist was a gold watch, probably worth more than what Paul made in a year, but now it was junk, as the ghoul could no longer tell time.

As Paul took the lead, he decided to save a bullet, and as he reached the business man, he swung the butt of his rifle up and under the zombie's chin.

The loud *crack* filled the street and the ghoul went flying backwards, its jaw now shattered. Falling to the pavement, the business man spit teeth and blood as Paul and Richard moved on, not caring if the zombie was down for good or not.

Richard ran around the squad car and jumped into the passenger seat again while Paul moved for the driver's door. But when he was about to open the door, a hand shot out from under the car and grabbed his left ankle.

He looked down quickly to see the eyes of the severed woman who had been begging for help minutes ago glaring up at him. She didn't look the same as before however. Because the undead gang members had gotten to her and began feeding before she revived, she now had large portions of her face, arms and neck missing. Her eyes, once a beautiful blue, were now bulging out of her red skull, the visage resembling the orbs in a toy skull, where the eyes would flick back and forth as the mouth gaped open and clicked.

Drawing his revolver, he aimed it at her head, wanting to put her out of her misery and Richard reached over and opened his door a crack from inside the car.

"Paul, what's taking so long, we need to go!"

That shook Paul from his fugue state and he shook his head to clear it. Deciding there was no reason to shoot the woman, he kicked out with his boot, kicking her in the face. The ghoul was pushed back under the squad car, and with Paul free, he opened the door the rest of the way and climbed in, slamming the door closed.

"What was that about?" Richard inquired as he stared at the large man next to him, seeing something different in his expression compared to only a second ago. There was now a darker brooding aspect that though always there, sometimes came out stronger than other times.

"It's nothing, man, we're cool." He turned over the engine and shifted the transmission into drive, then drove off.

As the squad car began to roll, rocking slightly due to the flat tire, there was a heavier bump under the left back tire, like a speed bump.

Richard turned to glance at Paul, wondering if the man knew what he'd run over, but the dark trooper said nothing, his eyes focused on the road ahead. Because of the flat tire, the steering was harder to control.

Richard checked his watch. It was ten to nine. They still had time, only barely, to reach the police dock and hopefully, their transportation to escape a dying city.

Behind the squad car, the crushed skull of the bifurcated woman spread out onto the pavement, the hands still twitching as the nerve endings finally ceased.

Overhead, the moon stood watch over the death and carnage, the only remaining witness to what had occurred.

* * *

The next twelve minutes were a tenuous thing as Paul drove through the streets of downtown Philly. At the first possible chance he had, Paul pulled over and quickly changed the flat. Luckily, the spare tire in the trunk was good and with Paul working fast and Richard watching his back, they had the tire changed in four minutes flat. Paul barely tightened the lug nuts before they were moving again, leaving the jack, the flat tire, and tire wrench behind. The new tire only had to stay on for a few miles and then it wouldn't matter.

At each intersection Paul and Richard both kept waiting to get to the one crash or pile-up that wouldn't allow them to make it through.

A few times Paul had to double back and try a different route and then, only just, were they able to make it.

All around them the city was in chaos, people running about while others were looking to loot what they could from the shops and stores.

"Why are they out here like this?" Richard asked incredulously. "They were told to stay indoors."

Paul shook his head slightly. "Yeah, but then they changed that and told people to get to rescue stations, remember? Only thing, those damn stations are probably as bad or worse than if they had stayed in their homes." He swung around a panel truck and continued forward. The police dock was a few minutes away, and as he turned a final left, he reached the edge of the city and the road that would take them to the nearby marina.

"You were right to want to run," Paul said. "It's the only chance we've got. We stay here we're all dead for sure."

"Yeah, that's what I figured," Richard replied. He glanced to Paul. "Glad you're along for the ride, I can use the backup."

"Oh, yeah? What about this friend of yours...Stewart. Can't he do that for you?"

Richard smirked, thinking of his friend. "You'd think so, but no. Stewart is a cracker jack of a helicopter pilot but he's not that good with a gun. I took him to the range once." He shook his head thinking about Stewart's abysmal score. "Let's say he's at his best when he's flying."

Paul actually grinned then. It was slight, only the left side of his mouth curling, but it was a smile nonetheless.

"I hear ya." Paul gestured with his chin to the road ahead of them. "We're almost there."

Richard looked forward again to see they were on an open road that wound around the coast to bring them to the marina.

And thank God! Richard thought as the squad car drew closer. There was the yellow and white WDNN traffic copter, sitting on the police dock, its running lights blinking as it sat under the one lamp post that illuminated the dock and its single gas pump.

Other than that, he couldn't see a thing, the darkness complete.

Paul stepped on the gas now, finally clear of the city and minutes later they had reached the police dock.

"There's somethin' goin' on," Paul said suspiciously as he put the black and white in park and grabbed his gear, Richard doing the same. Paul left the keys in the ignition, figuring maybe some other poor bastard could use it. He knew they wouldn't need it.

"Yeah, they look like cops, too. Hey, there's Stewart," Richard said.

Paul looked harder and he could see a man with a leather jacket and short brown hair. He looked to be pushed into a corner, one of the cops holding him there. But if the cop was interrogating him or just trying to grab a ride was unknown at this time.

"Paul, let me handle this," Richard said as he slung his rifle over his shoulder, closed the passenger door to the squad car, and casually walked the few feet to the dock so he was closer to the cop and Stewart. He saw there were a few other men on the dock, too, all wearing police uniforms.

"What's the problem here, officer?" Richard asked politely, though his hand was hovering over the grip of his revolver. In the ride over, he'd reloaded and was now ready for whatever would come next.

"I caught your friends here stealin' some company gasoline," the cop said, a bandolier filled with bullets covering his chest and wearing large handguns that weren't police issue on his hips.

"Friends?" Richard said innocently.

"They know, Richard," Stewart said hesitantly, figuring there was no reason for this charade.

It was then that the cop with bandoliers proposed that no one should be shooting at anyone. They were all cops after all and were on the same team. It didn't hurt either to help the cop come to this decision when Paul walked up with his rifle in his hands, prepared to be fired, and his intimidating presence.

Richard agreed and an uneasy truce was met, the other cops gathering crates and supplies as they loaded them into a small police launch. They were running, too, and they told Stewart they were trying for an island.

When Stewart asked the cop what island they were trying for, the reply was, "Any island we can find."

While Stewart was getting ready to go, Richard and Paul went back to the squad car to retrieve the rest of their gear. Paul noticed that from a distance and from the front, you couldn't tell the squad car had been in a firefight. All the bullet holes were on the driver's side and the trunk.

With their supplies in hand, the two troopers headed back to the helicopter. Once there, Richard smiled when he saw Susan, glad to see that Stewart had talked her into coming. In all the excitement he hadn't had time to talk to her. She smiled back and climbed into the back seat of the helicopter, leaving the front passenger seat for Richard. Paul stowed his gear in the small compartment in the rear of the helicopter and climbed in next to Susan.

"Who's he?" Stewart asked Richard as he gestured to Paul who was loading gear into the helicopter.

"A friend," Richard said as if that was enough of an answer.

Down below in the water, the cops were getting ready to push off their launch, hollering about where to go and what to do. As Richard watched them, he wondered how they would fair out there. From the looks of things, they weren't working as much of a team, and if they couldn't leave the dock with any form of coordination, that bode badly for their future.

But then Stewart was climbing into the helicopter and preparing to leave.

"You have any trouble getting here, Richard?" Stewart asked as he flicked switches and the rotors began to pick up speed.

"Nah, Stewart, it was a piece of cake," he replied. He cast Paul a glance and the large trooper only nodded, a slight grin creasing his normal countenance of stoicism. What had happened to the two troopers on their way to the police dock was between them, a bond of battle that had brought the two men closer. No one else needed to share in it.

One of the cops asked the four companions for smokes, but no one said they had any. As the young cop ran back to the launch, screaming if anyone had any cigarettes, Stewart lifted off from the police dock.

As the helicopter rose into the night sky, the lighted windows of a skyscraper behind the copter began to blink out as the power grid began to fail.

Philadelphia was dying, and it was a painful thing to watch.

As the helicopter soared off into the darkness, the four survivors knew their future was bleak, but at least now they had a chance.

The rest would be left to fate.

WALKING WITH THE DEAD

Richard Dearborn slowly opened his eyes and looked around the room.

It was bright white, the lights blinding him with the intensity of a supernova. He blinked a few times, and ever so slowly, shapes came into focus.

Heads covered in white masks were hovering over him and he could hear people yelling at one another.

Medical terms were being tossed around, and in his fogged state, he didn't understand what had happened to him. He tried to get up, but he couldn't move. His arms, neck, and legs were strapped to something.

A table?

He felt cold, no wait, he was hot.

That was odd.

It was like someone had placed an air conditioner on his lower half and a heater on his upper half.

He tried to move his head, but it wouldn't move.

Talk, he thought. *I need to talk, tell these people I'm okay, that they don't have to fuss over me so much.*

Opening his mouth, only gargles came out. Then he coughed, blood shooting from past his lips to fall back onto his face.

"I'm losing him!" a voice screamed from somewhere far away.

Losing him? What did that mean? Was the voice talking about him? Was he dying?

But how could that be? He tried to remember what he had done that day, but it was all a tangled mess.

Wait, I do remember, he thought.

I was driving home from work. It was a little before five and I snuck out early when the boss was in another office chewing some poor slob out about the week's financial report.

I took the interstate home and then the off ramp. I remember stopping at the local gas station for a pack of smokes and a gallon of milk.

Susan had told me to get her a gallon of milk and some bread.
Oh, great, I forgot the bread!

But I figured I could go out and get some later after I ate dinner.

So I left the gas station and then drove in the direction of that intersection everyone living in my city hated. It was a four-way intersection with a blinking red light in the middle that was about as good as that one bulb that always wouldn't work on my Christmas lights every year.

No one stopped at the four-way and it was always a free-for-all to get through it.

So I approached the intersection and then…

And then it all goes blank.

"Give me a shot of adrenalin, now, nurse!" a voice screamed, but in his struggle to remember, Richard barely heard it.

Now what happened at that intersection that I can't remember? he wondered.

Then he did remember and his breath stopped in his chest.

He was waiting at the intersection, and when he thought he had a chance to go, he'd taken it, but there had been a cement truck coming way too fast on his left, and at the last instant, Richard realized the driver wasn't going to stop.

He was able to look out his driver's side window and see the man was talking on a cell phone and he wasn't paying attention to where he was going.

In the flash of an eye, Richard remembered thinking it was the cigarettes he smoked that he thought were going to be the death of him, not an overweight truck driver with too many cell minutes on his calling plan.

Then there was a crescendo of crashing glass and twisting metal and he was tossed across the car seat and pummeled by the air bag when it went off.

Nothing then, nothing but darkness.

Until now.

"I need the paddles, now, give me those paddles!" a voice screamed, the same one as before.

"Here, Doctor, take them, ready when you are," a woman's voice said.

Was it Susan's? Was his wife here?

"Clear!" the doctor yelled.

Suddenly, he felt nothing but pain and his vision darkened as electricity shot through his body. His heart trip-hammered in his chest and he sucked in a breath, but then lost it.

There was a beeping sound coming from nearby, then it went steady, like a low hum.

"He's not responding, Doctor." It was the woman's voice again.

"Up the juice, let's hit 'em again!"

"But, Doctor..."

"Do as I say, nurse, I'm in charge in this trauma center, not you!"

"Yes, Doctor."

"Clear!"

Voltage surged through his limbs, feeling like acid was coursing through his veins.

"No, it's not working, his heart is too badly damaged!" the doctor yelled. "Nurse, get me the experimental drug!"

"What? But, Doctor, it's still in the trial stages. It hasn't even been tested on humans yet."

"I don't care, this man's dying and if I don't at least try then he's a goner. Do you want to tell his wife we didn't even try? She's right outside in the waiting room."

There was silence with the exception of people moving about and then the nurse spoke again.

"No, Doctor, I... I guess you're right."

Richard didn't know what was happening, he tried to talk but only garbled grunts came out. Then he felt a piercing stab right where his heart was. There was a warmness that suffused his body as his heart pumped whatever the doctor had injected inside him.

"Okay, now give me the paddles again," the doctor said. "The juice on top of the drug should be enough to repair his heart."

"But, Doctor, you don't know that," the nurse said.

"Listen, nurse, unless you know something about nanites, you need to keep your damn mouth shut and do as I say or I swear to God, you'll be cleaning bedpans for the rest of the year by the end of your shift tonight. Do I make myself clear?"

"Yes, Doctor," the nurse replied, her answer now more confident. She had pushed it as far as she could without damaging her career.

"All right, charge the paddles now!"

There was a whining sound.

"Clear!"

Richard's body jumped off the gurney and he felt a pain so great he thought he was going to die and in truth he was correct. Though the voltage shot through his heart, and the drug coursed through his system, he was gasping his last breath. The beeping stopped and a fateful steady droning filled his ears.

It was the last sound he heard.

"Call it, nurse, 6:22 p.m. I can't believe we lost him, I really thought he had a chance."

"It's not your fault, Doctor, he simply suffered too much trauma, there was really no chance," the nurse said. "He looks like he's gone through a meat grinder as it is."

The doctor tossed his bloody gloves on top of the table next to Richard's corpse and shrugged out of his once white lab coat, which was now a bright scarlet, like the man had tie-dyed it.

"Well, I might as well go tell his wife," he said. "Have this room cleaned up and get the body to the morgue."

"Yes, Doctor, I'll see it's done immediately."

Nodding curtly, the doctor left the room, his heart weary. He was now going to do what he hated most in his job profession.

He had to tell a grieving family member their loved one was gone forever.

* * *

Richard opened his eyes and looked around, seeing nothing.

He was cold, really cold.

It was utterly silent, not so much as a cough or a footstep to break the silence.

Quite a change of pace from where he was a few seconds ago.

Or so it seemed to him.

He didn't know how he could have gotten to where he was so fast, but he was here now so he might as well deal with it.

Moving his head, he could hear the soft rub of material and he realized there was a sheet over him. Reaching up, he pulled the sheet off his face, but it was still dark.

With a choice of laying in the dark or getting up, he chose the latter, so with slow, jerky movements he sat up and slid himself to the side.

His feet were now hanging off the side of the table, and in the total blackness, it felt like if he slid off whatever he was sitting on, he would fall into a black hole. But of course that was ridiculous. If there was a void below him, then how could the table or bed or whatever he was on be there at all?

With a leap of faith, he slid off the table and his bare feet slapped the cold floor.

Stumbling forward, his hands were out in front of him as he tried to find his way around like a blind man. He bumped into something and it moved with him, so he pushed it out of the way, whatever it was rolling across the floor until a metallic bang told him something had stopped it—a wall perhaps?

It was so dark he couldn't see his hand in front of his face.

He reached a wall and slapped it, not feeling the cold surface of the metal with his fingertips. In point of fact, he felt nothing at all. It was like he was in one of those temperature controlled meditation chambers.

His head was foggy, too, and he couldn't think straight.

He moved about the room some more and bumped into another obstacle. Was this one the same one as before?

He reached out and felt what it was. Though his sense of touch was almost gone, he was barely able to detect the curves and softness of what had to be an animal or a body.

A body?

But if that was so, then that could only mean...

No, impossible, hospitals don't make mistakes like that.

Suddenly, there was the sound of a latch being pulled and then bright, white light flooded into the room, temporarily blinding him.

He blinked multiple times and then realized he could see better. Turning around, he now saw the obstacles were bodies on gurneys, each one with a sheet over them and a small tag on each of their left big toes.

He glanced down at his own left foot and saw a tag there as well. And he saw he was naked.

None of this made sense. He wasn't dead. He was standing up, feeling fine. Sure, he was not at his peak, but who would be after what he just went through?

Someone was gonna pay and pay big, he thought. Maybe a big lawsuit, or better yet, a large cash settlement.

After all, what hospital would want it getting out they had placed a living patient in the morgue and left him alone, right down to placing a toe tag on his foot?

For the first time, he realized he wasn't alone in the room. A man was standing in the open doorway with light spilling into the room from the hallway behind him, and the man wore the uniform of a security guard.

An armed security guard.

The man was shaking as he screamed and pointed at Richard, and Richard tried to speak, to tell the man he was all right, that this was all a big mistake.

Then Richard watched the security guard do something he would never have believed possible, at least not to him.

The man pulled his gun and aimed it at Richard.

Richard tried to speak again, but only garbled noises came out. He reached for the security guard, trying to calm him down, not wanting him to do anything rash. And then Richard took a few steps toward the man while still trying to speak.

Hal Stevenson opened the door to the morgue and his eyes popped out of his head. The guy they had brought in two hours ago was walking around! And he was buck naked!

That was impossible. He had seen the guy with his own eyes when they rolled him into the cooler. Half his face had been bashed in and the body had had a massive hole in its abdomen from where a piece of metal had impaled the man when he'd been struck by the cement truck.

Hal knew all about Richard's accident. He loved hearing about the really gory cases in all their glorious details. He was a big horror fan and this was the best he could get for action in his quiet job in the hospital.

But what was standing in front of him was way more than he bargained for. Hal had seen enough horror movies—zombie movies in particular—to know one when he saw one.

And the naked corpse was doing exactly what a zombie should do.

He was stumbling around, moaning and groaning, and then he even raised his arms in the air like Frankenstein as he shambled at him.

Well, Hal wasn't gonna be lunch for a zombie, that was for sure.

So pulling his gun, one he had never fired before, he flicked off the safety and screamed at the zombie.

"Stay back, you, you, *zombie!* I'll shoot, so help me!"

But the zombie ignored his warning as a zombie was supposed to do and continued forward.

Well, what did he expect?

So Hal closed his eyes and fired his revolver three times, each shot striking the zombie in the chest and torso.

When he opened his eyes, he screamed in fear because the zombie hadn't stopped and had now reached him. Hal dropped the gun in sheer terror, wet himself in fear, and tried to run away, only the zombie had other plans for him.

Richard felt the rounds striking him and he grunted with each impact, but the funny thing was they didn't hurt.

That was odd.

Glancing down to his chest, he saw there was no blood either, only three round holes like someone had poked their finger into a mound of clay.

The security guard was yelling at him and Richard found himself growing angry, and then more angry than he could ever remember.

This man had shot him!

He was a patient for God's sake and he had just gotten shot.

He moved closer to the guard, and when he was no more than a foot away, something happened to him, something he couldn't explain.

He felt hungry.

Not just a little peckish, like he could go for a salad, but so hungry it was like he had been lost in the woods for three days and hadn't had a thing to eat—that kind of hungry.

And as he stared at the security guard, he saw the veins pulsing on the man's neck, each pulse equal to his beating heart, and it was like someone was ringing the dinner bell.

What Richard did next happened so fast he couldn't have stopped himself if he'd wanted to. He grabbed the security guard by the arms and leaned into the man's throat, his teeth opening wide as he bit deep.

Blood flowed down his throat and the guard screamed, but Richard's grip was like iron. He chewed like a homeless man eating a free turkey leg on Thanksgiving, tearing hunks of the man's flesh out with each bite. As for the guard, he jerked in his arms as his blood seeped from his wound in scarlet pints.

But as the blood went out, so too, did the same nanites infesting Richard's body go into the guard—now giving the dead man new life.

Richard continued feeding and soon let the body drop to the floor where he knelt down and began gnawing on the guard's right arm.

He did this for more than ten minutes until the guard began to stir again.

Richard didn't know why, but for some reason the instant the man stirred, the flesh became unappetizing. Standing up and backing away, Richard watched the guard stand on wobbly legs. The man's head was at a slight angle now, thanks to all the tendons and flesh Richard had eaten, but the man could function well enough.

Richard was hungry, the feeling of starvation still there. Though he had quelled it for a short span of time while munching on the security guard, the hunger was already coming back worse than before.

Turning to head down the hallway, he began to walk in plodding steps, not really knowing where he was going.

Behind him the security guard followed.

The dead man named Hal didn't know why he was following the naked man, but there was nowhere else better to go at the moment so his dead brain said, "Why not?"

At the end of the hallway was the elevator that would lead to the main floors of the hospital.

The first floor was for the emergency room, the second pediatrics, and the third was for rehabilitation. When Richard approached the elevator doors, they cycled open.

Whether it was coincidence or some remaining intelligence from when he was alive, he stepped inside. The security guard followed like a lost puppy, and when both zombies were inside the elevator, the doors closed softly.

For three minutes, the two zombies stood in the elevator, not moving, merely staring at the lighted numbers on the panel.

But then the elevator began to move, being called from another floor.

With a soft jolt, it rose silently while the two newborn ghouls waited patiently.

*　*　*

"Come on, Rose, push, you can do it!" the doctor yelled forcefully while standing at the foot of the hospital bed in room 632 on the second floor of the hospital.

In front of him, Rose Rodriquez was in pain, the baby in her body refusing to come out and embrace the world.

"Come on, Rose, I can see the head, it's almost out," the doctor said, but in his mind he knew if the baby didn't come out soon, he would have to consider a C-section. The woman had been partially dilated for almost a day and he was growing more worried with each passing minute. And to top it off, the woman had refused an epidural, citing she wanted a natural, drug-free birth. He applauded her strength, but if he had been a woman, and in her shoes, he would have been screaming for drugs and as many as they would give him.

"I can't, Doctor, I can't!" Rose screamed at him in a thick Spanish accent. She was all alone in this birth, her husband and family back in Mexico. Her eyes were closed and sweat covered her face in rivulets that dripped down her body to soak the sheets in puddles.

"Yes, you can, you just need the proper motivation," the doctor said.

And then a naked man covered in blood and a security guard with half his neck gone and a large part of one arm missing stepped into the room, both looking like they'd been through a war together thanks to the amount of blood covering both bodies.

The doctor stood up, staring at the two men, anger fuming inside him.

"What in God's name are you two doing in here? This woman is having a baby! Get out of here! Nurse, nurse, where's the nurse? Someone call security, I mean more security." He pointed at Hal. "This man's obviously sick and wounded!"

Richard raised his arms and moved closer, as the doctor raised his hands to push him away.

"Do you know who I am? I'm the head of pediatrics, damn it. This is my floor, now get out of here before I have you arrested!"

But his threats fell on deaf ears and whatever he thought might happen next, he never expected what did happen.

It shocked him to the bone.

Richard pushed past the doctor's hands and grabbed his head, pushing him to the bed right between Rose's open legs. Richard's jaw opened so wide it threatened to unhinge and came down faster than the doctor could have imagined. Teeth clamped on flesh and the doctor found he was now very much in need of a doctor of his own.

The security guard moved in, as well, sinking his teeth into the doctor's meaty right thigh.

The doctor screamed and pushed Richard away from him, and as he stood up, the blood from his carotid artery shot outward, bathing Rose in warm blood. She screamed in terror, and just as the doctor had said, all she needed was the proper motivation to give birth.

In her panic and terror at the bleeding doctor and the two men now eating him, Rose pushed as hard as she could and the baby popped out like it was a baseball from an automated pitching machine.

The doctor was writhing on the floor, and the baby bounced off his stomach, the jolt causing the baby to animate and a high-pitched scream filled the room.

"My baby! Where's my baby!" Rose screamed as she tried to see her child.

But Richard saw it first. Ignoring the doctor, the security guard now getting the screaming healer to himself, Richard reached out and picked up the baby by one tiny leg.

Rose screamed like she was about to die, and in truth she was, but first it was her baby's turn.

Richard never slowed, never halted. If he had still been human, he may have had a second thought about eating a newborn baby, but as a zombie, well, meat was meat.

Teeth clamped on small fingers and ripped them off like they were frog's legs. He grabbed both small feet, and with one in each hand, he pulled them apart, ripping the screaming baby in two. The screaming ceased and tiny organs and viscera splashed to the floor. Richard ignored them, chewing on the soft flesh like it was veal.

Rose screamed and tried to get up, but she was too weak from childbirth. Tears filled her eyes and she shook her head back and forth. If she wasn't going insane, she should have been. She had just witnessed her newborn baby, barely a minute old, drawn and quartered in front of her eyes.

Her screaming got Richard's attention, and with his face and torso covered in newborn blood, he turned to Rose.

She screamed louder still, barely seeing Richard or anything else in her madness. She was lost in a world of loss and horror where the only way to ever ease her pain would be to kill herself.

Richard was going to help her with that.

Stepping the three feet to her bedside, he reached out and grabbed her face with his bloodied hands. Still she screamed, her mouth open, her tongue flapping around.

Richard reached in and grabbed her tongue, the woman's screams abruptly stopping when she realized she was under attack. With the strength of the dead, Richard yanked her tongue from her mouth, blood shooting out like a small fountain. While the woman tried to scream with pain and fear, she began to gag on her blood as it slid down her throat.

Richard ignored her for a moment, chewing on the tongue like it was a delicacy. The soft, slippery meat slid down his throat like tripe and in his dead brain he realized he liked the tongue. But then he was curious for more and so he pushed Rose down on the bed, and while his left hand held her forehead down, the woman's arms thrashing wildly in agony, he went for her right eyeball. He slid two fingers to the side of the orb, and when they were in deep, he flicked them upward. The eye popped out like a marble that was stuck in a hole and he brought it to his mouth. Small threads of ganglia and nerves were drooping from the bottom of the orb, and when Richard had separated it enough from the socket, they snapped.

He popped the little ball into his mouth and chewed, a small amount of eye juice slipping out of the corner of his mouth. If he could describe the sensation of that *pop* when he bit down, it would be like eating a plump cherry tomato or a large grape.

Enjoying the taste, he went in for the next eye, but just before he did, three security guards arrived at the doorway, guns drawn and yelling about what was going on.

Behind the men, a charge nurse screamed at the men to just shoot, and though they shouldn't have listened to a nurse, and immediately called for backup, an order was an order, and in the chaos of the moment they just wanted to be told what to do. Each man fired three rounds into Richard and the dead security guard, but nothing seemed to work.

It was Richard who turned first, and as the three men stared at the abomination in front of them, one guard turned and ran, deciding that for $7.80 an hour, he didn't need this and he'd rather go work at McDonalds.

The two remaining security guards fired repeatedly and Richard's torso swayed with each round. Then Richard had reached the first security guard, and when the man tried to escape, he backed into his partner. Richard reached out, grabbed the man by the curly black hair on the top of his head, and yanked back, exposing the neck.

Scarlet teeth flashed in the light of the room and then the guard was screaming as a three inch piece of his jugular was torn free. Blood shot to the ceiling and trickled back to the floor and the guard was dead in seconds. The second security guard fired again, three bullets hitting Richard in the arm, leg and one grazing his forehead. Then Hal, who was finished with the doctor, was on the guard, too, and he and Richard tore the man apart.

The hospital room was in shambles; blood coating everything like someone had entered with a garden hose and just sprayed red everywhere.

While all this was going on, the hospital staff just stood in the hallway at the entrance to the room, transfixed.

What were they supposed to do?

The security guards had guns, they should have been able to subdue the crazy men and end whatever was happening.

By this time Rose was very dead, and the doctor was done twitching on the floor. Richard was feeding on the guard he'd grabbed by the hair and his stomach was becoming bloated as he packed more and more meat into it. It was only a matter of time before it simply ruptured.

Five minutes passed and the hospital staff stared in utter shock at the carnage in the birthing room. The police had been called, but they still hadn't arrived and until they did, there was nothing anyone could do.

No one was going back inside that room.

As the minutes passed, Rose revived and her lone eye began to twitch, flicking back and forth in its socket. With a garbled moan, the doctor slowly rose from the floor, now missing pieces of his face, neck and arms, plus a hunk from his thigh, making him resemble an anatomy project gone horribly wrong.

There were now three security guards in the small room, and as the one Richard still held in his arms reanimated, he let the man go. Rose slid off the bed and took a moment to pick up a small, newborn arm lying on the floor. She began chewing on it, the small, fragile bones crunching in her mouth. If she had any qualms about eating pieces of her baby, she gave no sign. Her missing tongue was forgotten—she had nothing to say anyway.

With the six zombies standing around and hungry, Richard turned and stepped into the hallway.

The staff screamed in panic and a few bolted while others tried to get the nearby patients to safety. With five ghouls behind him, Richard reached out and grabbed a nurse as she ran screaming by him. With her blonde hair in his hand, he twisted his arm and tossed her to the dead doctor.

With a gleam in his dead eyes, the doctor immediately dove in and ripped off the nurse's nose with his clean white teeth. She screamed and begged for mercy, but would receive none.

Richard began walking down the hallway, on the prowl for more food. The rooms were lined with expectant mothers, and down the hall, after a set of double glass doors, the nursery waited.

It would be a good feast. One any zombie would be proud of.

And best of all, there was enough food for everyone. No one would go hungry today.

When Richard was halfway down the hallway with Rose and Hal behind him, the police arrived. Five officers in blue uniforms and weapons drawn charged into the hallway.

They took one look at Rose and Hal, and a naked, blood-covered Richard, and their mouths fell open. They looked past them to see the doctor feeding on the nurse, the woman's uniform now torn open and her breasts exposed. As the police officers watched in horror, the doctor dove in, clamped his teeth down on one pert nipple, and tore it off, blood shooting from the wound to splash his face crimson.

As the nurse passed out from shock, the doctor looked up at the policemen, chewing happily on the flesh, almost swallowing the nipple whole before going back for more.

The cops looked back at the three zombies in front of them, and the three ghouls behind them feeding on the hospital staff, and they began shooting, cutting into the zombies like they were targets at the firing range.

But it seemed that no one had ever seen a zombie movie so no shots were aimed at heads. With the zombies taking each shot easily, they soon reached the policemen who tried to fight back. But how do you subdue an attacker that wants to eat you?

It didn't take long for the unprepared police officers to become zombie chow and soon enough they joined the ranks of the dead.

Richard was still first, and the rest followed him like he was their leader.

In no time, the rest of the floor was being eaten, killed, then re-animated, and after that hour had passed they entered the south stairwell and went upstairs and then downstairs, swarming through the hospital and killing everyone they found. Patients who were laid up in bed, some from operations, cancer, or broken legs, were all easy targets, trapped in their beds while the zombies ripped them apart.

Some escaped, but not many.

No one understood what was happening and expected the authorities to arrive and save the day. But the police officers on the scene never managed to get a call back to dispatch and warn others what was happening.

If someone had stood in the front of the hospital and gazed up at the windows, they would have seen macabre shadows of moving figures. They would have heard screams of terror and pain as innocent people were slaughtered in their beds. The hospital, once a place of healing, was now a place of death, and as the day passed to night in the small rural hospital in the middle of nowhere and everywhere, those same shadows from the windows began to reappear in the first floor lobby by the main doors.

With darkness falling across the parking lot and the street lamps flickering on, the first shambling bodies emerged into the crisp, night air.

Richard was in the lead, still naked and covered in gore. His upper torso was riddled with bullet holes and his stomach was extended to the point of popping like an overfilled balloon.

Behind him, Rose walked drunkenly, and next to her came the doctor. Security guards came up next and the rest of the hospital staff followed. Undead patients hobbled out on crutches and some with walkers. The ones with broken legs crawled along on the ground, the last in line.

Richard stopped when he reached the front of the hospital, then turned and stood in the middle of the street, swaying back and forth like he was listening to soft music that calmed him.

The cool breeze dried the blood on his naked body but he didn't feel it. He didn't feel anything anymore.

He only felt the *hunger*.

In front of him, about a quarter mile away, stood the city, filled with lights from a hundred buildings, looking like the stars had fallen to earth, a blanket of shimmering light that was a beacon to his dead brain.

Richard took one step forward, and then another down the middle of the street, while behind him, his army of the undead slowly followed.

The hospital was just the beginning.

Soon the city would know the gentle caress of death, and after that the entire state, and perhaps in time...the world.

The night was just beginning, and either way it didn't matter.

For the dead have all the time in the world.

WRONG PLACE, WRONG TIME

Night had recently fallen. Casting the area in darkness, as John Maxwell opened his eyes and looked around, not understanding where he was.

The last memory he had was of being in the prison, in the medical ward.

He had been brought there for some unknown reason and the guards had strapped him to a bed. Then the doctor had arrived with a hypodermic needle in his hand.

John tried to fight, knowing there was no need for a shot, for he felt fine, but strapped down, he had no choice but to endure the abuse. His head grew foggy and he passed out, and as he now opened his eyes, he saw he was definitely not in the prison any more.

He was lying on the ground, and as he sat up, ignoring the small bout of nausea filling him, he saw he was on the wrong side of a large wall, built of stone.

As he studied the wall, he saw cameras mounted on top, and the closest one blinked red at him, letting him know he was being watched.

As he checked himself, he saw a note was pinned to his shirt, his bright orange shirt courtesy of the prison system, and he plucked it from his breast, ripping the corner.

The words **Start walking**, were written in bold script.

Crumpling the paper in his fist, he tossed it to the ground, where it blew away to stop as it reached the wall.

Though he never did what he was told, a rebel till the end, which was why he raped and killed that woman he'd found in the park last year, he decided there was nothing else to do *but* walk.

So he set out, not understanding where he was or how he'd gotten here, but soon realizing he was in a town, and as he slowed in front of a dilapidated building, looking as if it had been condemned for years, he spotted the shadow of a figure from across the road.

"Hey, where the fuck am I? Hey, you, come here and help me out?" He wanted to add, "Or I'll kill ya," but left that out as he was in unknown territory.

The figure stopped abruptly and seemed to shift slightly. John tried to peer into darkness and see who he was calling out to but the figure remained hidden in the shadows.

John heard a noise from behind and he spun around to see another figure across the road, also lost in the darkness. Another sound caused him to look left to see more figures appearing from the nearby building and adjacent alleyway.

"Hey, who the fuck are you people? Where am I? I want some answers or so help me..."

His words were cut off in mid-sentence when the closest figure stepped into the wan moonlight cast down from above. John was shocked to see the figure, though in the shape of a human, was far from it in actual appearance.

The face was hanging in strips of dead flesh, as if it was a rubber mask now old from time, the rubber now cracked and decayed. The figure's hands were pale, and as it moved closer, John saw different color fingers on its hand, as if black, white and Hispanic had all donated their digits.

"What the fuck? What are you?" John gasped but the figure said nothing, only moved closer.

John glanced to the figure's other hand to see the it carried a large knife, the steel reflecting what light there was.

John took a step backwards, realizing for once he was the prey and no longer the hunter.

"Stay away from me, you freak, I'll kill you." he warned but the words were idle for he saw no fear in the figure's eyes—eyes that were two different colors, one brown, the other blue.

As he backed away, he felt hands grab him from behind and he realized he had forgotten about the other figures skulking about behind him.

Before he could so much as fight them off, rough hands grabbed him and forced him to the ground, where he tried to fight but was quickly overpowered.

As he lay there, struggling to be free, he saw the other figures were in a similar state of disrepair, as if they had taken body parts from other people and somehow connected them to the each other, like a bizarre human jigsaw puzzle. The figure with the different color eyes raised the blade over its head as and knelt down over John, its mouth twitching into a rictus of a grin.

And that was when John let the fear growing within him out and he screamed for help and mercy, but there was no mercy here, only death.

The blade came down and tore into his chest, cracking the ribcage and cutting downward. With the crude incision made, other hands dove in, pulling open the chest cavity like he was a baked lobster, hands digging in deep to pull out organs and other choice parts.

John could only shriek in agony as his arms were pulled off, his legs separated, each part going to a figure that needed it.

A woman who only babbled, as she had no tongue, reached in and plucked John's from his mouth in a geyser of blood. She jammed the tongue into her own mouth, and the new organ weaved into her orifice, becoming one with her. As she began to speak, the words were slurred, as she needed to get used to her new one.

By now, John was beyond hearing as his ears were ripped from his skull, a knife digging out his eardrums. His eyes were plucked out with little care and went to two different figures as his skin was peeled from his torso to then be laid over others.

When the group of mismatched killers were finished, there was nothing left of John Maxwell, for every part had gone to a well deserving figure.

With his blood staining the road like spilled paint, the figures turned and shambled away, soon to be lost in the darkness and shadows to wait for another victim to arrive

A CORPSE OF HOT COCOA

Barbara Bennet sat silently in the first pew of the United Methodist Church.

Sitting beside her was her daughter Terry and her son Thomas.

Behind her, in the other pews, was the rest of her family.

On the podium in front of her, the minister droned on about life and the hereafter.

But none of that was what mattered to Barbara.

The only thing that mattered was that the bastard was finally dead.

She glanced to the right of the minister to see the open casket with her now very deceased husband lying within. From her vantage point, she could just see the tip of his nose, the rest of his visage hidden behind the mahogany.

Oh, yes, her son and daughter had spared no expense for their dearly departed father. Barbara thought it was all a waste of money. If she'd had her way, the bastard would have been dumped into a hole upside down and covered with dirt.

She cast a furtive glance at her son and daughter, seeing the tears welling up in the corner of their eyes.

Neither of her offspring knew about their father, neither knew that he beat their mother time and again, sometimes for the simplest of things.

Of course, he had never left any visible marks, always making sure to leave her face alone, but her lower torso was covered in bruises.

So she was glad he was dead, and couldn't wait until his evil corpse was cremated the following day.

So the minister droned on about loss and Barbara nodded, looking sorrowful. She did it for her children and other family members, who didn't know her husband was an inhuman monster.

But he was dead now, she was finally free.

But though she was free from present pain, spiritual marks would remain. She couldn't help but remember the last time he'd hit her, which had been less than a week ago. He had come home late from work and she had dinner waiting for him on the table like always. But he didn't give her time to warm it up, sitting down and digging in immediately. The potatoes had been cold, and before she knew what was happening, he was punching and kicking her like she was an inmate at the county jail as she rolled around on the kitchen floor.

Of course she had re-heated the potatoes, while tears ran down her cheeks. He had eaten in silence, then, secure in his manhood.

The mass ended and everyone began to stand to leave. Terry moved next to Barbara and touched her arm.

"I'll handle the arrangements with the cremation, Mom, are you okay?"

"Yes, dear, I'll be fine, trust me, I'll do just fine without your father."

"Are we still coming over for Sunday dinner next week, Mom?" Thomas asked.

"Yes, Tom," Barbara replied. "Be there around one. And your Aunt Tracey and Uncle Bert are coming, too. It's going to be a more private affair to remember your father, not the fancy one we're all going to go to now at the VFW."

Thomas nodded, understanding.

After the funeral, everyone was invited to the VFW, her husband's favorite hangout. The staff at the VFW had set up a buffet and all the guests would get their fill for paying their respects.

With Terry on one arm and Thomas on the other, Barbara began to walk down the center aisle of the church. She cast a glance one last time at her dead husband, hoping he would burn in Hell for all eternity for what he'd done to her. But either way she knew by tomorrow, when he was cremated, he would roast just fine, it was just a shame he couldn't feel the pain of the fire.

Later that night, she finally returned home, and when she stepped into the empty house, she sighed happily. It was a wonderful feeling. She was truly safe from him.

Deciding she wanted to celebrate, she went to the kitchen and reached up to the top shelf of the cabinet over the sink and took down a clay jar.

Inside the jar she kept her homemade mix of hot cocoa. It was an easy recipe: cocoa, instant milk and sugar. She made it by the bulk and then used the jar to store it in. The clay jar worked wonderfully as it breathed, not letting moisture buildup like it could with plastic or glass.

Setting a kettle on the stove, she heated the water and had a seat at the kitchen table. She stared at the refrigerator, and as the water slowly began to boil, and though she was glad he was gone, she soon found herself crying.

But whether they were tears of happiness or loss, she truly didn't know.

Getting ready for bed, she set her now empty cup of hot cocoa on her bedside and climbed into bed. It was weird; the bed didn't feel right. It was too empty.

But as she stretched out, the feelings that overwhelmed her earlier were now under control, and she knew that with a hot cup of cocoa and her strength of will, she would be just fine.

Turning off the light, she wrapped herself in her blankets and went to sleep.

The next Saturday, Terry arrived to see Barbara with a package, but her mother wasn't home.

That was okay, as she knew where the spare key was hidden and she didn't want to leave the package unattended on the front porch.

So she let herself in and carried the package to the kitchen, where she set it on the counter.

She wrote her mother a note, telling her about the package, but then decided she should handle it herself, so she set the note on the counter and proceeded to look around for something to use as a storage container.

She found one on the top shelf of the cabinet above the sink; a clay jar.

But it had what looked like hot cocoa in it. Shrugging, Terry grabbed a bowl and emptied the contents out, then she opened the package and poured the contents into it.

Checking her watch, she saw she was late for an appointment. She had agreed to have lunch with a friend from work and didn't want to be late.

So leaving the clay jar on the counter, she figured the note would suffice. Not wanting to be messy, she put the bowl of hot cocoa on a shelf to the right of the sink; it could be dealt with later, for now she had to run.

She left the house and closed the door behind her, the wind of the slamming door catching the note and blowing it to the edge of the counter where it slipped into, and fell, between the crack separating the refrigerator and the counter.

Now all that was there, sitting inconspicuously, was the clay jar.

The next day, Sunday at one p.m., all of Barbara's family had arrived for Sunday dinner. As she puttered around the kitchen, cooking, the clay jar still sat there, but now it was pushed to the back of the counter so Barbara had room to work. She had never given the jar much thought, figuring she'd placed it there after having a cup of cocoa the other night, so she worked hard to get dinner on the table so everyone could eat.

She was in high spirits, her husband dead for almost a week, and though she was a little lonely, she was already going out and meeting new people and having fun with her life.

The dinner went well and soon everyone was in the living room, sitting and talking as she prepared to get dessert ready. Pastries, cakes and an apple pie were just some of the treats on the menu today.

Coffee was made and she asked if a few of her family would be in the mood for hot cocoa instead.

She was surprised when everyone said yes, that would be wonderful, forget the coffee. After all, there was a slight chill in the air and the cocoa would hit the spot after a wonderful meal.

Barbara had nodded and had gone into the kitchen to prepare the beverages.

Ten minutes later, she returned to the living room with a tray of piping hot mugs of cocoa. She had added some whip cream to the top of each and the family dug in with laughter and smiles.

Barbara was so happy; she didn't think anything could make her day better.

Everyone took their drinks to the dinner table and dug into the desserts as everyone talked and shared memories of her late husband.

Then her sister Tracey asked about the cocoa, saying it didn't really taste all that chocolately. That was when she took a sip and saw she had a point. There was still the faint taste of cocoa but it wasn't as strong as the last time she had enjoyed a cup.

Getting up, Barbara went to the kitchen and picked up the clay jar, carrying it back to the dining room.

"I tell you, Tracey, I just don't understand what's wrong with the cocoa?"

Terry's mouth fell open as she set down her cup of cocoa.

"Mom, are you telling me you made our hot chocolate with what's in that jar?"

Barbara nodded. "Of course, dear, why wouldn't I? This is where I store my cocoa mix."

"But, Mom, didn't you get the note I left for you yesterday? I came by but you weren't here so I left it on the kitchen counter."

"No, dear, I never saw any note. You came by? What time was that?"

Terry waved the question away. "It doesn't matter, Mom, but what does is what's in that jar."

Barbara went back to her chair and set it down as everyone continued to eat and drink their cocoa. Her son, Thomas, and her brother-in-law, Bert, were making odd faces now as they drank their cocoa.

Barbara took a sip of her cocoa and looked down at the clay jar. "Terry, dear, what on Earth are going on about?"

"Mom, that's not hot cocoa mix in that jar. When I came by yesterday it was too bring you Dad's ashes. I didn't know where to put them so I found the jar and put them in there after dumping the contents into another bowl. I didn't want you to have to deal with it. I figured we could transfer the ashes to something else later or if you were going to scatter them somewhere it wouldn't matter. I...I just didn't want to leave him in the plastic bag and box the funeral home stuck him in."

As Terry's words sunk in to the dinner guests, suddenly everyone was spitting out their hot cocoa, splattering the table with a dark, watery-gray substance.

"Holy shit!" Thomas yelled. "You mean to tell me we're drinking Dad?"

Terry nodded as she felt her stomach go queasy, knowing she had drunk over half a cup. "Yup, it's Dad's ashes in that jar. Mom made the drinks from the remains of our father?"

Bert gagged and turned blue. "Oh my Lord, I think I'm gonna be sick," he said as he got up to stumble for the bathroom.

"Not before me you're not," Tracey spat as she, too, jumped up and dashed for the bathroom.

Thomas and Terry also stood up. "Oh my God, I *drank* Dad!" Thomas screamed.

Terry felt her stomach spin inside her and she dashed for the kitchen, planning on using the sink to eject her eaten dinner. Thomas bolted for the upstairs bathroom, leaving Barbara all alone at the table.

She could hear her family heaving as they tried to eject her late husband, but all she did was smile.

Picking up her cup of hot cocoa that was actually the ashes of her dead husband, she took another sip and grinned widely.

"Needs more whipped cream."

THE HEAD WORKS BEST

"What are we supposed to do with her?" Brett, a pimply faced teenager asked.

"I don't know, we could shoot her, you know, like in the movies," Carl replied. He was a year older and so was the leader of the group.

"You mean like in the head?" Tim, the last of the group asked. He was a tall skinny kid with enough acne to make a pizza look bare. He had just been upstairs, getting a drink of water, and had just returned to hear the conversation.

"Sure, why not?" Brett asked. "The guy on the news said to shoot 'em dead when you see one. We did one better, we caught one."

Carl and Tim looked at their friend with trepidation.

The dead had been walking for more than a month now. No one knew how or why, but if you were recently dead, such as had a heart attack, then after you dropped to the floor, you got back up, simple as that.

"I could get my dad's gun," Carl suggested as he scratched his head. The dead woman was tied to a chair, her eyes pale white, her yellow teeth gnashing, only wanting to bite one of them. The stench of the woman was horrendous, like a garbage truck filled with maggots wrapped in a rotting corpse, right down to the bloated abdomen as putrid gases attempted to escape.

"Or maybe we could like, you know, cut her head off," Carl mused as he stared at the dead woman.

"No way, that would make a big mess. My parents would kill me if I got blood all over the cellar floor," Brett said.

"And what do you think is gonna happen if we shoot her in the head?" Carl asked blandly.

After catching the dead woman stumbling around in the street, they had managed to wrangle her and get her into Brett's cellar. It had seemed a good idea at the time, but now they didn't know what to do with her.

"Maybe we should just call the cops and let them handle this, guys," Tim suggested. As he stared at the dead woman he was growing sick to his stomach. Right now all he wanted to do was take an antacid and go lie down.

"No way, she's ours, we caught her fair and square," Brett said as he turned to the other two boys, anger flaring in his eyes. "'Sides, I want to kill one before they're all gone."

Unlike in the movies, the dead hadn't taken over the world. With guns, explosives, and body armor, the police and didn't find it hard to contain them.

They were more of a nuisance now, like stray dogs.

"We should cut her head off," Carl said, "definitely."

"No, I think shooting her in the head is better. I could put some plastic behind her to catch the blood splatter," Brett said.

"Cut off her head," Carl demanded.

"Shoot her in the head," Brett replied, the two now turning to face one another.

Suddenly there was a crash from upstairs and a SWAT team came flying down the stairs with full body armor and rifles moving, searching for a target. The lead officer saw the dead woman in the chair, raised his rifle and fired at almost point blank range The dead woman's head exploded in a circular mass of bone fragments and brain matter, gobbets of flesh flying off to strike each boy in the face and chest.

Bits of brain dripped down their cheeks and hung on their noses.

For a second there was utter silence as the blood dripped from the low ceiling.

Brett turned to Carl and nodded his head slightly.

"Okay, you're right, shooting her in the head is better."

DEAD DOG TIRED

Rufus rolled over in bed, smacking his lips as he tried to figure out what had woken him. His eyes were still closed, and as he slowly cracked them, bright white light sliced into his retinas, causing him to snap them closed.

His head began to pound and he knew he'd drunk too much again.

A squealing came to his ears, and he opened his eyes once more, turning away from the one window in the room with the ragged shade and no curtain. This time his eyes adjusted as he slowly sat up, the room spinning as his hangover took over his consciousness.

Rubbing his head, he looked around the room, smacking his lips once more. It felt like he'd chewed on sandpaper and then spit it out and tossed in a handful of dirt for good measure. The room looked the same as it always did; dirty laundry piled everywhere, a few crushed beer cans lying in one corner, the spouts gaping at him like one-eyed cats.

There was the distinct smell of unwashed bodies in the air, but Rufus didn't notice. He thought he smelled fine, and besides, it was still three more days till the standard weekly bath.

Standing up, he scratched his butt and stumbled to the bathroom, which looked like someone had carried in a bucket full of shit and had then begun tossing it in every direction. A Rorschach painting of feces, Rufus would have thought; if he had the brain power to think in such terms.

But Rufus had managed all of the second grade, and in his family he was considered a college graduate.

After finishing in the bathroom, and not deciding to flush—the water was only a little yellow, he'd wait till it was a full brown—he felt his head pulse with pain as another bout of squealing floated into the house.

Looking around, he knew what it was immediately, and he waddled to the kitchen to look out into the backyard.

"Damn dog, always complainin'," he said to himself as he grabbed his jacket and opened the back door. Stepping outside, the chill air caused his testicles to crawl up inside him and he shook off the cold, watching his breath coalescing in front of him like a miniscule wraith.

Across the yard was his dog, chained to the old oak tree with gnarled branches and a rotting core. The tree should have been taken down years ago, but at the cost, it wasn't worth it. Better to let it die, and when a good storm came, Mother Nature would see to upending it right out of the ground. Of course, if it fell the wrong way Rufus might find out he had a new sunroof, but he wasn't bright enough to think that far ahead.

The dog, a rather large pitbull, woofed its displeasure at being chained up for the entire night.

"Shut up, ya damn mutt," Rufus snapped. "The only reason you're here is 'cause I made sure my bitch of an ex-wife didn't getcha in the divorce."

The dog woofed again and whimpered. Though a large animal, the ribs of the dog poked through from lack of food and its paws were raw from where it had scratched the frozen earth to escape its chain. The collar to which the chain was affixed had dug into the fur until it could barely be seen. Sores festered around the collar where the leather was biting into the animal's flesh and flies buzzed about; feeding on the spots of blood that would appear each time the dog flexed or pulled on the chain.

Attached to the color, hanging under its neck, was a dog charm. The charm looked like an upside down ampersand, and had small writing scrawled along the metal. Rufus didn't know what it was as it was from his ex-wife, the woman having bought it from some old voodoo shop in town.

The dog lowered its head and growled low, sensing Rufus wasn't here to help it. The two had never gotten along, and when Rufus' wife had filed for a divorce on the grounds he was a lazy, good for nothin', wife beating, vagabond—her words—he had made sure to get a lawyer with enough teeth to stick it to her good.

So what if he'd slapped her around now and then. It was only when she deserved it, such as when dinner wasn't ready or the house wasn't clean. A woman needed to know her place and Rufus' knew they needed it, craved it. Though they might not admit it, women like to be dominated by their man, to be told what to do and when to do it.

Well, he had fixed her wagon in the end, the bitch going and spreading lies and rumors about him.

The only thing she had ever loved while with him was the dog and he had made sure to get it in the settlement. He got the house, too, and to this day he didn't know what his divorce lawyer had managed to do to get away with that one. Last time he checked, his ex was living in a studio apartment in the city—not the good part, either, and she had a job waiting tables at some dive of a diner on the east side.

Rufus didn't work, thanks to a disability check from the government. In his file, it said he was mental, though in reality he was just an asshole.

Couldn't work with others, didn't listen to orders, and couldn't complete tasks given him. That's what it said on his discharge papers from the army.

None of that had to do with him getting his brains fried in the war, though it could have. No, Rufus was just an asshole who thought he knew better than everyone else.

Still, he took the check and cashed it once a month and smiled while he did it.

The dog growled again and Rufus chuckled at it. The dog had been his for all of a week and he had fed it twice when feeling charitable. But now, with his head pounding, he could give two-shits for the damn mutt.

"Shut the hell up, you mangy dog, or so help me I'll come out here with my shotgun and end you once and for all."

The dog lowered its head so low to the ground its chin scraped the soil, its small tail pointed down. The eyes were creased in what seemed to be anger, and as Rufus chuckled malevolently, the dog lunged for him, only the chain stopping it from tearing out Rufus' throat.

As for Rufus, he jumped back and screamed like a girl, falling in the mud beneath him. He quickly looked around to make sure no one had seen him act the coward. Of course there was no one, the next yard more than five hundred feet in each direction.

Slapping the mud under him with his hands, the cold water soaking into his pants, he raised a muddy fist at the dog and snarled, "You'll pay for that, you no good mutt, just try and get another meal out of me."

Pulling himself to his feet, he took a step forward, just to the limit of the dog's chain, and sent a kick into its right shoulder blade. The dog rolled across the dirt and jumped up a second later, only to lunge and become halted by the tight snap of the chain once more.

Rufus spun around and headed back into the house with an evil grin creasing his lips. He glanced over his shoulder once to see the dog watching him, its hackles still raised. But Rufus wasn't scared. The chain holding the dog had inch thick metal links, and as the dog grew weaker from hunger, he knew the fight would go out of the animal.

It was just a matter of time.

The next four days were one of absolute suffering for the dog as it slowly starved to death.

Rufus would sit on the back porch and watch the dog whimpering as its ribs became more pronounced. As the dog slowly died, he imagined it was his bitch of an ex-wife he was making suffer.

A pile of beer cans lying on the porch showed how much time he'd spent watching the dog succumb to death.

One time, when he was feeling particularly evil, he had taken a cooked chicken leg leftover from his dinner and placed it exactly six inches from the dog's face. Though the animal tried to stretch the chain to get at the food, it was an impossible task.

Rufus chugged another beer and laughed hysterically as the dog tried to reach the chicken leg. Its eyes rolled up into its head as it whimpered with desperation, but it could never quite reach the food.

Finally, when Rufus became bored, he kicked the chicken leg into the dirt, where it rolled and came up against the fence. The dog's eyes followed it roll, then lowered its head and whimpered like a sad boy who had dropped his ice cream cone.

Rufus had laughed and went back into the house, and as he lay in his bed, he drifted off to sleep hearing the melody of suffering that was his ex-wife's dog.

On the fifth day he woke up to hear only silence.

Scratching his butt as he made his way to the kitchen, he grabbed a beer out of the fridge and went out to the backyard. The beer tasted sweet, and though it was only ten in the morning, he finished it off and planned on getting another. But first he wanted to check on the mutt and see if it was dead yet.

As he crossed the denuded yard, he saw the animal was lying on its side, its mouth open, the tongue hanging out. The eyes were wide and glazed and dozens of ants were crawling on the carcass.

Rufus took a swig of beer and nodded to himself, seeing the dog had died sometime in the middle of the night.

Finishing his beer, he wiped his mouth with his sleeve and went to get a shovel.

Deciding the less work the better, he dug the hole only two feet from the dead dog. It took him almost an hour, as he had to rest continuously. Manual labor was not his forte, and by the time he was finished, he was sweating profusely and panting the same way the dog had done when it tried to get the chicken leg.

The hole was three feet deep, and he figured it was good enough for a dumb mutt.

Bending down, he unclipped the chain and carelessly kicked the body into the hole. The dog landed muzzle down and to add insult to injury, Rufus unzipped his fly and pissed on the corpse, spraying his stream up and down the matted fur.

When he finished, he zipped up and filled in the hole, slapping the dirt a few times when he was done. He had some leftover dirt now so he spread it around the yard, using it to cover the few piles of feces the dog had left before finally unable to expel anything, as there was nothing going inside its stomach to fuel the machine.

He tossed the shovel to the side and let it clatter to the ground, forgotten as soon as it landed.

Letting out a burp, he stumbled back into the house to grab another beer. He idly wondered what he was going to do now to keep himself occupied now that the tortured dog was dead.

But for now he wanted to go lie down. The digging of the whole had tuckered him out and he was dead dog tired.

There was a thunderstorm that night.

The wind buffeted the trees around Rufus' house as lightning crackled in the sky. The rain came down in sheets, washing the earth clean.

In the backyard of Rufus' home, the muddy soil began to shift and undulate, as if a giant worm was just under the surface.

Like a light switch had been flicked, the rain stopped and the thunder ceased, the storm over, now only the smell of ozone and the drenched soil left behind.

As the leaves on the large oak tree sagged with moisture, the soil below it continued to move.

Ever so slowly, a mud-covered paw broke through the mud to flail back and forth, as if searching for a hand to pull it free. But there was no one in the shadow-enshrouded yard, the moon hidden behind the clouds, and the porch light off.

As the paw flailed back and forth, another paw soon shot forth, looking like a spear stabbing the earth in reverse. In between the two paws, the mud still shifted, and ever so slowly, a dog's head appeared, the muzzle oozing mud as the tongue flicked slightly, resembling a snake tasting the air.

Ever cautious, the dead dog wiggled back and forth as its paws began to scrape the mud, carving long furrows in the wet soil as it began to haul itself out of its shallow grave.

The eyes seemed to glow with a hatred unknown to this earth, and the talisman on its collar moved slightly, as if it was an appendage, a third tale, that twitched when the dog was pleased or angry.

The muzzle cracked and mud spilled forth, the dog puking up more than a gallon of foul water and soil, all that had seeped into its maw as it lay in the sodden grave.

With a groan, the dog stood on its four legs and shook itself, mud flying off in all directions as the matted fur managed to keep some of the soil within its knotted clumps. The dog looked up at the night sky and howled, a long mournful wail, one of loss and frustration.

As the cloud cover began to break apart, the moon sliced through and illuminated the yard, casting the back porch in its pallid glow. The dog's head swiveled toward the back porch, and when it saw the rear door, its hackles raised and its growl vibrated from within it like a cyclone ready to explode.

There was a beer can on the ground and the dog leaned down and sniffed it, not detecting a scent thanks to the rainstorm, but despite this, the animal knew who the can belonged to.

Legs cracked as rigor mortis began to fade, and with halting steps, it began to stumble drunkenly towards the back porch.

As it moved closer to the house, thunder rolled from the north, the storm now out of range, but soon about to pummel another part of the county.

With eyes glowing with hatred and hunger—a hunger for vengeance—the dog padded toward the back door and the oblivious sleeping Rufus waiting within.

The back door was made of cheap wood, with a brown baize on the inside. With its left paw the dog began to scratch at the wood, its sharp claws digging in and scratching long gouges into the facade. This continued for more than hour, each swipe of its claw slowly taking away more of the wood. On the inside of the door, the brown material began to slowly undulate as pressure from the opposite side increased.

Then the baize ripped and the paw could be seen as it wiggled back and forth, tearing and pulling at the edges.

By the time the hole was large enough for the dog's head to fit, the paw that had done the scratching was a bloody nub with bone protruding at the tip, gobbets of flesh and fur hanging from it to slap the porch as the dog continued to worry at the door.

With a hole now present, the dog forced its head inside, then slowly began pulling its torso through the opening. But the edges of the hole were jagged, thick wooden splinters jutting at odd angles, and as the dog slowly crawled into the kitchen, the wooden daggers sliced into its fur, its flesh, tearing large gashes that seeped congealed blood like cold maple syrup on a winter's day.

One such dagger, jutting at an odd angle, managed to pierce the dog's left eye. The spear sliced into the orb, penetrating more than an inch; a pinkish ooze seeping out of the socket to drip onto the floor.

Finally, the dog's hind legs were through the hole and it plopped down on the floor. The animal lay there, acting as if it was catching its breath, which was the farthest thing from the truth; for it no longer breathed.

As it lay there, covered in mud, large gashes in the animal's hide, one eye now missing, it paused, for a moment not moving, as if it had returned back to death's door.

For the space of half a minute, the dog was immobile. Then a snore carried through the house from the opposite end, causing the dog's head to snap up. Slowly, it pulled itself to a standing position.

It now stood at an odd angle due to the missing paw, now nothing but a bloody stump, and as it began to walk through the house, there was an odd, *slap, slap, click, slap, slap, click*, for each time the exposed bone connected with the kitchen floor.

The snoring called to the animal and it slowly made its way through the house, not rushing, silent as death itself.

At the doorway to where the snoring was emanating, it paused, then used its muzzle to cautiously push the partially opened door wider. The room was wretched in darkness, only a wan spear of moonlight creasing the shadows, cutting through the tattered window shade of the lone window.

The dog entered the bedroom and moved to the bed, where Rufus lay in a drunken stupor.

The dog woofed once, softly, as if it was warning its victim, giving Rufus a chance to wake up and defend himself, but even if the dog had barked with its loudest volume, Rufus was out for the night.

The dog glared at the man who had tortured it, killed it, its on eye seeming to glow in the dull gloom. Then it placed the worn nub of its leg onto the bed and pulled itself up, its rear paws kicking and scratching the bed frame for a second as it hopped onto the mattress.

It slowly walked over to Rufus, standing so its legs were one either side of him, its head even with Rufus' face, and it stood immobile, looking down on the man who had killed it, had let it starve to death for the simple joy of being cruel.

The hours passed silently, the dog never moving, only the viscous ooze from its gouged eye dripping onto the pillow next to Rufus' head. As the night began to recede and the first hint of dawn touched the sky, the mangled body of the dog remained still.

It was waiting for something to happen, but what that might be was locked in its dead brain.

Dawn slowly vanished to be replaced by full morning, the rainwater slowly drying as the grass blades glistened with moisture.

It was going to be a beautiful day, and as Rufus slowly opened his eyes around 11:30 in the morning, his alcohol-tinted orbs gazed up at the muzzle of the dog—the one he'd buried only yesterday.

At first he thought it was a dream, something from his drunken binge that had seeped into his mind, perhaps a small kernel of guilt at what he'd done.

But no sooner did the idea flood his mind then he pushed it aside. He wasn't remorseful. Hell, he'd do it again if he could have figured out how to bring the damn dog back from the dead.

But he never had to consider that again, for something or someone had done that for him.

As his eyes pushed away the grogginess of sleep, he stared up at the muzzle of the dog he'd killed, its teeth flaring in what seemed like anger. Bits of mud dropped off the dog's face to sprinkle Rufus' cheeks and brow, and he realized he was staring up at a horror he could never have imagined— and it was now real.

He had time for one long scream before the dog's jaws darted onto his throat, tearing out a fist-sized, bloody chunk of flesh. The head snapped back, and the dog swallowed the meat whole, to then dive in for more; Rufus' shrieks of pain growing in volume. Blood geysered from the man's wound to spray the wall behind the bed crimson, and the dog's face was washed in scarlet as it dove in yet again, teeth gripping tendons and tearing, using its powerful neck muscles to work at the gaping wound continually.

By the time the dog was finished, Rufus' head had been severed from his shoulders, the jagged neck stump squirting blood in all directions, the top of the bed now a deep red as the liquid soon began to drip onto the floor. Rufus' arms twitched spastically for a few seconds before going limp, the legs kicking a staccato drumbeat into the mattress before stopping.

The dog chewed at the exposed stump, finally filling its empty belly, finally getting the food Rufus had denied it in life.

The dog fed for almost an hour, and by the time it was finished, the neck and parts of the shoulders were missing, as well as a large hole ripped in Rufus' torso, where the dog had fed on his moist organs, chewing on the heart and kidneys as if it was the finest veal money could buy.

The entire time, Rufus' head lay on his pillow, his eyes still open, as if he could see his body being consumed and was helpless to stop it.

Suddenly, the dog stopped feeding and its head snapped up. Its ears pricked to the side and the dog woofed twice. Swiveling on the bed, the dog jumped off and padded through the house, Rufus' corpse now forgotten.

The animal went to the back door and crawled through the hole again, woofing each time its ears would prick up. Unknown to human ears, a dog whistle had been blown, and the dog recognized the caller, having been trained when it was alive.

After pulling itself through the hole, and sustaining a few more tears to its flesh from wooden splinters, it hobbled around the house and to the front yard, where a woman in a large flowered hat waited for it.

Excited to see the woman, it began to move faster, its nub of a tail wiggling happily.

When the dog reached the woman, she knelt down on one knee, and with a handkerchief pulled from her purse, she quickly wrapped the bloody stump of its front leg.

"Look at you, you're a mess, you poor thing. Oh and look at your eye. Well, we can get that fixed up once I get you home."

She patted her hip playfully and began to walk, the dog hobbling behind, looking as if it had just been in a hit and run.

"Once we get you home, we'll get you all cleaned up," Rufus' wife said as she paused, knelt down and clipped a leash onto the dog's collar, her hand caressing the talisman hanging from the dog's neck. "There you go, my baby, there's a leash law in this town and I wouldn't want to get a ticket."

The dog woofed once, as if it understood what she was saying.

The dog and its rightful owner walked away from the house, and as the woman reached the end of the driveway, she turned slowly and gazed back at Rufus' home, at the house of the man who had beat her, treated her worse than a slave, and she smiled widely.

"I win, you drunk bastard," she said softly.

Turning, she continued on, her loyal companion padding right beside her, its blood-coated muzzle trailing small red droplets of blood in its wake as it hobbled along at its master's side.

ATLANTIS RISING

The schooner Sultana cut through the ocean waves like a giant knife, the cold spray splashing onto her decking and washing it clean. The ship was returning from a long journey abroad and the crew and passengers were anxious to return home to Chestertown, Maryland.

In the bow, two men stood staring off into the horizon.

One man, the captain of the ship by his uniform, lowered his telescope and turned to his companion.

"It's still there, sir. It's not a mirage then."

Michael Pearson nodded as he looked out on the barren ocean, only the one small spec on the horizon visible to the naked eye.

"That land mass shouldn't be there, Captain. I checked the charts and this entire area is void of either islands or reefs," Pearson said thoughtfully.

"Then what is it, sir?" the captain asked.

"That is what I aim to find out. If there has been volcanic or earth tremors on the ocean floor, then it is quite possible a new land mass has arisen."

The captain's eyebrows went up in curiosity. "Are you serious?"

"Of course, Captain. This entire region is well known for its instability. We could be on the verge of discovering an entirely new land mass. Imagine, we could either be the first people to step on the soil of that island ever or perhaps the first in thousands of years. We have to investigate."

"I don't understand, sir?"

"You see, Captain, the earth is constantly shifting and land masses have risen and sunk constantly over the millennia. Mind you, this happens over thousands of years, but it still happens." He gestured out to the small spec. "That could be a historical find as great as Columbus' discovery."

"But, Mr. Pearson, we've been on the sea for almost four weeks now. Our supplies are low and the crew needs rest. Plus, my ship is old, sir. She will be retired when we reach port. This is her final voyage. Her old bones are weary. And I have to tell you honestly, sir, the sooner I have off-loaded your cargo, the better."

The captain turned around to look down onto the deck of his ship. The Sultana was a strong ship, but after more than sixty years, her keel was faded and her decking was worn. She stretched from bow to stern a total of ninety-seven feet, her decking fifty-three feet. Her deck was made of fir and her keel white oak. Her two masts and four full sails caught the wind and pulled her along at ten knots.

On her decking, her crew moved about, half of the twenty-five keeping her running as best they could, the rest belowdecks. But though every ship creaked as it sailed, the Sultana creaked with age, like an infirm woman with arthritis.

The ship was near the end of its life and the captain knew it would be hard to say goodbye. But it was out of his hands and he knew it.

That was why he had taken the risky cargo onboard his ship.

In the schooner's hold, there was more than two thousand pounds of explosive. The fragile dynamite was old as well, and one good jarring on an errant wave could see his ship retired earlier than he planned. That was why he had taken on the risky cargo. The money made on this voyage would help him put a down payment on a new ship. For he was a man of the sea and if he wasn't on it, working for his living, he might as well die right now.

"But we have a duty to the world to see this thing through, to investigate," Pearson was still talking and the captain came out of his thoughts to look back at the man.

"I'm sorry, sir, my mind wandered away for a moment. You were saying?"

Pearson frowned but continued. "Yes, Captain. We need to go to that land mass and investigate."

The captain shook his head. "No, I'm sorry, Mr. Pearson, but you paid me to get your cargo to Maryland and that is what I'm going to do."

Pearson frowned and the captain could see his mind working behind his Harvard educated brow. Then Pearson spoke up. "I can pay you more if it's about money."

The captain paused then, dollar signs floating in his vision. "How much, sir?"

Pearson pulled out a small book and began to flip through the pages. Finally he stopped, closed the book, returned it to his pocket, then looked the captain in the eyes.

"I can give you three hundred now—all I have on me—and five hundred when we reach port in Maryland."

"Eight hundred, eh?" the captain said. "That is a generous offer, sir, you must really want to go to that island, if that is what it is."

"Yes, Captain, I do. I am a man of science and that land mass could have all my peers fawning over me for years. I have to take the opportunity that's in front of me. Why, this could be the biggest find of 1935."

"Very well, sir, I'll take you to your island, but if I see so much as a rock out of place, I will turn about and head to port. And you will still pay me my due. Is that agreed?"

Pearson smiled as he shook the captain's hand. "Agreed, Captain, and trust me, you won't regret this. Why, some day they will speak about your name and this ship in the history books."

Pearson turned and left the bow, jumping onto the main deck as he no doubt headed off to see his fellow passengers and share the news.

"We shall see about that one, sir, we shall see indeed," the captain said as he turned and looked through the telescope once more at the land mass on the horizon.

That island wasn't supposed to be there and the captain wasn't a man who liked either mysteries or unexpected events.

And that island was both.

He couldn't help but wonder if he had asked for too little to go to the island, and should have asked for more.

The schooner reached the island as the sun was setting, casting the world into darkness once more. Pearson and a fellow traveling companion were both eager to go ashore regardless of the night, but the captain was able to talk them out of it.

"We don't know what could be over there, sir, surely you must realize that," the captain pleaded.

"But, Captain," James Caruthers rebutted, one of the other passengers, who was also a man of science, "that land mass was under water not too long ago as no other ships have reported sighting it. What can possible be there but a few crabs and perhaps some seagulls?"

"Doesn't matter, sir, I will not risk any of my men. You will just have to wait for sunrise. Now if you'll excuse me, I have to check on my men and make sure the ship is battened down for the night." He turned and walked away, leaving Caruthers and Pearson standing alone together.

"The captain thinks to highly of himself," Caruthers said to Pearson.

"Perhaps, but he is in charge of the ship."

Caruthers grinned, his teeth flashing in the gloom of dusk. "Ah, but he isn't in charge of me. Tell you what, Pearson, old boy. You paid to get us here so I will pay to hire a few of the crew that want to make some extra coin. With them I will sneak onto the island tonight and see what is afoot. That way in the morning, when you come ashore, I will already have a portion of the island covered."

Pearson couldn't argue with the logic. The captain had said they could have the afternoon of the next day, and then he was setting sail, and whoever wasn't on his ship would be left behind. This way more ground could be covered.

Finally, Pearson nodded. "That is an excellent plan, Caruthers. But please, be careful. In the dark, who knows what sinkholes or other catastrophes could befall you."

Caruthers waved the warning away. "Oh, please, Pearson, 'tis an island in the middle of the ocean, what could possibly happen?"

"Indeed," was all Pearson could say as Caruthers walked away to see who of the crew was willing to make some money on the side to come along with him.

Just past midnight, when the captain was in his cabin sleeping, Caruthers and six armed crewmen set off from the schooner, rowed to the island, and went ashore. Pearson watched from the port side of the ship as Caruthers expeditionary team lit torches and set off.

He watched the torches bob up and down for almost ten minutes before they finally disappeared around some rock bed or obstruction hidden in the complete darkness.

With nothing left to do, he went to bed, already anxious to awaken to find out what Caruthers had found upon his return.

The next morning, Pearson was awoken by the angry voice of the captain, who was berating his crew in a tirade that had most of the men quaking in their boots.

Rubbing his eyes, Pearson left his cabin and climbed the small ladder that led to the upper deck. Stepping out, he glanced to the island to see it was now plainly visible.

He now saw the obstruction that had caused Caruthers party to disappear was a copse of weeds, which seemed to lead deeper onto the island.

"You, Mr. Pearson!" the captain roared when he saw him step on deck.

"Captain? Good morning to you."

"Don't give me that, Mr. Pearson. Six of my men are gone and so is your friend, Caruthers."

"Sir?" Pearson said, trying to act innocent, but the captain would have none of it.

"Don't even try, Mr. Pearson. I gave implicit orders that no one was to leave the ship. That at first light the island could be investigated. Now I have six men missing as well as a passenger." He glared at Pearson, as if waiting for a rebuttal, but when none came, he continued. "So now I have no choice but to send in a search party." He jabbed a finger at Pearson. "And of course you are coming, too."

"Of course, Captain, I wanted to go ashore anyway. Whatever I can do to be of service, I am at your disposal."

"Indeed," the captain said. "Then go get your gear as we will be leaving in less than an hour. As soon as we have what we need, such as weapons and supplies, we'll set off."

"I'll be ready, sir," Pearson said, and before he could say more, the captain had dismissed him by turning back to his men, barking orders and informing his second-in-command what would he happening and what he wanted done.

With nothing else to do, Pearson went down below to get ready for the search party, and though there was a sense of concern over the missing Caruthers and the six crewmen, there was also anticipation for what magnificent discoveries might await.

An hour later, with the sun high in the sky, the search party set out.

Besides Pearson and the captain, there were seven crewmen, which left eleven crewmen to watch over the ship as well as the six remaining passengers.

They used the same boat that Caruthers' team had used. The captain had ordered one of his men to swim to the island, reach the boat, and by using a rope, pull it back.

As the men rowed ashore, Pearson studied the land before him. All he could see were rocks, most of them coated with dried mud from when the island was on the ocean floor.

But as they got closer, he also saw fresh growth. Seagulls had brought seeds in the form of their excrement. As the seagulls rested on the island and prodded the muddy soil, the seeds they ingested were left in the feces to then fertilize and begin to grow in the rich soil. Small seedlings looking at least a month old were scattered across the area that he could see and he had no doubt in a month's time there would be more.

In a year's time, the entire island would be a lush sanctuary to the birds and sea life able to reach it.

Arriving on the shore, the captain stepped out as his men pulled the boat onto the rocky beach. Pearson climbed out of the boat, grateful for not having to get his boots wet, and looked around again.

The captain walked back and forth and then pointed to footprints in the mud.

"Here, they went this way!" he called out as he waved the sword in his hand in the direction he was heading. A pistol rode his hip and a dagger was in his left boot. The rest of the crewmen also carried weapons, and only Pearson was unarmed. He was slightly uncomfortable with this, but then he knew even if he was to carry some sort of weapon, he would probably end up either cutting or shooting himself. He was a man of science, not violence.

By natural means there was a path through the largest rocks and it was here that the captain went first. The footprints of Caruthers' team were less than ten hours old and it was so plain a child could have followed it.

With care for the unknown surroundings, the search party moved deeper onto the island. For more than an hour they saw nothing but rocks, birds and fresh growth, but then, as the captain rounded a bend on the natural path, he stopped short and raised his right hand.

"There's someone ahead of us," he said as he drew his sword once more, sensing danger.

Either too stupid or too ignorant to understand the potential for danger, Pearson slid up next to the captain, wanting to see what was ahead.

"Get back, man, are you daft?"

Pearson said nothing, but did take a step back. But he had seen what he had wanted to see. The captain had spotted a pair of boots and lower legs inside them on the path up ahead. The rest of the body was hidden around the bend on the path.

The captain pointed to Pearson and his men. "You stay here, I'll check this out myself," he said. He pointed at Pearson with his sword and then turned and slowly crept up the path, his free hand on his pistol.

When he reached the boots, he ever so carefully peered around the outcropping of rocks and let out a small gasp at what he found.

Though not a squeamish man, the sight before him was enough to make him force his morning's breakfast back down his gullet or risk spewing it over the path. For before him, were the lower legs of one of his crew, but that was where it ended. From the waist up there was nothing, as if the body had been ripped apart to leave the waist and legs. As he studied the pants, he knew it was definitely one of his crewmen, and as he took a step past the legs to see what lay beyond, he spotted a severed arm. Stepping over the legs and to the arm, he used his boot to nudge it. As the arm rolled to the side, he saw a tattoo on the bicep and he knew that tattoo well. It belonged to one of his men, a burly fellow with a woman in every port. But despite his reputation with the ladies, he was a faithful son and the painted heart with the word MOM sprawled across it left no doubt to the owner. There was a pistol a few feet away from the open hand and the captain picked it up, seeing it was empty. This man had used his weapon on something.

He heard steps behind him on the path, and he spun, the sword coming up, prepared to take off the head of the attacker, but at the last second he halted his swing. Pearson, now with wide eyes, stared down at the sword an inch from his throat.

"I told you to stay behind," he snapped as he removed the offending blade from Pearson's throat. Pearson couldn't help but rub his neck, imagining what might have happened if the captain had been a bit slower.

"Sorry, Captain, but I was just too curious. That poor man. Any idea how this happened?"

The captain shook his head. "No, none, but I damn sure plan on finding out. Go get the men and tell them to follow. And tell them no dawdling. On our way back to the ship we'll take our fallen man with us."

Pearson nodded, went back to the other men, and a moment later they were with the captain once more. They talked amongst themselves, all unnerved by the death of one of their own.

The mood was unsettling as they made their way down the path once more. Fifteen minutes later, another body was found, only this one was relatively intact. But where the crewman's chest should be there was nothing but a gaping chasm, looking like something had exploded out of the torso. The man's eyes were wide open in death and the mouth locked in a perpetual scream. The captain knelt down beside the corpse, closed the crewman's eyes, and shook his head.

"There is something foul on this island, Mr. Pearson, if I didn't need to know where the rest of my men were, I would sail away and leave this cursed place to rot."

Pearson said nothing, seeing the anger in the captain's face.

They moved on and an hour later came to a massive boulder, easily the size of the ship left floating off shore.

Following the footprints, the search party found a small opening, no more than a foot wide in the boulder. One at a time, the men crawled through, having to stretch their arms, one in front and one behind, so they would fit.

One of the crewmen, a hefty fellow weighing over two-sixty, actually got stuck and a few heaving boot prints on his arse plus a tug on his forward arm, were enough to see him through with only a few minor scratches.

Though the mood was morbid, even the captain had to chuckle at the crewman's disposition upon popping out of the opening.

"Think you need to lay off the pork bellies, Jack, my boy," the captain joked, which had the rest of the crew laughing heartily. For these were men who lived for the present, and though saddened by the loss of their fellow crewmen, were still normally high in spirits; the reason being simple. They were still alive and sucking in breath which was more then could be said for their brethren. Such was the temperament of the average man of the sea.

They continued on for another twenty minutes and the captain called a halt at yet another body lying on the natural path. Actually, it really couldn't be called a path anymore, but was just a convenient opening between the rocks and mud.

Upon moving closer, the captain could see this wasn't one of his crewmen, but was Caruthers, his missing passenger.

"Jack," the captain called out, "keep Mr. Pearson here with you, and as for the rest of you, take five but keep your eyes and ears open. I'm going to see if this body is in the same condition as the last two."

"Aye, Cap'n, I got it," Jack said and turned to the other men. "Take five, boys, while the Cap'n sees to the next poor bastard."

The men did as they were told, some rolling smokes while others took off their boots to rub their feet.

Meanwhile, the captain walked down the path and knelt down once more in front of the body.

The eyes on the face were closed, and as he examined the corpse, he didn't see any signs of trauma. The body had all its limbs and no blood could be discerned, and he was about to get up and return to the others, when Caruthers eyes snapped open and he reached up and grabbed the captain's left arm.

The captain fell back onto his haunches, amazed to see the man alive, and was about to call out for help when Caruthers began to babble incoherently, only a few words making sense.

"Lost...city...amazing...jewels...was...under...ocean...something ...here...*kill... beware...run...*" then his eyes fluttered and his hand let loose of the captain's arm and dropped to the ground. The captain leaned over and checked the man again and this time was confident he was dead.

He sat back on his butt and stared at the body, trying to decipher the words—the last words of a dying man. The only ones he remembered, as in the only ones that stood out to him were *lost, city* and *jewels*.

He was just getting to his feet, his interest now more piqued to continue on, not for his missing crewmen but for the mystery of the dying man's words, when Caruthers' stomach began to *stretch*.

The captain stopped short of walking away and stared at the strange sight. As he watched, the man's abdomen began to pulse, in and out, in and out, again and again. Not understanding what was happening, the captain used his sword to slice the buttons off Caruthers' shirt, thus exposing the flesh of his torso to the air.

Now that the abdomen was exposed, he could see the undulation was more prominent. It was like a mini wave was inside the corpse, slowly moving from his chest to his groin, then back again.

"What in the nine Hells?" the captain muttered under his breath. Behind him, his crewmen talked and chatted as they enjoyed the moment's respite.

Still curious, the captain leaned down, wanting to inspect further, having an opinion on what was happening. Surely a rat or some other small rodent had somehow managed to get into the corpse and now was trying to escape. But if so, then why had Caruthers still been alive and not screaming in agony?

And then, as the captain stared with wide eyes, the corpse seemed to explode outward, the abdomen blowing out as entrails and blood sprayed in all directions.

The captain cried out and fell back as he shielded his eyes with his arm, and when he turned back to see the corpse, he saw something from his nightmares.

There, sitting in the jagged belly of the body was a large, slug-like creature covered in slime. It had eyes, but they were small, and as he watched, the creature opened its mouth, exposing two rows of jagged teeth. Five more of the foul creatures popped out of the gore, each one hissing as if in anger.

The captain heard his men running up behind him and he held up a hand to stop them from coming too close. Only Pearson refused to listen, as he didn't have to take orders from the captain. As the man of science walked closer, one of the creatures swiveled in the gore that was Caruthers and hissed louder.

"My word…" Pearson began but was then held in shock when the creature seemed to catapult out of the corpse to fly through the air on a direct course with Pearson's face. The man had no time to move, the slug-thing heading right for his open mouth, which was wide open, resembling a lid with a bad hinge, when there was a blur of metal and the slug was sliced in twain in mid-air.

The separate halves fell to the earth and wiggled about ineffectually.

Turning, the captain used his sword to slice in twain the other creatures, a few trying to escape only to be flattened by the soles of his boots. They wiggled about even though carved in two, that is until the captain stepped on and stomped each one with his boot.

He crushed the small, gore-covered bodies with his heel, grinding the meat into the dirt, then he turned to Pearson.

"I said to stay back, Mr. Pearson. If you want to live to see home again, I suggest you listen to me when I speak."

Pearson could only nod, learning his lesson.

"What the 'ell were those things, Cap'n?" Jack asked as the rest of the crewmen also voiced their opinions, each wanting to be heard over the rest.

Finally, the captain raised his hands in the air and yelled, "Enough! All of you, quiet. Now, I have no idea what those little sea monsters were but I do know two things. One is that we have missing men on this island, and two is that before this fool died," he pointed to Caruthers mangled corpse with the tip of his sword, "he spoke of jewels and lost cities, and I for one like the sound of that. So, enough of what has transpired here and let's continue onward. Besides, t'was nothing but eels."

"I never seen eels do that to a man, Captain," one of the men said.

Jack punched the man on the shoulder. "Didn't you hear what the Cap'n just said? He said there are jewels around here somewhere, if that man spoke the truth. That is worth fighting off a few killer eels, ain't it?"

"Aye, of course it is, I ain't a coward," the crewman replied, offended.

"None of you are," the captain said. "Now, no more talk, we need to find our missing men, hunt out whatever treasure is to be found, and leave this cursed place in our wake, but only much richer than when we arrived. Are you with me, men?" He raised his sword over his head and was rewarded with claps and a shaking of fists.

"Move out then," he said and they began to walk, the men taking a wide berth around both the corpse and the crushed slug-creatures.

"Captain," Pearson called as they walked. "I know what eels look like and those were definitely not eels."

"Maybe so, Mr. Pearson, but they were still easily killed and if they can be killed then there's nothing to fear. So enough talk, we may have found your friend worse for wear but I still have four missing men on this island."

Pearson opened his mouth to reply but the captain picked up his pace and outdistanced him. With no one to talk to, Pearson closed his mouth and concentrated on walking.

Twenty minutes later they came to a large, steaming chasm.

As the men gathered around, Pearson explained what it was. "So you see, there is probably magma under our feet even now."

"But are we safe here, Mr. Pearson?" the captain asked.

"Yes, Captain, I believe we are. Whatever caused this land mass to rise is still active, but the surface of the island seems safe enough."

"What's down there, sir?" Jack asked. "Lava?"

Pearson chuckled. "No, Jack, lava is what's on the surface, magma is what is underground." He peered into the chasm, the steam causing him to sweat profusely. "Down there is enough power to fuel a thousand ships for a decade, if not more."

"Maybe so, sir," the captain said, "but I have men to find so let us continue, eh?"

Nodding, Pearson stepped back from the chasm and they headed off once more.

Another hour later brought them to the base of a large hill.

After resting for a while, they proceeded up the incline. The captain, like always was on point, and was the first to crest the hill. When he did, he stopped short, staring off into the distance. Pearson was next, and he was about to ask the captain what was wrong, when he too crested the hill and had his first look at the vista before him.

"It can't be," Pearson said, his mouth hanging open once more.

"Aye, sir, indeed it is," the captain replied as his men gathered behind him, each one letting out a gasp of amazement of what lay before them.

In a large valley were the ruins of a massive city.

From where the search party stood, they could only see a small portion of the city, the rest lost behind the crumbling structures of marble and stone, but each man had the impression it went on for miles.

And in the sunlight, for all to see, jewels glistened, reflecting the rays and letting them dance across the facades of the crumbled buildings.

Before the captain could speak, his men were running past him, bounding down the hill as they called to one another in their greed.

With excitement in his eyes, Pearson turned to look at the captain who returned his gaze. "Well, Captain?"

"Well, what, sir? It seems we found a city of some sort. Any ideas what it could be?"

Pearson nodded. "Actually, yes. A few suppositions are at the front of my mind, but I don't want to speak them until I'm sure."

"Sure of what?"

Pearson waved the question away. "Captain, if what I think is true, then we may have stumbled across the greatest find of the nineteenth century, perhaps of all time."

"Really," the captain stated blandly.

Pearson nodded, his excitement only fueled to greater heights as he imagined his theories were correct. Then he turned and moved down the hill, following the path the crewmen had taken.

With nothing else to do but follow, the captain headed off, his mind already working on ways to carry back the treasure he's seen. At least his money problems were over, and then some. Why, when he returned home, he would buy himself an island of his own somewhere and retire in style, only sailing on the sea for pleasure instead of for wages.

As his eyes took in the glittering jewels that seemed to be embedded in every structure, every wall, he imagined himself buying a country instead of merely an island.

By the time the captain reached the limits to the ruined city, he saw his crew was already looting everything they could get their hands on.

"Look at 'em all, Cap'n," Jack said as he held up an emerald ruby the size of his palm. It sparkled in the sun and even being underwater for ages had done nothing to mar its beauty. "And they are everywhere. The entire place is full of 'em." Jack moved next to the captain and handed him the ruby. "For you, sir."

"Well, thank you, Jack. That's mighty generous of you," he said as he held the hefty jewel in his hand. It fit his palm nicely and was worth a king's ransom.

Jack laughed as he waved his arms around him. "Hardly, Captain, as I said, the place is lousy with 'em. We're all rich men! The hard part is going to be how to get it all back to the ship!" He turned and ran back to join the other crewmen, who were making a large pile in the center of what had once been a road.

Pearson was studying some strange markings on the side of a building, the structure now nothing but rubble. Seaweed and fish skeletons could be seen scattered amongst the ruins, not to mention dried mud and silt.

As the captain eyed the ruins, even he could tell that the island had been above water for at least a few weeks as the mud was all but dried everywhere he looked.

Suddenly, the island began to shake and a few standing structures toppled. The crew let out a yell and jumped back as a large pillar fell to the road, nearly crushing one of the men. When it subsided, all eyes looked about warily as stone dust floated in the air like fog.

"What in the name of all that is holy was that?" the captain asked warily.

"This land mass is unstable, Captain," Pearson said as he picked himself up. "The same eruption that sent this island to the surface could just as easily send it back down. Remember back at the large gap with the steam?"

The captain nodded.

"Well, the fact it was exposed and magma still exists and hasn't cooled yet to rock could mean this land mass is far from settled. If the tremors grow worse, I recommend we return to the ship immediately."

"Good advice, Mr. Pearson," the captain said. "So, sir, do you know what this city is? It seems ancient, but there should be nothing like this out here."

Pearson nodded as he touched the etchings on one of the buildings' foundations. "You are correct, Captain. But though it may sound impossible, I believe this city, these ruins, are the fabled lost city of Atlantis."

The captain blinked twice at what he'd heard. "Surly you're mad, sir. Atlantis? Why, that is merely a fairy tale. A story about hidden treasures such as the one about the lost city of gold." He waved his hand about him. "I, sir, do not see gold, do you?"

Pearson nodded. "No, Captain, I do not. But these gems," he picked one up, lying at his feet like gravel, "how do you explain them? Only a city such as Atlantis was even rumored to have streets paved with gold or rubies. Perhaps the myth has changed over the years. But this is real enough."

The captain was about to reply when one of the crew called out. "Cap'n, we found the rest of the lost men! Come quick!"

Dismissing Pearson and shoving the emerald ruby still in his hand into his shirt, the captain jogged away, Pearson following close behind. At the cry from the crewmen, the rest of them gathered around the captain as he followed the first crewman through the ruined streets. It appeared the men had been branching out, trying to cover as much territory as possible. Roughly two blocks away from the location Pearson and the captain had discussed Atlantis, the crewman stopped and pointed to what appeared to have once been some sort of town square.

Even with the rubble scattered about, the circular impression was there, and in the middle was what had once been a beautiful stone fountain. Mermaids and seahorses were carved into the sides and the eyes of the sculptures were large diamonds, at least two inches in width. It was obvious by some of the gaping eye sockets on the sculptures what the crewmen had been doing here.

The captain pieced together what had happened. Caruthers must have tried to return on his own with two of the crewmen as escorts, but they never made it. The rest had stayed behind to loot what they could.

As the captain and the others moved through the small square, the corpses of the dead crewmen were strewn about like discarded trash. Each torso was torn open from the inside and more than one body was missing a head.

As the captain knelt down next to one of his dead men, he used the tip of his sword to jab at the exposed organs. As he pulled the sword back, there was a gelatinous slime on the tip.

"This looks to be the same substance that we saw on that eel thing that was in Caruthers," the captain said as he wiped the tip of his sword on the pants of the corpse.

Pearson knelt down by one of the corpses and inspected it, though his face turned a shade whiter as he fought to control the urge to vomit. "I would concur with your assessment, Captain," he said.

"All right then. Listen up, men!" the captain yelled. "We found our missing crewmen and they are dead, and it looks like it was the same little beasties we found on the path leading here. So this is what we do. We gather as much treasure as we can and then we leave this place in our wake. Are you with me?"

Cries of "yes" and "hell yes" floated in the air as the men got back to work.

The captain called Jack to him.

"Aye, sir?" Jack asked.

"Pick one more man and take care of burial duty for these men, Jack. We can't bring them and the treasure back with us, and if it's a choice, then the dead will have to take this island as their final resting place."

"Aye, sir, I'll get it done."

"Oh, and Jack," the captain, called.

"Aye?"

"Take what clothes from the bodies that you can. They will make good sacks to carry the jewels back in."

Jack's eyes went wide as he figured out what the captain meant. "Aye, Cap'n, damn good idea. I'll see right to it." He trotted off to get to work.

"I'm sorry about your men, Captain," Pearson said as he watched Jack and another crewman begin to drag the bodies to the side where they began stripping and covering them with rubble. The rest of the men went back to looting the ruins.

"They knew the risk when they signed on with me, sir. Though I doubt they ever imagined their demise would be from little beasties that look like eels."

"I would love to be able to capture one of them, Captain. To bring it back for analysis," Pearson said.

The captain snorted in disgust. "After what those little bastards did to my men? No, sir, if I see one of those damn things again all I will do is kill it. And I won't allow one on my ship." He turned to glare at Pearson. "Do you understand me, sir?"

"Yes, Captain, completely."

"Very well, then, sir. I suggest you see to what you want to because as soon as those bodies are buried and we have enough jewels collected to live as rich men for the rest of our lives, we're heading back to the ship."

"Very well, Captain, I will be ready when you say so."

"Good, see that you are." He turned and walked away to see to his men, and to see about making a pile of jewels for himself.

Thirty minutes later, the captain called out to his men that it was time to leave. Each man had two full sacks of jewels; one for themselves and one that would be divided amongst the rest of the crew waiting back on the ship.

The captain had a sack for himself and even Pearson had a small one, though he was adamant that it was to be used for research and not for personal gain.

No one cared what he did with his share as long as they got theirs.

As they trekked through the rubble of a dead city, all eyes went up to admire the stone columns. Each was as thick as three men pressed together, and Pearson was reminded of ancient Greece.

At the end of the line, three of the crewmen walked silently. Since they had returned from searching for their treasure, neither man had spoken, each man now holding a dullness in their eyes, as if they were sleepwalking. A few of the men had tried to strike up a conversation, but when ignored, had muttered a curse and gone to another man who was interested in talking. Spirits were high, each man counting his money in his head, and though burdened by the weight of the sacks of jewels, no man complained, and in fact wanted to take back more. It was the captain's reasoning that had stopped this.

How many lifetimes worth of treasure does one man need? The captain had reasoned to them. One, two, three? How many is enough? They would have enough money to never work again, it was enough.

"I tell you, Captain, I can't wait to come back here with a larger expedition," Pearson said jovially as he walked. "What a marvelous find. Do you realize we will go down in the history books as the people who actually found the fabled lost city of Atlantis?"

"You can take another ship back here, Mr. Pearson, that is all I know. When we get back, I'm going to buy me a new ship, get me a good woman, and sail off to an island and sip drinks on the beach till the day I die. Maybe build me a nice house too. Hell, with all the money I have now, I'll build a damn castle. Right, boys!" As he called out to his men they all cheered—all but the three men at the tail end of the line.

By the time they reached the city limits of the rubble of Atlantis, the scenery had grown wearisome to all but Pearson. The impressive stone monoliths no longer were repaid with open-mouthed stares as each man was anxious to return home and begin spending their newfound treasure.

At first, no one knew anything was amiss, that is until the screaming began.

The captain and Pearson, along with Jack and the other crewmen, all turned as one to stare at the three trailing crewmen, the ones who had said nothing since returning.

The three men were now sprawled on the ground, their backs arced, their faces carved into a rictus of agony as their stomach undulated like tiny waves were trapped within their flesh. Shrieks of anguish escaped their cracked lips and all eyes stared at them in shock, the sacks of treasure lying on the path ignored.

Pearson went to take a step forward and the captain grabbed his arm.

"Wait, sir, stay back. This is familiar, is it not?" He called out to Jack. "Did you see those men the entire time we were in the city, Jack?"

"No, Cap'n, I didn't. They went deeper to search for more jewels and then returned before we left."

The captain nodded, realizing what was transpiring with the men immediately. What had gotten inside Caruthers was now inside his men.

Before he could call out to his men and tell them to get back, the three writhing, thrashing bodies exploded like they were balloons filled to the breaking. Gore and blood went in all directions, spraying every man scarlet. As each man turned away, blinking blood from their eyes, they turned back to see more than two dozen of the slug-like creatures pouring out of the body cavities.

Some seemed to jump while others slid across the ground like super fast snails without shells. A man near Pearson suddenly yelled out as one attached itself to his cheek. As he batted it away, another jumped from between his feet and slid into his open mouth.

Pearson fell back in horror as the slug wiggled into the crewman's mouth, then a bulge appeared in his throat as the slug forced its way down his esophagus. The man began to choke and he fell to the path, writhing in the same way the other three men had been doing only moments before.

The captain had his sword drawn and he was stabbing at the slugs as fast as humanly possible, but there seemed to be more with each passing second. Flicking his eyes to the three bodies, the captain saw more slugs coming out of the cavities, their small slime-covered bodies leaving a trail behind them.

Jack was to his right and the man had a slug held in each hand. Squeezing them tightly, blood squirted out of each small carcass and Jack tossed them away from him. But no sooner did he turn then three more launched themselves at his face, and though he knocked two away, the third found his mouth and slid inside, to begin its journey down his throat. He fell to the path as he clawed at his neck, his eyes wide and bulging.

Pearson felt a slug jump onto the back of his neck and he reached up and brushed it off, screaming as he did so. The captain had five slugs on him and Pearson watched as the man used the sword to remove them, receiving a few shallow cuts for his trouble. Pearson had to wonder if the cuts would become diseased as the slime made contact with the open wounds, but then he was fighting off another half dozen that were seeking his face.

As the seconds passed and the men fought for their lives, it came down to only Pearson and the captain still standing. Pearson was still alive only due to luck, while the captain was a shrewd fighter who had figured out the slugs wanted to enter his body and had therefore kept his mouth closed, his teeth gritted as he spit epitaphs at the foul creatures.

"Keep them away from your face! They want to get inside ya!" the captain yelled through sealed lips.

Pearson said nothing, but jumped behind the captain, who seemed to be his only chance of surviving the little creatures.

As the captain fought off the last of the slugs, his men stopped writhing and slowly crawled to their feet. Their eyes were glazed and their mouths slack, slime dripping out of the corner of their lips.

"By God, they look like zombies!" the captain yelled. "Those things are inside them and I bet they would have tried to reach the ship if something hadn't gone wrong."

Pearson's eyes lit up, always the man of science. "Of course, Captain, it makes perfect sense. The men are like hosts and there must be an incubation period once ingested. But the creatures didn't know how long it took to return to the ship and multiplied too early!" He moved closer to the captain. "You can't let these men back on the ship, Captain, if that creature was to make it back to the mainland, why, the entire population, nay, the world could become infected."

The captain nodded, seeing the reasoning in Pearson's logic.

"Aye, sir, I had already come to that conclusion myself." He looked at Jack as the man turned forward, arms outstretched like some human monster from a pulp novel. "Sorry, Jack, but it has to be like this," the captain said as he brought his arm back and swung the sword, almost beheading Jack in one swipe.

But the neck was harder to sever than it looked and the head was only half severed. As blood geysered from the stump, the head flopped to the side like a torn pocket on an overcoat.

Horrified that Jack was still standing, the captain drew his pistol and shot Jack in the chest. The man went down and as the arms thrashed, then the stomach exploded outward and the slugs tried to escape its fallen host. But the captain was there and he stepped on them before they crawled four feet, squashing them into gobbets of flesh.

A moan came from behind him and the captain spun to see one of his men coming for him. Raising the pistol, he shot the man in the left eye, the body falling heavily to the path.

Spinning on his boot heels, the captain made short work of the rest of his men. With sword and pistol, it was child's play to destroy the unarmed attackers.

As the bodies lay writhing on the ground, the captain grabbed Pearson and picked up his sack of jewels, grabbing one more for good measure as he began running down the path.

"I think it is time we left this cursed island and its damn ruins, Mr. Pearson."

"I couldn't agree more," Pearson said as he turned and followed the captain.

The two men made their way back to the ship, barely slowing to rest. They passed by the smoking crevasse where the magma still roiled below the earth and finally they came out to the shore, making the return trip in a fraction of the time it took to travel to the city ruins. As the two men reached the boat that would take them back to the ship, the captain studied his vessel warily.

"Where is everyone? Where is my crew?" he asked, speaking more to himself and not expecting an answer from Pearson who offered one anyway.

"Below decks?" Pearson suggested.

"Perhaps, but I can't understand why. Well, either way we need to get back." He tossed his sacks of jewels into the boat and gestured for Pearson to get in.

The two men rowed the short distance to the ship, and as they climbed aboard, they were met by nothing but silence.

And then they saw the first one, crushed and flattened on the main deck.

Moving to the small creature, the captain kicked it with his left boot.

"They are here, too? But how?"

"Does it matter, Captain?" Pearson asked.

"I suppose not, but my crew and the passengers..."

Walking to the hatch leading below decks, the two men climbed down the ladder to the crew's quarters, pausing at one of the cabins for the passengers. Upon opening it, the two men saw one of the passengers supine on their bed, the eyes closed and the abdomen roiling like small waves were within. Closing the door and locking it, they continued onward, finding the same thing in each of the other cabins.

Moving to the crew quarters, the captain let out an angry snarl to see his men all in their bunks, their torsos undulating.

"The damn things have infected the entire bloody ship!"

"Captain, we need to get off this ship right now, before they hatch" Pearson said.

"Aye, sir, we will, but not before I take care of some unfinished business."

He turned and marched away, Pearson following him.

"What are you going to do, Captain?"

"I'm going to make sure this damn island can't capture any more unsuspecting people, Mr. Pearson, that is what. And get some revenge at the same time."

He made his way to the ship's storage hold where the dynamite was still waiting to be brought to port. He took three boxes, as much as he could carry, and then handed two boxes to Pearson."

"What do you want me to do with this?"

"Carry it, sir, and follow me."

The two men returned to the main deck where they quickly loaded the dynamite into the small boat, then rowed back to shore. Once there, the captain set off back the way he'd previously traveled, Pearson following and continually asking questions.

"Before I was a ship's captain, sir, my father was an explosives man. I know a thing or two about dynamite and I also know a thing or two about magma and such."

Pearson looked at the captain in a new light, wanting to ask questions, but the captain shut him up.

"Just follow me and I will make sure this damn island goes back into the ocean where it belongs."

The two men made their way back down the path and finally came to the smoking crevasse once more, both now exhausted and wanting nothing more than to rest, but knowing there was no time. The captain set his boxes of explosives down and pointed to the crevasse as Pearson did the same, careful not to jar the dynamite.

"Set your load by the edge, sir, and when I give the word, push it in the hole and run for dear life."

"But I..." Pearson began.

"Look, Mr. Pearson, do this or don't, but stand aside and let me do what needs to be done. You just said a while ago that these things can't make it back to America, and I have a debt to pay this place for killing my crew. So help or don't, but stand back."

"No, Captain, I'll help you, just say the word."

The captain nodded and then he pushed his boxes to the edge. One slight nudge to each box is all it would take to push them into the crevasse and the waiting magma below.

"Ready, sir?" the captain asked and Pearson nodded.

"Then on three," he said and counted. On three, the two men kicked their boxes full of dynamite into the crevasse. As Pearson watched them fall to be lost in the steam and smoke, he heard fast moving footsteps behind him and turned to see the captain running for all he was worth.

"What did I just say, sir, run for your damn life!"

Pearson heeded the warning, spun around, and ran for his life.

The two men hadn't made it more than fifty yards before the first explosion shook the crevasse and had the ground vibrating below their feet. Keeping their balance, the two men ran on as the explosions behind them became more intense and the magma shifted and the fragile substructure of the land mass began to crack.

By the time the two men reached the shore once more, the island was on the verge of exploding, already the far side slipping back into the ocean.

As the two men climbed into the small life boat, the shore was half the size it was before and slowly losing land with each passing second.

With massive explosions now thundering throughout the island, the captain and Pearson rowed back to the ship.

But as they climbed onboard, they found the situation had changed again for the worse.

As the captain planted his boots on the deck, a massive horde of slugs came pouring out of the openings in the decking to swarm across the wooden planks.

"By God, they hatched!" Pearson yelled as he fell back. "What do we do?"

"Get back into the boat, I know what to do," the captain said and dashed off and down into the storage hold. As he ran, he swatted the slugs away from him. With his mouth closed, they couldn't find a way to infect him and he battled through them like he was wading through water. By the time he went below decks, Pearson saw over a score of the creatures covering his body.

Pearson crawled into the boat to wait restlessly, but no sooner did he look up at the edge of the ship, then the slugs began to swarm over the side and fall into the boat with him.

With no other option, he jumped into the water and swam away, treading water as he looked up at the ship.

He waited for what seemed like an eternity, but was in fact only minutes. The slugs still lined the deck rails but they had stopped falling into the water. Pearson noted the slugs didn't seem to like the seawater and sank like lead weights. He said a silent prayer for small favors.

Then Pearson heard running footsteps, sometimes deadened when the same boots landed on slugs, crushing them, and then the captain appeared at the deck rails, covered in slugs from head to toe.

The man ran straight at the deck rails, arms flailing, and toppled over, falling into the sea with a splash that had slugs falling behind him.

Pearson didn't know what to do and he called out to the captain, who still hadn't surfaced.

It was as his mind was trying to decide what to do, the island behind him already beginning to break up and sink back into the ocean, that a thunderous explosion began from inside the ship, one so massive it hit Pearson like a giant hand and had him slipping under the surface of the water, dazed.

As he sank into the ocean, he was able to look up at the surface to see the ship explode into nothing but wood splinters and large fragments of the masts and decking. Wood and debris flew out in every direction as a massive fireball rolled across the surface of the water, making Pearson glad he wasn't still floating on the surface, for he would have been burned to death in an instant.

As he swam back to the surface, his lungs wanting air, the explosion waned and he came back up to see the ship and the small boat were gone, only flaming wooden pieces floating about as the few slugs still alive struggled to stay alive. But as the fire forced them to abandon their floatations, they plunged into the seawater where they sank to the bottom of the ocean.

Pearson swam to a piece of the cracked mast, about eight feet long, and wrapped his arms around it, spitting water and breathing heavily. He looked around to see he was alone, and his heart sank, for he was surely doomed.

As the island began to sink behind him, clouds of dark black smoke and gray pillars of soot floated into the air, and bubbling water that pushed him and the debris out into the clear ocean, he slowly began to drift.

It was as his heart was about to give up hope that a head split the surface of the water and Pearson cried out in shock and happiness.

"Captain! Oh my Lord, I can't believe it's you!"

"And who else would it be, sir?" the captain asked as he swam to the mast and wrapped his arms around it. "I expected a large explosion when I set off the dynamite in the ship's hold, but that was more than I planned on." His face was covered in round red circles, from where the slugs had attached themselves to his face.

Pearson winced when he saw the captain's face. "Does it hurt?"

"Not really, reminds me of a sunburn." He began to wiggle and made a face and he reached inside his shirt to pull out one of the slugs, now dead after being exposed to seawater. Casually, he tossed it away and grinned back at Pearson.

He looked over the man's shoulder to see the island sinking, only the tallest boulders now still in sight. Pearson looked over his shoulder and sighed.

"What a shame, Captain, that was the greatest find of our century. We would have been considered heroes, right up there with Columbus."

"Perhaps, Mr. Pearson, but for now I will take my life to live." He move around the mast until he was next to Pearson, then he began to kick with his feet, propelling them along. "Come along, Mr. Pearson, get kicking, it's a long way back to Maryland."

"How far away do you think it is, Captain? Back to Maryland?"

"Oh, I would say a hundred miles give or take, but don't worry, long before that we should come across another ship. We weren't too far off from the shipping lanes when we found your island, I figure four or five days will see us found and saved."

"Four or five days? How will we ever live that long?"

The captain smiled heartily. "How did we live through the ordeal we just experienced, sir? Where there is a will there is a way."

Pearson was quiet then and the two concentrated on kicking, but eventually Pearson grew tired of the silence and spoke up.

"I wanted to tell you how sorry I was about your ship and your men, Captain, and for losing all that treasure."

The captain smiled as he kicked harder. Then he slowed and the two paused to rest. The captain wrapped an arm around the mast as he reached into his shirt. He pulled out a shiny red emerald, as big as his palm. It was the one Jack had given him, and it was worth a king's ransom all on its own.

"I think I will be just fine once we get home, sir, don't worry about me. That old ship was heading for the scrap yard when we got back anyway. Now enough rest, it's a long way home and I want to get there before we die of thirst."

"I have to agree with you on that one, Captain, I can only promise to do my best by your side."

"A man couldn't ask for a better partner, sir," he paused then and looked out to the sea, Pearson following his gaze.

"What do you see? Is it a ship?" Pearson asked hopefully.

"Not sure, is that a shark fin?"

Pearson's heart skipped a beat and he turned to see where the captain was looking, then back at the man to see a wide grin on the captain's face.

"Don't even joke about something like that, Captain, please."

The captain let out laugh that belayed their predicament, and despite the dire circumstances, Pearson was filled with hope for their survival.

So he began to kick, and so did the captain, the two continuing on to the horizon and beyond.

DEAD RAGE

by Anthony Giangregorio
Book 2 in the Rage virus series!

An unknown virus spreads across the globe, turning ordinary people into bloodthirsty, ravenous killers.

Only a small percentage of the population is immune and soon become prey to the infected.

Amongst the infected comes a man, stricken by the virus, yet still retaining his grasp on reality. His need to destroy the *normals* becomes an obsession and he raises an army of killers to seek out and kill all who aren't *changed* like himself. A few survivors gather together on the outskirts of Chicago and find themselves running for their lives as the specter of death looms over all.

The Dead Rage virus will find you, no matter where you hide.

CHRISTMAS IS DEAD: A ZOMBIE ANTHOLOGY

Edited by Anthony Giangregorio

Twas the night before Christmas and all through the house, not a creature was stirring, not even a. . . zombie?

That's right; this anthology explores what would happen at Christmas time if there was a full blown zombie outbreak. Reanimated turkeys, zombie Santas, and demon reindeers that turn people into flesh-eating ghouls are just some of the tales you will find in this merry undead book. So curl up under the Christmas tree with a cup of hot chocolate, and as the fireplace crackles with warmth, get ready to have your heart filled with holiday cheer. But of course, then it will be ripped from your heaving chest and fed upon by blood-thirsty elves with a craving for human flesh! For you see, Christmas is Dead! And you will never look at the holiday season the same way again.

BLOOD RAGE

(The Prequel to DEAD RAGE)

by Anthony Giangregorio

The madness descended before anyone knew what was happening. Perfectly normal people suddenly became rage-fueled killers, tearing and slicing their way across the city. Within hours, Chicago was a battlefield, the dead strewn in the streets like trash.

Stacy, Chad and a few others are just a few of the immune, unaffected by the virus but not to the violence surrounding them. The *changed* are ravenous, sweeping across Chicago and perhaps the world, destroying any *normals* they come across. Fire, slaughter, and blood rule the land, and the few survivors are now an endangered species.

This is the story of the first days of the Dead Rage virus and the brave souls who struggle to live just one more day.

When the smoke clears, and the *changed* have maimed and killed all who stand in their way, only the strong will remain.

The rest will be left to rot in the sun.

The Zombie in the Basement
by Anthony Giangregorio
Illustrated by Andrew Dawe-Collins

The spooky house at the end of the street was the one all the kids avoided. With its overgrown shrubs and weeds, the place was a modern day haunted house. Especially at night. So when Ricky sneaks into the yard to retrieve his favorite ball, he comes across something he'd only seen in movies and bad dreams. He sees a zombie in the basement window of the old house, but when he tells his friends, no one believes him. Ricky knows what he saw, that something lurks in the old house, something that isn't supposed to exist.

With his best friend Eric by his side, Ricky will find out the truth and prove to everyone that zombies are real. And when the night is done, everyone will know about the zombie in the basement.

Note: This book is for young adults and for those who are young at heart.

DEADFREEZE
by Anthony Giangregorio
THIS IS WHAT HELL WOULD BE LIKE IF IT FROZE OVER!

When an experimental serum for hypothermia goes horribly wrong, a small research station in the middle of Antarctica becomes overrun with an army of the frozen dead.

Now a small group of survivors must battle the arctic weather and a horde of frozen zombies as they make their way across the frozen plains of Antarctica to a neighboring research station.

What they don't realize is that they are being hunted by an entity whose sole reason for existing is vengeance; and it will find them wherever they run.

VISIONS OF THE DEAD
A ZOMBIE STORY
by Anthony & Joseph Giangregorio

Jake Roberts felt like he was the luckiest man alive.

He had a great family, a beautiful girlfriend, who was soon to be his wife, and a job, that might not have been the best, but it paid the bills.

At least until the dead began to walk.

Now Jake is fighting to survive in a dead world while searching for his lost love, Melissa, knowing she's out there somewhere.

But the past isn't dead, and as he struggles for an uncertain future, the past threatens to consume him. With the present a constant battle between the living and the dead, Jake finds himself slipping in and out of the past, the visions of how it all happened haunting him. But Jake knows Melissa is out there somewhere and he'll find her or die trying.

In a world of the living dead, you can never escape your past.

DEAD MOURNING: A ZOMBIE HORROR STORY
by Anthony Giangregorio

Carl Jenkins was having a run of bad luck. Fresh out of jail, his probation tenuous, he'd lost every job he'd taken since being released. So now was his last chance, only one more job to prevent him from going back to prison. Assigned to work in a funeral home, he accidentally loses a shipment of embalming fluid. With nothing to lose, he substitutes it with a batch of chemicals from a nearby factory.

The results don't go as planned, though. While his screw-up goes unnoticed, his machinations revive the cadavers in the funeral home, unleashing an evil on the world that it has not seen before. Not wanting to become a snack for the rampaging dead, he flees the city, joining up with other survivors. An old, dilapidated zoo becomes their haven, while the dead wait outside the walls, hungry and patient.

But Carl is optimistic, after all, he's still alive, right? Perhaps his luck has changed and help will arrive to save them all?

Unfortunately, unknown to him and the other survivors, a serial killer has fallen into their group, trapped inside the zoo with them.

With the undead army clamoring outside the walls and a murderer within, it'll be a miracle if any of them live to see the next sunrise.

On second thought, maybe Carl would've been better off if he'd just gone back to jail.

ROAD KILL: A ZOMBIE TALE
by Anthony Giangregorio
ORDER UP!

In the summer of 2008, a rogue comet entered earth's orbit for 72 hours. During this time, a strange amber glow suffused the sky.

But something else happened; something in the comet's tail had an adverse affect on dead tissue and the result was the reanimation of every dead animal carcass on the planet.

A handful of survivors hole up in a diner in the backwoods of New Hampshire while the undead creatures of the night hunt for human prey.

There's a new blue plate special at DJ's Diner and Truck Stop, and it's you!

ANOTHER EXCITING CHAPTER IN THE DEADWATER SERIES!
DEAD CITY by Anthony Giangregorio
NEW PERILS IN AN UNDEAD WORLD!

After narrowly surviving an attack by a large pack of blood thirsty, wild dogs, Henry and his companions stumble upon an enclave that has made its home in an abandoned shopping mall.

Hoping for a respite from the perils of the walking dead, Henry and the others plan to settle down for the winter, safe in the company of fellow survivors of the zombie apocalypse. But unknown to the group is the dark secret the enclave keeps, a secret that could threaten to destroy the companions and anyone else unfortunate enough to be caught in the trap.

In a dead world the only thing still living... is hope.

THE DARK
by Anthony Giangregorio
DARKNESS FALLS

The darkness came without warning.

First New York, then the rest of United States, and then the world became enveloped in a perpetual night without end.

With no sunlight, eventually the planet will wither and die, bringing on a new Ice Age. But that isn't problem for the human race, for humanity will be dead long before that happens.

There is something in the dark, creatures only seen in nightmares, and they are on the prowl. Evolution has changed and man is no longer the dominant species. When we are children, we're told not to fear the dark, that what we believe to exist in the shadows is false.

Unfortunately, that is no longer true.

SOULEATER
by Anthony Giangregorio

Twenty years ago, Jason Lawson witnessed the brutal death of his father by something only seen in nightmares, something so horrible he'd blocked it from his mind.

Now twenty years later the creature is back, this time for his son.

Jason won't let that happen.

He'll travel to the demon's world, struggling every second to rescue his son from its clutches.

But what he doesn't know is that the portal will only be open for a finite time and if he doesn't return with his son before it closes, then he'll be trapped in the demon's dimension forever.

SEE HOW IT ALL BEGAN IN THE NEW DOUBLE-SIZED 460 PAGE SPECIAL EDITION!

DEADWATER: EXPANDED EDITION
by Anthony Giangregorio

Through a series of tragic mishaps, a small town's water supply is contaminated with a deadly bacterium that transforms the town's population into flesh eating ghouls.

Without warning, Henry Watson finds himself thrown into a living hell where the living dead walk and want nothing more than to feed on the living.

Now Henry's trying to escape the undead town before he becomes the next victim.

With the military on one side, shooting civilians on sight, and a horde of bloodthirsty zombies on the other, Henry must try to battle his way to freedom.

With a small group of survivors, including a beautiful secretary and a wise-cracking janitor to aid him, the ragtag group will do their best to stay alive and escape the city codenamed: **Deadwater**.

DEAD END: A ZOMBIE NOVEL

by Anthony Giangregorio

THE DEAD WALK!

Newspapers everywhere proclaim the dead have returned to feast on the living!

A small group of survivors hole up in a cellar, afraid to brave the masses of animated corpses, but when food runs out, they have no choice but to venture out into a world gone mad.

What they will discover, however, is that the fall of civilization has brought out the worst in their fellow man.

Cannibals, psychotic preachers and rapists are just some of the atrocities they must face.

In a world turned upside down, it is life that has hit a Dead End.

BOOK OF THE DEAD 2: NOT DEAD YET

A ZOMBIE ANTHOLOGY

Edited by Anthony Giangregorio

Out of the ashes of death and decay, comes the second volume filled with the walking dead.

In this tomb, there are only slow, shambling monstrosities that were once human.

No one knows why the dead walk; only that they do, and that they are hungry for human flesh.

But these aren't your neighbors, your co-workers, or your family.
Now they are the living dead, and they will tear your throat out at a moment's notice.

So be warned as you delve into the pages of this book; the dead will find you, no matter where you hide.

ANOTHER EXCITING ADVENTURE IN THE DEADWATER SERIES!

DEAD SALVATION

BOOK 9

by Anthony Giangregorio

HANGMAN'S NOOSE!

After one of the group is hurt, the need for transportation is solved by a roving cannie convoy. Attacking the camp, the companions save a man who invites them back to his home.

Cement City it's called and at first the group is welcomed with thanks for saving one of their own. But when a bar fight goes wrong, the companions find themselves awaiting the hangman's noose.

Their only salvation is a suicide mission into a raider camp to save captured townspeople.

Though the odds are long, it's a chance, and Henry knows in the land of the walking dead, sometimes a chance is all you can hope for.

In the world of the dead, life is a struggle, where the only victor is death.

INSIDE THE PERIMETER: SCAVENGERS OF THE DEAD
by Alan Spencer

In the middle of nowhere, the vestiges of an abandoned town are surrounded by inescapably high concrete barriers, permitting no trespass or escape. The town is dormant of human life, but rampant with the living dead, who choose not to eat flesh, but to instead continue their survival by cruder means.

Boyd Broman, a detective arrested and falsely imprisoned, has been transferred into the secret town. He is given an ultimatum: recapture Hayden Grubaugh, the cannibal serial killer, who has been banished to the town, in exchange for his freedom.

During Boyd's search, he discovers why the psychotic cannibal must really be captured and the sinister secrets the dead town holds.

With no chance of escape, Broman finds himself trapped among the ravenous, violent dead.

With the cannibal feeding on the animated cadavers and the undead searching for Boyd, he must fulfill his end of the deal before the rotting corpses turn him into an unwilling organ donor.

But Boyd wasn't told that no one gets out alive, that the town is a death sentence.

For there is no escape from *Inside the Perimeter*.

DEADFALL
by Anthony Giangregorio

It's Halloween in the small suburban town of Wakefield, Mass.

While parents take their children trick or treating and others throw costume parties, a swarm of meteorites enter the earth's atmosphere and crash to earth.

Inside are small parasitic worms, no larger than maggots.

The worms quickly infect the corpses at a local cemetery and so begins the rise of the undead.

The walking dead soon get the upper hand, with no one believing the truth. That the dead now walk.

Will a small group of survivors live through the zombie apocalypse?
Or will they, too, succumb to the Deadfall.

LOVE IS DEAD: A ZOMBIE ANTHOLOGY
Edited by Anthony Giangregorio
THE DEATH OF LOVE

Valentine's Day is a day when young love is fulfilled.

Where hopeful young men bring candy and flowers to their sweethearts, in hopes of a kiss...or perhaps more. But not in this anthology.

For you see, LOVE IS DEAD, and in this tome, the dead walk, wanting to feed on those same hearts that once pumped in chests, bursting with love.

So toss aside that heart-shaped box of candy and throw away those red roses, you won't need them any longer. Instead, strap on a handgun, or pick up a shotgun and defend yourself from the ravenous undead.

Because in a world where the dead walk, even love isn't safe.

ETERNAL NIGHT: A VAMPIRE ANTHOLOGY
Edited by Anthony Giangregorio

Blood, fangs, darkness and terror...these are the calling cards of the vampire mythos.

Inside this tome are stories that embrace vampire history but seek to introduce a new literary spin on this longstanding fictional monster. Follow a dark journey through cigarette-smoking creatures hunted by rogue angels, vampires that feed off of thoughts instead of blood, immortals presenting the fantastic in a local rock band, to a legendary monster on the far reaches of town.

Forget what you know about vampires; this anthology will destroy historical mythos and embrace incredible new twists on this celebrated, fictional character.

Welcome to a world of the undead, welcome to the world of Eternal Night.

BOOK OF THE DEAD
A ZOMBIE ANTHOLOGY VOL 1
ISBN 978-1-935458-25-8
Edited by Anthony Giangregorio

This is the most faithful, truest zombie anthology ever written, and we invite you along for the ride. Every single story in this book is filled with slack-jawed, eyes glazed, slow moving, shambling zombies set in a world where the dead have risen and only want to eat the flesh of the living. In these pages, the rules are sacrosanct. There is no deviation from what a zombie should be or how they came about. The Dead Walk.

There is no reason, though rumors and suppositions fill the radio and television stations. But the only thing that is fact is that the walking dead are here and they will not go away. So prepare yourself for the ultimate homage to the master of zombie legend. And remember... Aim for the head!

REVOLUTION OF THE DEAD
by Anthony Giangregorio
THE DEAD SHALL RISE AGAIN!

Five years ago, a deadly plague wiped out 97% of the world's population, America suffering tragically. Bodies were everywhere, far too many to bury or burn. But then, through a miracle of medical science, a way is found to reanimate the dead.

With the manpower of the United States depleted, and the remaining survivors not wanting to give up their internet and fast food restaurants, the undead are conscripted as slave labor.

Now they cut the grass, pick up the trash, and walk the dogs of the surviving humans.

But whether alive or dead, no race wants to be controlled, and sooner or later the dead will fight back, wanting the freedom they enjoyed in life.

The revolution has begun!

And when it's over, the dead will rule the land, and the remaining humans will become the slaves...or worse.

KINGDOM OF THE DEAD
by Anthony Giangregorio
THE DEAD HAVE RISEN!

In the dead city of Pittsburgh, two small enclaves struggle to survive, eking out an existence of hand to mouth.

But instead of working together, both groups battle for the last remaining fuel and supplies of a city filled with the living dead.

Six months after the initial outbreak, a lone helicopter arrives bearing two more survivors and a newborn baby. One enclave welcomes them, while the other schemes to steal their helicopter and escape the decaying city.

With no police, fire, or social services existing, the two will battle for dominance in the steel city of the walking dead. But when the dust settles, the question is: will the remaining humans be the winners, or the losers?

When the dead walk, the line between Heaven and Hell is so twisted and bent there is no line at all.

DEAD HISTORY: A ZOMBIE ANTHOLOGY
Edited by Anthony Giangregorio

The history of the walking dead is a long one.

Since before man walked the Earth, the dead have been with us. Rotting, decrepit animated corpses have existed, and in many places, have helped create the evolution of the very history we all know as fact, but yet they have always remained hidden from mankind as the sands of time flowed through the hour glass.

From Egypt, to London, to the first moon landing, to the old West; zombies have been a part of our culture, our very lives, though each time it has been erased, eradicated from our history.

Perhaps in these lost tales of our past is the hope for our future. In these stories might very well be the answers of what to do when the zombie apocalypse finally arrives. So read these tales quickly and learn from them. For even in the past, the dead walk, and if they did once before, it's a fact they will do so again.

The only question is: When will that be and will you be prepared?

THE CHRONICLES OF JACK PRIMUS
BOOK ONE
by Michael D. Griffiths

Beneath the world of normalcy we all live in lies another world, one where supernatural beings exist.

These creatures of the night hunt us; want to feed on our very souls, though only a few know of their existence.

One such man is Jack Primus, who accidentally pierces the veil between this world and the next. With no other choice if he wants to live, he finds himself on the run, hunted by beings called the Xemmoni, an ancient race that sees humans as nothing but cattle.   They want his soul, to feed on his very essence, and they will kill all who stand in their way.   But if they thought Jack would just lie down and accept his fate, they were sorely mistaken.

He didn't ask for this battle, but he knew he would fight them with everything at his disposal, for to lose is a fate worse than death.

He would win this war, and he would take down anyone who got in his way.

THE WAR AGAINST THEM: A ZOMBIE NOVEL
by Jose Alfredo Vazquez

Mankind wasn't prepared for the onslaught.

An ancient organism is reanimating the dead bodies of its victims, creating worldwide chaos and panic as the disease spreads to every corner of the globe. As governments struggle to contain the disease, courageous individuals across the planet learn what it truly means to make choices as they struggle to survive.

Geopolitics meet technology in a race to save mankind from the worst threat it has ever faced. Doctors, military and soldiers from all walks of life battle to find a cure. For the dead walk, and if not stopped, they will wipe out all life on Earth. Humanity is fighting a war they cannot win, for who can overcome Death itself? Man versus the walking dead with the winner ruling the planet. Welcome to *The War Against Them*.

DEADTOWN: A DEADWATER STORY
B OOK 8
by Anthony Giangregorio

The world is a very different place now. The dead walk the land and humans hide in small towns with walls of stone and debris for protection, constantly keeping the living dead at bay.

Social law is gone and right and wrong is defined by the size of your gun.

UNWELCOME VISITORS

Henry Watson and his band of warrior survivalists become guests in a fortified town in Michigan. But when the kidnapping of one of the companions goes bad and men die, the group finds themselves on the wrong side of the law, and a town out for blood.

Trapped in a hotel, surrounded on all sides, it will be up to Henry to save the day with a gamble that may not only take his life, but that of his friends as well.

In a dead world, when justice is not enough, there is always vengeance.

END OF DAYS: AN APOCALYPTIC ANTHOLOGY
VOLUMES 1 & 2

Our world is a fragile place.

Meteors, famine, floods, nuclear war, solar flares, and hundreds of other calamities can plunge our small blue planet into turmoil in an instant.

What would you do if tomorrow the sun went super nova or the world was swallowed by water, submerging the world into the cold darkness of the ocean? This anthology explores some of those scenarios and plunges you into total annihilation.

But remember, it's only a book, and tomorrow will come as it always does.

Or will it?

Eternal Night

A Vampire Anthology

Edited By
Anthony Giangregorio